War of the Fae

Book One

The Changelings

Elle Casey

All names, places, and events depicted in this book are fictional and products of the author's imagination.

Elle Casey
PO Box 14367
N Palm Beach, FL 33408

Website: www.ElleCasey.com
Email: info@ellecasey.com

ISBN/EAN-13: 978-0-9856071-3-5

First Edition

Dedication

This book is dedicated to my daughter Skye ... my kickass little fae-blooded girl who never ceases to amaze me with how awesome she is.

Other Books by Elle Casey

War of the Fae: Book One, The Changelings
War of the Fae: Book Two, Call to Arms
War of the Fae: Book Three, Darkness & Light
War of the Fae: Book Four, New World Order

Clash of the Otherworlds: Book 1, After the Fall
Clash of the Otherworlds: Book 2, Between the Realms
Clash of the Otherworlds: Book 3, Portal Guardians

Apocalypsis: Book 1, Kahayatle
Apocalypsis: Book 2, Warpaint
Apocalypsis: Book 3, Exodus
Apocalypsis: Book 4, Haven

My Vampire Summer
My Vampire Fall

Wrecked
Reckless

War of the Fae
Book One

The Changelings

Elle Casey

Chapter One

I CAN'T TAKE MUCH MORE of this high school nonsense. I feel like I'm not supposed to be here. Where would I be if I weren't here? ... I don't know. All I *do* know is I'm in the middle of all this crap, going to class, taking tests - but I'm on autopilot, going through the motions, waiting for life to start happening.

I'm sitting in World History, and there's a girl one row over who's the polar opposite of me. She's staring attentively at the teacher, her pen poised above an already nearly full page of notes, eager to write down every nugget of educational wisdom he's throwing our way. She loves it here, and she has big plans for moving on to college next year. She has cheer practice after school and a boyfriend named Mike who plays wide receiver on the football team. *Ugh.*

I own a pen. I probably have some paper somewhere in my backpack too. Today, however, I'm using my pen to draw symbols all over my right hand - temporary tattoos. I write and eat with my left hand but do just about everything else with my right. My own body is confused with what it's supposed to do.

I'm in the minority in this school. It seems like just about everyone else knows exactly what they're doing now and what they're going to be doing until the day they die. Me? I don't have a clue. All I know is, *this* isn't it. Today the bathroom scale said I'd lost another two pounds. I was literally wasting away with boredom. Maybe I was going to just disappear altogether. I wondered if anyone would miss me.

"Jayne? May I ask what you're doing?"

Uh-oh. I'd been spotted by the droner. I tucked my hand under my desk, hiding my artwork.

"Um, nothin' ... just taking some notes." My face was the picture of innocence. Or so I thought.

He walked over and stopped at my desk, looking down at its empty surface. "Where are these so-called notes?"

I reached up with my non-tattooed hand to tap my temple, looking up at him. "Right here, Mr. Parks; it's all riiiight here." I gave him a saucy wink just because I knew how much he'd hate it. Sometimes I do that kind of stuff - my mom calls it cutting off my nose to spite my face. I'm not sure why I do it; maybe to make life more interesting, give myself more of a challenge ... or maybe I'm just a glutton for punishment.

I looked over at the girl sitting next to me, noticing her scowl out of the corner of my eye. I stuck my tongue out at her because I'm not all that mature and I still enjoy doing the things that cracked me up when I was ten.

She doesn't get me at all. I'd heard girls like her call me a waste before. I couldn't say that I disagree with that comment - I am definitely wasted on this school.

"Cute ... I wonder if the assistant principal would agree." Mr. Parks went back to his desk, bending down to write out a referral slip. "Take this up to the office and see what he thinks about your mental note-taking program."

I slid out of my chair, standing to walk to the front of the classroom with a loose grip on my nearly empty backpack. Bringing books to class was something I didn't normally bother with. My locker is better equipped than my shoulder to manage twenty pounds of blah, blah, and blah.

"Thanks ever so much," I said sweetly, taking the slip from him and turning my head to look at my classmates. There would be no leaving with eyes cast down and a heart full of shame for this girl.

I caught the eye of my best friend, the biggest dork on the entire planet, Tony Green. I blew him a kiss with the referral slip held between my middle finger and thumb so he and the rest of the class could enjoy my one-finger salute. His face turned bright pink and he sunk low in his chair, shaking his head and refusing to meet my eyes. He was probably worried I was going to get him a one-way ticket to the principal's office too. They don't know him there like they know me.

Tony has been my friend, not necessarily willingly, since he ended up having the extraordinarily good luck to sit in front of me in Analytic Geometry, two years ago. He was so pitiful - still is really. Skinny as a sack of bones with crazy, unkempt and un-styled brown hair, wearing clothes I know for a fact his mother bought for him in the little boys' section at Wal-Mart, and shoes with weird, thick rubber soles. The bright pink pimples he always had on his pale white skin did nothing to help this package. It's not like I'm miss beauty queen or anything, but I know bad fashion choices when I see them. The first day I saw him, I couldn't help latching myself right on. He was like a scraggly little puppy who'd had its ass kicked.

I preferred the casual look for myself - usually jeans, purple Converse sneaks, and cute t-shirts ... hoodies in the winter. It never gets too cold in south Florida where we live, so my fashion choices are somewhat limited. I keep my brown hair long because it's so thick; the few times I got it cut short, I ended up having a big, puffy hair triangle on my head. Not cool. But sporting a thick, long, wavy mane in Florida is crazy hot, so my hair is usually up in a rubber band, out of the way. I've been told that I'm pretty or, more often, cute. I don't wear a lot of makeup, mostly eyeliner and mascara, occasionally lip gloss. Adults always comment on my big green eyes and heart-shaped lips, whatever that means. I'm shorter than about half the girls I know, so I guess that makes me average height.

Every day I went into Geometry that semester, I'd ask Tony when we were going to start hanging out together. I don't know why I did it; he just seemed so shy and cute, scared to death of everything around him. I wanted to toughen him up or something, maybe break him out of his lonely shell.

As the school's winter dance got closer, I took to leaning forward and whispering all kinds of stuff in his ear. First it was things like, 'When are you going to ask me to the dance?' And then it kind of devolved into, 'Hey, Tony, whaddya say you and I go hang out after school and smoke some dope or something?' I don't do drugs, but I liked shocking the crap out of Tony - who I was calling Tony Baloney by this time. Or Tones. Or Tone-Tone.

Tony had other friends, but they were all computer geeks, and none of them were girls. I know a bit about computers, but I mostly use them to research places I'd rather be than school. I have no idea how to program anything other than the alarm on my cell phone. I had other friends - girls - but they were always busy doing homework and making their parents proud. We didn't have a lot in common, and their parents tended to discourage friendships with me. I'm apparently what some might consider a 'bad influence'. As far as I was concerned, they were the fun police.

Tony's ability to blush on command was unrivaled. All I had to do was say 'boobs' or 'dick' and instantly his face would be scarlet. I made the mistake of telling my mom about my antics with him one day, and she went off, telling me I was bullying the poor boy. She made it a point to remind me that I sometimes don't realize how persistent I can be. I think when she said 'persistent' she really meant 'annoying' or 'pain-in-the-ass-ish'. My mom's asshat boyfriend was more than happy to chime in on that conversation. He practically lives with us now, which is why I avoid going home as much as possible.

After my mom said that about Tony, I felt a little bit bad. I looked back on everything I'd said to him and thought that maybe people could see it as bullying if they didn't realize that I was actually quite fond of the guy.

Over the weeks and months of my 'persistence', Tony kinda warmed up a bit. We talked about things. He learned to brush off my inappropriate comments, even laughing at them on occasion when they were particularly crass. We walked between classes together sometimes. We hadn't started hanging out after school, but I had a feeling it was going to happen some day soon.

After the talk with my mom, I decided I needed to clear the air with old Tony Baloney. I didn't want to think about him going home and crying because some mean girl at school was making his life a living hell. Lord knows my father, long gone from the household but still haunting me via court-ordered visitation, had given me that credit enough times over the years.

Before History class the next day, as we were waiting for our teacher Mr. Banks to arrive, I asked Tony if I was bothering him. The conversation went something like this:

"Hey, Tony. Am I bothering you?"

"Yes."

"No, I mean really, Tone-Tone. Am I *really* bothering you?"

"Yes, you really are."

"Okay, thanks, I feel better now. I thought I was really bothering you."

Sigh. "You ARE bothering me, are you deaf?"

"No, but I know what you really mean when you say 'yes'."

"Ah, so this is one of those 'no means yes' things we learned about in health class?"

"Uh ... kind of. Yeah, I'm pretty sure."

"Okay, whatever. Just stop bothering me."

Even though this verbal sparring was fun, it was getting me nowhere. I decided to get down to business. I had to let him know I wasn't a bully - just a socially inept girl trying to make friends with a nerdy dude in rubber-soled shoes.

"Hey, Tony, when you saying 'bothering' do you mean 'bothering' or 'bullying'?" I could see he was going to turn around so I put on the most innocent face I knew how to make. I tied it up with as sheepish a grin as I could manage too, just in case my innocent look wasn't as awesomely powerful as I thought it was.

He didn't say anything at first; he just looked at me. For the first time in our relationship, I felt uncomfortable, which for me is saying a lot. I squirmed in my seat a little bit and felt my smile faltering. I realized as he stared at me that I really, really didn't want to be bullying him. Tony was a cool dude, and it was possible I was the only one in the whole world who knew it. And it was also possible that he was the only person in the world who knew I *did* give a shit about some things. He was a perceptive guy.

"You're not bullying me, and you're not really bothering me, either ... Jayne."

It was the first time I'd heard him say my name. I guess I was a little surprised that he even knew it, though I shouldn't have been.

We'd been in this class for almost the whole semester. It was the look on his face, though, that blew me away. He looked so friggin serious, staring me right in the eyes. I felt like he was seeing into my head. My smile came back, but it was totally real this time.

I grabbed my pen and twirled it in my hand. "Well that sucks, 'cause I was kind of enjoying bothering you." Being a total smartass when in tight situations is one of my best skills.

"I could tell. So now that you know you're not bothering me, you can stop."

"Stop what?"

"Stop bothering me," he said as he turned back around in his seat.

"Okay, that makes perfect sense. So when are we going to hang out?" I expected him to do his usual - turn bright red and refuse to answer me. But he surprised me this time.

"How about today?" He still had the red face and neck, flaming with embarassment, but only a little bit of the shoulder hunching that always gave him the appearance of a turtle going into its shell.

"Don't you have chess club or computer club or calculus club or build-a-robot club or some other rule-the-world-someday club to go to?"

While I waited for his answer, the teacher arrived in class to start the show.

Tony turned sideways, pretending he was getting a book out of his backpack. "Chess club, but I'll skip it." He pushed his oversized glasses back up on his nose as he sat up, turning to face the front of the class again.

Did I mention Tony has the butt-ugliest, brown tortoise-shell glasses you've ever seen? They are not cool or fashionable, even in a statement-making sort of way. I swear he must have gotten them from the dumpster outside of Goodwill.

"Wow, living on the edge ... sure you can handle it, Tones?"

He sat up straighter than I was used to seeing him sit. "I can if you can," he whispered.

"Fine. I'll meet you at the front of the school after seventh period. Oh, and by the way, I saw that."

"Saw what?"

"You smiled ... I think you like me." I was staring at his back, but I swear I saw his scalp move.

"No I didn't, and no I don't."

"You don't?"

Sigh. "Jayne, shut up before you get me in trouble."

I smiled and stage-whispered, "Boooooring." But I left him alone for the rest of the period, sure he was anxious to bust out his notebook and take some awesome notes. I had tattoos to draw anyway.

And so, *The Year I Adopted Tony Baloney As My New Best Friend* commenced. Every day since, we have hung out after school and I've harassed him in every class I could. The following semesters we even tried to arrange our schedules so we'd have a lot of classes together. Apparently he'd grown quite fond of my harassment and persistent nature, not that I'd given him much choice. I'd found him, and he was mine - cute little bugger that he was, messed up glasses, funky shoes and all.

*****

As I arrived at the assistant principal's office and took my seat in the waiting area, I thought about all the time Tony and I had spent together these past two years. We hung out after school and got to know each other's screwed up families pretty well - my mother who couldn't think for herself and her asshat boyfriend, and Tony's parents who were almost never around.

Most of our time was spent walking around town and hanging

out at the library where Tony tried to study while I found new ways to make him crazy by not studying and making noise. Every once in a while we went to the movies, but usually we couldn't afford it. Tony wouldn't even consider sneaking in or trying to see more than a single movie on one ticket. He was a spoilsport that way, but he kept me out of trouble so I didn't complain.

Some people say it's impossible for a guy and a girl to be best friends, but I completely disagree. Tony and I are friends and that's it. I didn't like him in a romantic way - I preferred the bad boy type, and Tony was as far from being a bad boy as I was from being a good girl. I mean, what girl doesn't go for the bad boy really? Actually, most of the guys I knew around school were idiots with their heads so far up their butts I couldn't stand to be around them for very long. They had a lot to learn about how to treat a girl, and I didn't have the patience to train any of them. Case in point, Brad Powers, who was also sitting in the principal's waiting area; only he was probably there to kiss the principal's ass, not to be chastised by him. I barely spared him a glance. He had a rep for being a total douche to girls - using them and then throwing them to the curb. He was a kiss-and-tell kind of guy, if you know what I mean.

That's another good thing I can say about Tony - the guy is an absolute prince. He always holds doors for girls, pulls out chairs, offers them drinks and stuff. I don't think I've ever heard him burp. All this time hanging out with me has somehow not trained the manners out of him. I'm not sure how that's managed to happen, really. You'd think my powers of persuasion would be stronger than that.

Tony has his crushes, but he would rather walk over hot coals than actually ask a girl out. He prefers to crush from afar. I offered to help hook him up a few times, but the thought of me being involved in his love life nearly sent him into apoplectic spasms that were frightening to watch.

I did try once to get a girl I knew he liked to warm up to him. It was a disaster from the word go. As soon as I mentioned his name she got a disgusted expression on her face. "Tony? *Tony Green?!* Are you *kidding* me?" She just stood there looking like she'd smelled something bad.

"Um, yeah, okay, never mind." I realized it wasn't going well, so I bolted. I saw Tony later and confessed, although I left out the hairy details.

"You did WHAT?!" His face turned an interesting shade of reddish-purple and got all blotchy; even the whites of his eyes went a little red.

"Dude, chill. I didn't tell her you like her or wanted to get into her panties or anything."

"Wha ... ? Panti ... ? Wha ... ? ARRRRrrrgggg!" The strangled noises coming out of his throat didn't sound good. He bent over slightly, grabbing the door of his open locker, probably to keep himself from falling on the floor.

"Dude, holy shit, what is your problem? Breathe already, she's just a girl for chrissakes."

I started beating him on the back, hoping to get him breathing right again. His reaction struck me as over-the-top, especially for Tony. It crossed my mind that I could possibly be witnessing some psychological scarring happening right before my eyes. I did feel a measure of guilt over the fact that it was me who had caused it, but I assuaged this guilt by telling myself I was only trying to help the poor guy.

He was breathing deeply, trying to get a grip on himself. He elbowed my whacking hand off his back and stood, running his fingers through his hair until it stood on end. This was nothing new for Tony, as his hair was usually in a state of disarray.

"Do I even want to know what she said?" he asked, the look of hope in his eyes too pitiful to bear.

I sighed. "Not really, dude. She is too stuck up to even see you. I'm actually thinking about going back there and punching her in the face."

He looked stricken, his face now going white. "That bad, huh?"

I was afraid he was going to do that crazy breathing thing again. I put a serious look on my face. "No, actually. She just said your name; like, repeated it. She didn't say anything else. I just took off - I started thinking about the spasms you'd have if you found out I'd done it, and I got scared."

Tony knew my serious look was a load of crap. "You? Scared? That'll be the day." He closed his locker quietly, because Tony never slams his locker shut. "Let's go, we're gonna be late for class." He sounded really, really tired. Or bummed.

I felt like crap. Now I really wanted to punch that chick in the head, and I'm generally not a violent person. I talk tough, but I'm all talk and no action usually. I had to do something, though, to get him out of this mood.

"Oh boy, *biology*, hold me back. Tony, I'm so excited, I feel like *skipping* to class!" I grabbed his elbow and started skipping, dragging him along a few feet before he was able to wrestle himself away from me.

"Suit yourself!" I yelled, as I skipped my way through the crowds, annoying a few people on my way, no doubt.

"Skipping in a crowded hallway is antisocial, Jayne!" he yelled out after me.

"Perfect!" I yelled back.

Poor kid - thought he was gonna shame the maniac out of me. He should have known that was never going to work.

Just then the assistant principal opened his door, interrupting my reverie. He smiled at Brad who returned the smile and gave him a knowing look. Then he turned his head and saw me, scowling in recognition.

Perfect. I tried to duplicate the look Brad had given him, just for fun, but I'm sure my humor was totally wasted on this guy.

"Jayne Sparks, what a surprise. Come into my office and sit."

Just another day of lame-ass high school. All I could think about as he blathered on and on about responsibility and respect was: *When am I finally going to get the hell out of this place?*

*****

I met Tony in front of the school after seventh period so we could walk home together. He lives two streets over from me, less than two minutes on foot.

"How'd your meeting with VP Matthews go today?" he asked.

"Why fine, thank you so much for asking," I answered brightly as I kept walking. Fast.

Tony struggled to keep up with me, carrying his normal hundred pounds of books and wearing his ugly-ass Frankenstein shoes. "Stop screwing around, Jayne; did you get suspended or not?"

"Nope. Just lectured until I wanted to stab myself in the eye with my pen. I actually prefer a suspension - otherwise known as a mini-vacation."

"Well, you're lucky. Anyway, I have news ... *big* news."

I immediately stopped, since Tony never said he had big news ... *it must be really big,* I thought. My unexpected stop caused him to bump into me.

Next thing I knew, his stupid backpack had swung off his

shoulder and hit me in the arm, knocking me off the sidewalk to land in the grass on my butt under a big tree. Leaves cascaded down from its branches, landing all around and on me. I hadn't even touched the tree at all. Sad to think it was the percussion of my ass hitting the ground that had caused the tree to shed its clothing like that.

"*Aaarghh!*" I yelled out as I went down, "Tony what the hell is your problem?!"

"Oh crap, sorry!" He stopped struggling with his bag and rushed over to help me up. "Are you hurt?"

We both froze when we heard the next sound.

"Yo! Look at the two lovebirds under the tree. Whaddya doin' over there, dorks? Having a picnic?"

Brad Powers strikes again. He not only spends his time wooing the hearts of assistant principals and teachers everywhere, he also likes long walks on the beach, reading poetry, and making students who don't look like Barbie dolls feel like complete a-holes.

I stood up, brushing myself off. "Yes, Mr. *Flowers!* We *are* having a picnic! Why don't you come over here and join us? I have something special for you to EAT!"

Tony was sweating, the droplets of water beading up on his forehead as he pleaded with me. "Jayne, don't do it. Just shut up; he's going to pound us."

"Pound us? I highly doubt that. I'm pretty sure I can take him."

"What'd you say, *bitch?"* Brad was crossing the street, obviously planning to come join our picnic.

Tony went into full breakdown mode. "Jaaayyne, he's coming over heeere!"

"Shut up, Baloney, I can see that. Let me handle this."

Tony stood up straight, suddenly resolute, and no longer messing with his bag. "No way, Jayne, you'll get your butt kicked. Step aside."

I was in shock for a split second. My little boy was growing up before my eyes, but there was no time to ponder and sigh. First I had to save my life and the life of my best friend.

Before shit-for-brains could get too close, I stepped out to meet him partway. That was at the curb, where luckily I gained about five inches of height, making me only a few inches shorter than him instead of, like, eight.

He launched the first volley. "You got somethin' to say, *Freak?"* He stopped about two inches from me and engaged me in the high school fighter's stare down. I kick *ass* at that, so I gave him my best stuff. I can look crazy cool with my stare down. At least I think so, but Tony says it just stops at 'crazy' and leaves out the 'cool'.

"Yeah, I got somethin' to say, Flower Boy. *Go fuck yourself* ... how 'bout that?"

The next thing I knew, I was back on the ground under the tree with what felt like the aftershocks of a run-in with a bull, echoing across my chest. *Did he just touch my boobs? Crap, my butt is gonna be sore later.* More leaves sprinkled down around me. It was starting to look like Fall in that one small space next to the sidewalk, except the leaves were green.

Before I could think anything else even more ridiculous, I heard Brad say, "Whoa, hey little dude, just chill."

This is me now: head tilted to the side, confused look of the family dog on my face ... *Do I hear fear in the voice of my worstest enemy, aimed at my bestest friend?*

Yes, I did. I looked over to see my beloved Tone-Tone, pointing what was definitely a real, live nine-millimeter handgun, at Brad Powers. And he did all this standing on the sidewalk. In public. Not twenty yards from the front of the school.

Chapter Two

"TONY, WHAT THE HELL?!" I screamed, sounding like a freaked out girly-girl.

"Don't worry about it, Jayne; I got this one." His face was set with grim determination as he stared at Brad, the gun pointed right at his chest.

I'd never seen Tony look like that. Sweet little Tone-Tone. Shy little Tony Baloney. Frankenstein-messed-up-shoes wearing Tony Green - who right now looked very much like a small and skinny but still very badass Rambo.

"Um, Tony, I don't really know what the hell is going on right now, but you need to put that thing away ... like *now!"*

Brad's self-preservation instincts must have just engaged then because he chimed in with, "Yeah, Tony, you should put that away. You don't want to shoot me; you'll get kicked out of school."

Brad was nobody's dummy, apparently. I knew this line of reasoning would get to Tony for sure, or at least I thought it would.

"Screw school, and screw you too, *Brad.*" The last word was said with such venom, even I was a little scared at this point. Who was this kid, and what had he done with my best friend?

"Brad?" I asked carefully, "What did you do to Tony?"

"Nothin'! I didn't do anything to this little nut job ... he's freakin' out! It's got nothin' to do with me!" He was trying to back up without taking his eyes off the gun.

Tony responded very coolly. "He pushed you down, Jayne; he insulted you. He treats you like you're a piece of garbage all the time. That's not nothing."

To say that I was stunned would be an understatement; but the analysis of this interesting turn of events would have to wait for a time when I wasn't actually fearing that Brad Shit-For-Brains was going to die at the hands of my best, but misguided, friend.

"Tony, dude, it's nothing; he's not worth it. It doesn't bother me, I'm totally fine. Put the gun away and let's get the hell outta here."

I could see him relaxing a little bit, thinking. His grip on the gun loosened ever so slightly. Brad and I waited for Tony's next move.

"You heard her, Powers ... get the hell out." He gestured with the gun, encouraging Brad to move.

Brad didn't need to be told twice. He turned and sprinted away like I'm sure he does on the football field every week, not that I bother going to school games or anything.

Tony lowered the gun, bending over to pick up the backpack he had abandoned on the ground. He casually put the gun inside, zipping the bag up in one, quick motion.

I, on the other hand, was standing there frozen in place, still in shock over what I'd just witnessed.

"Come on, Jayne, let's go." He threw his bag over his shoulder and reached out to grab my elbow. I let him take it because my autopilot seemed to be jammed or something. It was easier at this point to let him call the shots. We walked together towards his house as my mind raced.

What the hell had just happened back there? I snuck a peek at him sideways. He still had that weird, determined look on his face, but otherwise he was old Tony Baloney in his dorky clothes again. I wasn't sure exactly what to say, and I was pretty sure I should be delicate about it, but as you probably have guessed by now, subtlety is not really my style.

"TONY!!!!" I screamed. I stopped walking, turning to face him. "WHATTHEFUCKWASTHAT??!!" I was definitely freaking out.

"Jayne, don't make a big deal out of it ... come on." He tried to urge me forward, but I wasn't having any of that crap.

"I am *not* leaving this spot until you tell me what the hell that was all about! I'm serious!" I crossed my arms for emphasis, as if this would scare my best bud who had now revealed himself to be some sort of commando ninja guy.

"We'll talk about it at my house, I promise. Can we just go? I don't want anyone finding me out here with this thing."

"Okay, yeah, that thing ... that *thing* that happens to be a *gun*. I could see why you wouldn't want to be caught with *that.*" We started walking again, me filling up the empty space around us with my hysteria.

"Because that would mean you'd go to jail and leave me at this shitty school by myself with all these losers who have nothing better to do than crap on me and my friends, not to mention my mother's asshat boyfriend who ... "

Oops. I'd almost spilled the beans there. I tried for a quick recovery.

"Anyway, you need to get rid of that thing. I'll back you up if Shithead tries to turn you in or anything." I focused really hard on looking straight ahead because I knew if I looked Tony in the eyes, I'd cave.

"What are you talking about ... your mother's boyfriend? What's he got to do with anything?" he asked pretty casually, all things considered.

"Nothing ... he's got nothing to do with anything. At all. Forget I said anything." The nervousness set in, making me feel sick to my stomach.

Tony stopped walking and grabbed my arm. "Wait, Jayne, stop for a minute. We should talk about this." He was speaking softer now and sounded so ... patient. And because he was being so sweet, it made me feel even worse, not better.

I stopped walking but kept my eyes straight ahead. He used his puny muscles to push my arm back, effectively turning me around so he could see my face. I refused to meet his eyes, and he knows me well enough to know that's a dead giveaway.

"Look at me, Jayne. Come on. Talk to me about what's going on."

I couldn't look at him. I didn't want to cry, and I knew if I saw his face I wouldn't be able to hold it back. I had this secret shame thing going on that I didn't even like thinking about myself, let alone talking about with Tony.

I took a deep, calming breath. Actually, it was more a wavering breath and not so calming, but I was giving it a try anyway. "I don't wanna talk about it now ... actually not ever, really. Let's get outta here."

I turned, walking away quickly, and Tony let me go. I felt him come up beside me a few seconds later, and we continued on together in silence the rest of the way to his house. I used that time to get a grip on myself.

Mission partially accomplished, autopilot engaged.

*****

Tony's place was empty as usual. His parents are workaholics; I almost never saw them. Tony's an only child who has tons of freedom and opportunity to get into trouble. Up until today, he's never taken advantage of that. I guess he was saving it all up for one, big event. With a gun.

"Wait here," said Tony, dropping his backpack on the ground inside the door. He ran upstairs to his room where I could hear him stomping around, slamming doors and scraping what sounded like furniture across the floor.

A couple minutes later he was downstairs with a bigger backpack in his arms. He dropped it next to the other one.

"Let's get something to eat."

"What's that big bag for?" I asked. "Does this have anything to do with the news you said you had, before we were accosted by Mr. Turdsville?"

He ignored me and went to the kitchen. I stared at the bag, hoping some sort of x-ray vision skills would kick in for me, but no such luck. The mystery bag stayed put, and I followed Tony to the kitchen.

When I got there, he was busy pulling things out of cabinets, laying them out on the counter.

"Um, I'm really not *that* hungry, Tony." I was still feeling queasy, even though the moment of madness had passed.

"That's okay, you'll be hungry later."

"Yeeaaah ... and then I'll have dinner, so I won't need all these ... " I picked up the nearest box he had set down, " ... granola power health bars."

"You're not going home for dinner," was his response.

Now I was confused *and* seriously concerned for my friend's mental health. Even more than I already had been.

"What do you mean, I'm not going home for dinner?"

"I mean, you're not going home for dinner. We're getting the heck outta here. We'll eat on the road."

"On the road where? What are you talking about?" I was trying to remember if we had planned on going to the library or something, but nothing was ringing a bell.

"We're leaving here, Jayne, tonight ... *now* ... so help me pack this stuff." He threw an empty grocery bag in my direction.

Yep. It was now confirmed. He'd definitely lost it.

"Tony, calm down. I know you're a little bit - or maybe a lot - freaked out about what happened back there with Powers, but it doesn't mean you have to leave town or anything. Don't worry, we'll figure something out. He probably won't even say anything to anyone. He won't want anyone to know you got the drop on him."

I was standing there with the empty grocery bag in my hand, hoping my words of reason were making an impact. Tony stopped waiting for me to cooperate and grabbed the bag out of my hand, filling it himself.

"Come on." He took me by the arm, and the three of us - him, me, and his bag of granola bars and juice boxes - walked quickly out of the kitchen and back to the front door by his bags. He shoved the groceries into his big bag and then unzipped his book bag. He took out the gun and threw it into the bigger bag too. He was obviously in total meltdown mode, probably worried about how he was going to be kicked out of the computer club or something.

As freaked out as I was about his behavior, I knew I couldn't leave him here like this. My best bet was to humor him until I could figure out how to calm him down. It never crossed my mind that I would be in danger from my loony friend, because that's what he was - my friend. My best friend, in fact. Today's knight-in-shining-armor-with-a-gun episode proved that.

"Okay, fine. I'm all ears. What's the plan? Where are we going?"

"Don't patronize me, Jayne, I'm serious. We're leaving here."

Hmmm. It appeared my plan wasn't working. Time to get all grown-up on his ass. I gently took his hand, lacing his fingers in mine so he'd quit stuffing things in his commando bag and look at me. He stopped with the packing, staring at our interlocked hands.

"Tony, come on. Look at me."

His eyes remained lowered. "Jayne, I know what happened with your mother's boyfriend; I know what he's done to you. We either have to leave, or I'm going to kill him. It's that simple."

The blood drained out of my face. I dropped his hand, feeling dizzy. *How did he find out?* This wasn't about Brad Powers. This was about my deepest, darkest, ugliest, filthiest secret. The shame. I couldn't deal with it, not now. Not knowing that Tony knew.

I stood up quickly, meaning to leave. Tony must have known my intentions because he jumped up too and ran to the door before I could get there. He stood with his legs and arms spread out wide, his back to the door, facing me.

"I'm not letting you leave without me, Jayne. We stay together; we're a team. We can do this."

I was crying now. I couldn't help it; it was too much. My awful secret was out there, floating in the air between us - unspoken but just as big and real as if I'd vomited it out all over the floor. "We can do *what,* Tony? *Shoot* someone? Show some douchebag who's boss? Because I don't think so! I don't think that's going to work!"

He took a step towards me with the most earnest look on his face ... I could hardly stand it. "We're not going to shoot anyone, Jayne. We don't have to if we leave. But if we stay, I can't promise that won't happen; and I'd like to go to college someday, and not online while I'm wearing an orange jumpsuit, if that's okay with you."

I half choked and half laughed at the visions his words created, and couldn't help but stop crying at the idea of him in an orange jumpsuit tapping away on a huge computer from the eighties with a glowing green screen. "You'd end up being some guy's bitch for sure."

"Yeah, I know. So let's go, get your stuff." He stepped away from the door to get his big bag, leaving the book bag where it was.

For some reason, this was when it really hit me how serious he was. He wasn't taking his school stuff.

I reached down to grab my bag. "Tony?"

"Yeah, Jayne?"

"What the hell?" I searched his eyes for some explanation of what was happening.

"Don't worry, Jayne. I've got it figured out ... well, most of it anyway. We'll get the rest figured out later."

The look on his face just blew me away. He totally meant it. He was so friggin brave and amazing in that moment, I couldn't help it - I leaned in and gave him a quick kiss on his cheek, surprised to feel beard stubble there. "You're my hero."

His face blushed bright red. "Yeah, whatever, come on." He held the door open for me, as usual. Same old Tony - but then again, not the same old Tony. Not the same old Tony at all.

"Does this mean I can't call you Tony Baloney anymore?"

He laughed. "You can call me anything you want, just don't call me late to dinner."

"Ugh, Tony, that is so old. You can do better than that."

"Okay," he said, walking down the front pathway to his driveway, "you can call me anything you want, just don't call me Freak."

"Word to your mutha, Tones."

"Talk about old."

"Whatevs. So, where to?"

"To the bus stop. We're going to Miami."

"What's in Miami?"

"I don't know ... more than what's here."

I shrugged my shoulders. *Might as well.* I pulled out my cell phone. "Okay, so what am I supposed to say to my mother?"

"Tell her we're going to the library to study late. We'll figure out what else to tell her later; we have a few hours."

I made the call really quick and then put my phone in my bag. She never asked questions anymore. I'm not even sure if she'd notice if I never came home; she'd probably be glad. I didn't want to think about why this had become the case at our house because it would harsh my new mellow, and I wasn't ready to get all bummed out again yet. There would be plenty of time for that on our little trip, because I knew Tony wasn't going to ignore my issues forever.

We walked a few blocks over until we got to the main street. We waited at the bus stop for about two minutes before climbing onto the one that took us to the Tri Rail station. We got off the bus and Tony stepped up to the vending machine, buying us two one-way tickets to Miami.

Chapter Three

"OKAY, SO WE'RE HERE ... NOW what?" I hitched my backpack up over my shoulder, looking around the Miami train station. I was hoping Tony had a plan because I sure didn't.

"You guys lost?"

Tony and I turned to look at the guy walking up to us. He seemed to be about our age, maybe a little bit older, definitely scruffier. I was immediately suspicious.

"No, we're not lost, but thanks," said Tony, brushing him off. He dropped his bag from his shoulder to the ground, fishing around in it for what turned out to be a map.

"Why do you need a map if you're not lost?" asked the guy, now standing over Tony's stooped form.

I seriously wasn't in the mood for this. "Dude, we've got a map, therefore, we're not lost. Do you mind?"

He held up his hands in mock surrender. "Yeah, hey, no problem. I was gonna offer you some help, but I guess you don't need it. See ya later." He strolled away, sitting down on a nearby bench and pulling out a cigarette.

"So where are we, Tony?" I asked in a low voice, keeping my eye on Mr. Helpful over on the bench, sure he was up to something.

Tony stood up next to me, showing me the map. "Well, we're here, at the station."

"And we're going ... ?"

"I'm not sure."

I left off monitoring Mr. Helpful to roll my eyes at Tony. "Whaddya mean, you don't know? Where're we going next?"

Tony shrugged his shoulders. "Wherever you want."

"Tony, this was *your* plan! Where are we going? I'm gonna have to call my mom and tell her, eventually."

"Well, to be honest, my plan was to get out of town. I didn't really think much beyond that; I figured you'd come up with something."

I put my fingers on the bridge of my nose, pinching it and squeezing my eyes shut, trying to stop the flood of swear words that were about to fly out of my mouth. "Tones, do you mean to tell me we came all the way down to Miami with fifty bucks between us and no plan at all?"

He looked at me through his impossibly horrible glasses, nodding soundlessly.

I glanced at Mr. Helpful who was smirking, blowing out obnoxious smoke rings.

"Sure you don't need my help?" he asked loudly, not even looking over at us.

I grabbed the map, frustrated, and went over to the bench, Tony on my heels. "Fine. You want to help? Tell us a good place to get some cheap dinner and maybe sleep too." I thrust the map towards him.

The weather was nice; I was thinking we could probably just find a nice spot on a beach somewhere and not worry about spending any money. It would be like camping in the Girl Scouts - not that I had ever done that or anything.

"You don't need a map, just follow me." He got up from the bench, rolling his cigarette between his two fingers until the ash fell off the end.

Tony and I looked at each other. Man, I wished I could speak telepathically with him because I really didn't want Mr. Helpful hearing what I wanted to say.

Tony didn't worry so much about that stuff, apparently. "I don't know, Jayne. We don't even know this guy."

"Oh yeah, sorry about that. Name's Jared ... Jared Bloodworth." Mr. Helpful held out his hand to Tony, putting the no-longer-lit cigarette butt in his front pocket with the other. "You've got nothing to worry about. I'll show you where I stay and you can decide if you want to stay there too or not; it's up to you. Sometimes there's food, too."

Tony took his offered hand, shaking it firmly. I continued to watch Mr. Helpful ... Jared ... trying to figure out if he had any ulterior motives hidden behind his dark brown eyes. I kinda suck at that though, so I gave up, shrugging my shoulders. Tony had his gun, and this guy didn't look too dangerous. He had kind of a freaky name, but that wasn't his fault. He was skinny and not much bigger than me, with brown hair swept around in a casual rocker kind of style. I was thinking I could take him if I had a little adrenaline rush going for me, which I probably would if he were trying to kill me. He looked like he could use a shower, but he didn't exactly appear homeless. His clothes were in decent shape. I still couldn't figure out the cigarette thing, though. Why did he put that disgusting filter in his pocket? I guess it was better than dropping it on the ground. Maybe he was a save-the-environment freak.

Jared strolled ahead of us, not seeming to care whether we followed or not. We walked a few blocks away from the train station, down some streets and alleys, into a commercial warehouse area. It was pretty rundown, some of the businesses having closed a long time ago. Our destination was in the back of a warren of single-story warehouses covered in graffiti.

Jared stopped in front of a beige metal door with a heavy-duty lock on it - the kind that has a thick metal plate over the latch area so no one can pick the lock or crowbar the door open. He banged on the door with his fist. "Open up, it's me, Jared."

Tony and I looked at each other. He put his hand in his bag, making me suddenly very nervous. The last thing I wanted to see was that gun coming out and Tony playing Rambo again.

We heard the lock click open. The door opened a crack while whoever was inside verified it was Jared standing there. The door opened a little bit more and then stopped. "Who the hell are *they?"* The female voice coming from within didn't sound very happy.

"Don't worry about it," said Jared, pushing on the door, opening it the rest of the way, the girl stepping back to make room. "After you," he said, gesturing to the gloomy dark interior.

Even though it was dark inside, the girl at the entrance was easy enough to see, illuminated by the light of the late afternoon Miami sun - bright and hot as hell. She was tall and skinny, a little dirty, hair almost scrappy-looking. None of this, though, could obscure her beautiful face.

Tony was awestruck. I elbowed him in the stomach so he would close his mouth, afraid he was going to drool on me. Tony's reticence about entering the dark warehouse disintegrated in the face of this Aphrodite standing in front of him. He stepped forward, entering the building and disappearing into the blackness within.

Jared stood looking at me expectantly. "What are you afraid of?"

Pfft. "Nothing," I said. False bravado is my friend. I stepped into the darkness behind Tony, hoping I wasn't about to become a teen runaway statistic.

Chapter Four

ONCE INSIDE, OUR EYES ADJUSTED quickly and we could see that Jared and Angry Girl weren't the only ones here. Three other teenagers were sitting on a couch and some chairs set up in the middle of the small warehouse. In the center of this not so cozy space was a banged up coffee table with a group of mismatched burning candles on top.

"Hey, Jared, what's up?" asked one of the kids sitting on the couch. He had a slight southern accent that I identified as coming from central or north Florida - a little rednecky in flavor. I immediately named him Tom Sawyer in my mind because he looked exactly like I always pictured that character - with straw colored hair and freckles, and a devilish look permanently stuck on his face. I could picture him sitting on a dock, fishing in one of central Florida's many gator-ridden lakes.

"Nothin'. Found some lost souls at the station. Meet ... " he gestured to us so we would introduce ourselves.

"Tony. Nice to meet you all."

"Jayne," I said. I wasn't sure yet if it was nice to meet them so I kept it short. Angry Girl was still making me feel a little unwelcome with the cold stare she was giving me. I gave her my hard look, hoping she scared easily. I've been told my hard look is not much scarier than a chipmunk's, but I do what I can.

Angry Girl shut the door behind us.

Tony stepped over closer to me, and I was glad for his nearness. I didn't feel threatened, but this wasn't my usual scene. The living rooms I was accustomed to had lights, electricity, and a house around them. I surveyed the room's vast openness and complete lack of decoration, thinking this would probably be a great place for a rave. I'd never been to one, but I'd seen them in the movies.

Jared asked the group sitting in the chairs, "Where's Spike?"

"He went out to play for a while, scare up some grub," answered Tom Sawyer.

"Spike's our resident musician. He plays over on Fifty-Fourth Avenue and usually makes enough money to buy a pizza and some coke," explained Jared. "Go ahead and have a seat, make yourselves at home." Jared turned his back on us to have a whispered conversation with Angry Girl.

Tony and I walked over and sat down on the couch next to each other and Tom Sawyer. Tony looked nervous, but probably no more than I did.

"So, Tony and Jayne, where are you guys from?" asked a small black-haired girl sitting in one of the chairs.

"West Palm," I said, not sure how much detail she wanted but unwilling to give more.

"Cool, I'm from Tampa. My name's Becky by the way. And that's Finn on the couch next to you from Apopka, Chase there is from Maryland, and Samantha at the door – she's from Miami. Nice to meet you guys."

"Finn?" I got a big grin on my face. I couldn't help it.

"What's so funny?" asked Finn.

"Oh nothing, just ... nothing. Nice to meet you, Finn."

Huckleberry Finn, that is. I had almost gotten it right.

Finn looked at me suspiciously, probably not believing I wasn't somehow mocking him, since I still couldn't get the goofy grin off my face.

The Chase guy just sat there, not saying anything. He didn't look mad - actually he seemed pretty zen. He was sitting down, so I couldn't see all of him, but even so, it was easy to see he was a big guy with broad shoulders and thick legs. His hair was blonde and cut in a military style. He looked like he'd just dropped out of boot camp or something.

Becky seemed pretty nice. I was feeling less nervous being around her. She was super little, so I was pretty sure I could bring her down if need be. She sat cross-legged in the chair, practically bouncing every time she talked. She was one of those types that was always enthusiastic and for no apparent reason. Normally those kind of people bugged me, but she seemed okay.

It got really quiet, so we could hear Angry Girl, otherwise known as Samantha, arguing with Jared. I couldn't really hear what she was saying, but my guess was, she wasn't happy about us being there.

Tony elbowed me in the ribs. I looked at him and he was gesturing not too covertly towards the far wall, off to our right. There were some flattened cardboard boxes, a couple of mattresses, and what looked like some grungy sleeping bags, all set out in neat little rows.

"That's where we sleep," explained Finn, no expression on his face.

Yikes. I wondered if we were going to be invited to sleep there. I was trying to figure out a polite way to turn them down when Samantha and Jared came over.

"Hi. I'm Samantha."

Obviously she'd been forced to play nice. Jared was standing casually off to the side. The pecking order was now becoming clear. Jared, Samantha, maybe Chase, Finn, Becky. *Done.* I wondered how long they had been here and what their stories were.

Tony pushed his glasses up higher on his nose. "Hi, Samantha, nice to meet you."

Tony was always so polite. He was my better half, if it were possible to have a non-romantically involved other half.

"So ... ," I stopped, unable to think of what to say next. I wasn't good with awkward silences.

Someone banged on the door, saving me from my sorry attempt at conversation. Samantha walked over and opened it, admitting a skinny guy with jet black, spiked hair and an acoustic guitar, also black. He walked in sideways, the last thing coming in being his right hand holding up a pizza like a delivery boy.

"Soup's on!" he said cheerfully.

Everyone smiled and offered him their congratulations. Apparently it's a big deal to come back from the streets carrying a pizza.

He brought the food and his guitar over to the sitting area, putting the food down on the table, saying, "Dig in; there's a piece for everyone, even the new guys." He smiled at Tony and me, holding out his now free hand. "I'm Spike. Welcome to our humble home."

Tony and I took turns shaking it. "Jayne and Tony," I said. *Man,* did Spike sure have a cute smile. And cool teeth, if it was possible to have cool teeth. They weren't movie star straight, but for some reason I dug them instantly. They suited his look perfectly - kinda messed up, friendly, sharp on the corners. As I was thinking it, I doubted my own sanity. I saw Tony staring at his smile too, though, so I made a mental note to ask him later what he thought of Spike's teeth . Tony wouldn't think I was crazy, I was pretty sure.

Everyone took a piece of pizza and ate in silence. Spike pulled a two-liter bottle of soda out of his backpack, and everyone but Tony and me took turns swigging directly out of the bottle.

"Worried about cooties?" asked Becky, giggling and then burping the cutest burp ever. *What is it with tiny girls and their tiny burps?* When I burp, I sound like a trucker.

I shrugged. I wasn't going to lie; and I also wasn't going to drink after six pretty scrappy-looking runaways.

I was assuming they were runaways since they looked the part and seemed to be living together here in this warehouse. I could see that they were some sort of cohesive group - maybe not a family in the traditional sense of the word, but they ate together, slept together, and apparently had some sort of agreement between them that Jared was the boss and Spike kept them fed. At least, he provided the pizza and soda, which are two of the four main food groups in my world. I wondered how long they'd been together and how long they'd been living here in this warehouse.

Tony searched around in his bag and pulled out a bottle of water. We shared it, trying not to be too obvious about our cootie aversion. "Trying to cut back on the sugar," I offered as explanation. I'm not sure that they fell for it, but at least they acknowledged my effort to take the sting out of our rejection.

I was starting to feel a little uncomfortable; not because of the company we were keeping but because I had to go to the bathroom pretty badly. We'd been in the warehouse a couple of hours by this time, and so far all I'd been able to see from where I was sitting was the living room, front door, and sleeping area ... no bathroom. Luckily, Tony has a weaker bladder than I do.

"Um, guys, is there a bathroom we could use around here anywhere?" he asked.

"I'll take 'em," said Becky cheerfully. She jumped up off her chair. "Follow me. It's not far."

We grabbed our bags, following her out the door and down the nearby alley.

"So, did you guys just get here from West Palm?" she asked.

"Yeah," said Tony, "just before we came here to your place."

"You gonna stay a while or are you headed somewhere else?"

I elbowed Tony, signaling him not to give our secrets away, even though we really didn't have any secrets.

"Not sure. We don't really have a plan. We were going to find a spot to sleep near the beach or something."

"You don't want to do that," said Becky, a warning note in her voice. "It's not safe. There are some pretty mean guys who go there looking for homeless people - several kids have been beat up pretty bad lately." She turned and walked backwards. "You can stay with us. We've been here a few weeks now. It's not much, but it's dry and safe ... none of those guys know we're here."

"Do you know them – the ones who beat people up?" asked Tony.

"Not *know them* know them, but we're pretty sure we know who they are; gangster types that deal drugs and have prostitutes down there. Some of the beaches aren't too nice at night." She shrugged her shoulders and then turned back around. "Here we are."

We were standing in front of a blue and white port-a-potty.

"It smells pretty bad and it's not the cleanest thing in the world, but it's better than going in the street." She reached into her pocket and pulled out a wadded-up napkin, handing it to me. "Here, use this. It's mostly clean."

I took the napkin, staring at it. *So this is what my life's come to. I'm a teenage runaway using an abandoned port-a-potty and a gently-used Burger King napkin to wipe my nether regions. Oh well. At least I'm not getting my ass kicked down on the beach by a drug-dealing pimp.*

"Thanks," I said, opening the door to the bathroom. "*Whoof!* Holy batballs ... what died in this thing?" I desperately waved my hand back and forth in front of my face, trying to get the smell away, but it just stirred it up worse. I was pretty sure the stink molecules had gotten stuck to my nostril hairs.

"Don't breathe through your nose. You'll get used to it."

I looked at her in horror. "*Used to it?* I think not." But I held my breath and went in anyway; I really had to go bad.

I tried not to touch anything, which was difficult because it was such a small space. I peed faster than I've ever peed before, and jumped out before I had even zipped up my pants. Tony had already done his business around the corner. This was not the first time in my life I wished I could pee standing up.

"Well, that was an adventure," I said, praying the smell of the craphole wasn't in my clothes or hair.

Becky smiled. "Life is never boring when you're on Jared's crew."

"Jared's crew?" I asked.

"We just call ourselves that, like a joke kind of. Jared is our unofficial leader. He found all of us and the warehouse. He's a good guy; he makes sure we stay safe and somehow get fed every day."

"How did he find all of you?" asked Tony, apparently as curious as I was about how this particular group of teens had ended up together.

"Oh, I don't know. He found me panhandling downtown. Samantha was in a fight outside a club one night when Jared found her."

"Surprise, surprise," I said. She seemed like a scrapper.

"She's not bad once you get to know her; she's just protective of our space. I think she's had some hard times ... we all have." She looked sideways at me. "Haven't you? Isn't that why you're here? Not many kids end up on the streets of Miami if they have a great life back home."

Tony opened his mouth to say something, but I didn't want this conversation going too far down confession lane, so I jumped in. "We just needed to get out of town for a few days, no big deal really. We'll be leaving soon."

Becky shrugged. "Whatever. Jared brought you to the warehouse, so that means you're part of the crew for as long as you want to be ... as long as you follow the rules anyway."

Okay, here comes the good stuff ... where they tell us we have to sacrifice a chicken or something to be a part of their club. "What rules?" I asked.

"No fighting, no drugs, no alcohol, no stealing, no bringing in strangers until Jared has checked them out ... and no littering."

I decided to test her. "What about the chicken sacrifices?" I wasn't sure exactly what the pass/fail on this question was, but it came out of my mouth before I could stop it, so I went with it.

Becky laughed. "No chicken sacrifices. No animals, actually; we don't want any barking or whatever telling people we're here. We have to lay low so we don't get kicked out."

"Seems reasonable," said Tony, obviously thinking out loud.

"Becky, will you excuse us a sec - I want to talk to Tony privately ... no offense."

"Oh, don't worry, none taken. I'll meet you back at the warehouse; it's just up there on the right." She smiled like a fool and then took off jogging towards the door we could see from where we were standing.

I stopped, grabbing Tony by the arm. "So, what do you think?" I asked.

"I don't know; they seem nice. They shared their dinner with us.

And they don't sacrifice animals, so that's a point in their favor." Tony smiled at me. "I can't believe you said that ... no wait ... I *can* believe you said that."

"Yeah, well, you would have been pretty upset if they were animal sacrificers and they just sprung it on us later."

Tony laughed. "You're nuts. So are we staying with them or what?"

I thought about it for about two seconds, but I couldn't come up with any better options. "At least for tonight, since you don't have a friggin' clue what we're doing or where we're going or even how we're going to afford to feed ourselves."

"Yeah, well, we had to get outta there. And we still haven't really talked about why, Jayne."

I had to shut him up because I didn't want to talk about this issue we'd been dancing around. "Yeah, you and your Rambo moves with a-hole Flowers ... "

It was too dark now for me to see Tony's face, but I knew he was giving me one of his parent looks.

"That's not what I was talking about and you know it."

I pulled my phone out of my bag. "I have to text my mom. I'm telling her I'm staying at your place."

"You've never stayed the night at my place before. Think she'll buy it?"

"She doesn't care, Tony, trust me."

I sent off the text and a few seconds later I got 'OK' in return from her number. That's it. I shoved the hurt feelings down deep because I was not ready or willing to deal with them right now.

I showed him my screen. "See?"

Tony shrugged. "I can't do that with my parents. I'm going to tell them I'm at Robert's house - he'll cover for me." Tony sent off the texts to his parents and his chess club buddy, putting his phone back in his bag once he'd received confirmation that everything was okay. "We're all set."

I walked towards the warehouse, and Tony followed, saying, "We have to talk about this other issue, Jayne."

"I'm not talking to you about that crap right now. What I want to know is, first of all, what is with the no littering rule? And second of all, do I have to sleep on one of those gnarly sleeping mats they had? Because I'm already feeling itchy just thinking about it."

Tony jogged to catch up to me. "I think Jared is a tree-hugger or something so that's why he doesn't litter; and so you know, I brought two ultra-thin sleeping bags from my dad's camping stuff. If you want, we can just grab a cardboard thing for insulation and sleep in the bags on top."

I threw my arm across Tony's shoulders. "*That* is why you are my best friend."

"Because I bring sleeping bags when we run away?"

"Yes. Because even when you have your head totally up your butt and drag me to Miami with only fifty bucks in your pocket, you still make sure that I have a nice, clean place to sleep."

"Did I mention that I also brought a blow up mini pillow for your head?"

"Did I mention that I love you?"

We reached the door and stood there in the near dark, facing each other.

"So we're doing this? We're going to sleep with Jared's crew tonight?" I asked.

"Yep, for tonight. Then we decide what to do in the morning."

I banged on the door for admittance. "It's us - Tony and Jayne."

The lock clicked open and the door swung in a few inches to

reveal Samantha standing in the opening. "Oh. You're back."

"Disappointed?" I asked, ready to call her bluff. I knew how this crew operated. Jared called the shots, not her.

She snorted, stepping aside, opening the door the rest of the way. I thought as I walked by I saw her smile, but I couldn't be sure. Her face was quickly hidden in shadows as she moved to close and lock the door behind us.

Chapter Five

"HOLY CRAP, TONES, MY BACK is killing me." I tried to move out of my sleeping bag, but my body didn't want to cooperate. The floor was concrete and the cardboard box that had been my mattress was useless. My teeth felt like they had sweaters on them, and my tongue was covered in some kind of heinous goo. *How do homeless people do this every day?* I decided then and there that I needed to *not* be homeless - or at least be homeless for as short a period of time as possible.

"Mine too," he groaned out. "I think this is what arthritis feels like."

Everyone around us was waking up. Jared had gone to the door, propping it open with a rock, letting the sunshine in.

"Another beautiful day in paradise," he said, pulling a cigarette pack out of his pocket.

I walked up to look out the door. "Those things'll kill ya, you know."

"We're all going to die sooner or later," he said, lighting the end of it. "Some of us much later."

"Better later than sooner," was Tony's reply as he walked by both of us and out into the sun. "Where's a good place to get some food for breakfast?"

The others joined us outside, rubbing faces and heads, trying to wake up the rest of the way. Finn was the first one to respond.

"There's a 7-11 four blocks thatta way." He gestured off towards the train station.

"Chase likes to go to the IHOP which is about a quarter mile that way; but it costs more money," said Becky, smiling already even though it was only eight in the morning.

Why is she so happy all the time? Sometimes happy people annoy me this early in the morning.

Chase just stood there saying nothing, swinging his torso left and right to crack his back. Samantha stood apart from the rest of the group, playing with the tip of a blade sticking out of her Swiss army pocketknife. She and Chase made a good couple - a silent, angry couple.

I looked around and realized someone was missing. "Where's Spike?"

"He'll be here soon. He's a night owl; he usually sleeps during the day," explained Becky.

Sure enough, no sooner were the words out of her mouth, when Mr. Dark and Sexy came around the corner, walking towards us.

"Hey, guys, what's up?"

"Nothin'," answered Becky. "Anything interesting happen last night?"

"Only this!" he said excitedly, pulling out a piece of folded-up paper from one of his pockets. He handed it to Jared, who put his cigarette in his mouth and went quiet for a few seconds, reading it.

"What is it?" asked Finn.

"A job we can all do, and it pays good too," said Spike.

"Where'd you find this?" asked Jared.

"It was hanging in the laundry place we use, the Wash-n-Fold over on fifty-second."

Jared took the cigarette out of his mouth and rolled it between his fingers, causing the entire end of hot ash to fall off. He put the butt in his pocket.

Why in the heck does he keep doing that? I was going to have to ask him one of these days.

Samantha walked over to stand by Jared's side, looking over his shoulder. "What is it?"

Jared read aloud from the paper.

"Institutional clinical trial, seeking physically fit test subjects to participate in fitness activities/focus group study. Compensation $500 paid to those who complete the test. Time required: five days. Must be eighteen or over to participate."

"What kind of fitness activities?" asked Samantha.

"Five hundred bucks? That's a lotta spendin' cash," said Finn, obviously impressed.

Jared continued. *"Informational meeting and pre-screening to take place on March third at one o'clock p.m., Miami Hyatt, Hacienda Meeting room. Sponsored by One Eleven Group."*

"That's today," said Becky.

Jared stared at the paper. I watched his eyes go back and forth, re-reading it several times. He sighed, folding it up and putting it in his back pocket.

"Whaddya think?" asked Finn.

Everyone waited for Jared's answer. I looked at Tony, and he shrugged his shoulders slightly. I was thinking about the five hundred bucks. Tony and I were pretty physically fit, probably him more than me, and it wasn't like we had anything else to do. Plus, we needed some money if we were going to work on that not-being-homeless thing, which was pretty high on my priority list right now.

"Let's have a meeting," said Jared, turning to go back into the warehouse. Everyone but Tony and I followed him in.

"What do you think?" I asked Tony.

"Might as well go to the informational meeting ... we need some money."

"Yeah, that's what I was thinking."

Becky stuck her head out the door. "Are you guys coming?"

Tony and I shared a look and then went inside. We weren't officially part of the crew, but I wanted to hear what they were going to do.

"So, show of hands, who thinks we should go check it out?" asked Jared.

Everyone but Chase raised their hands.

"Chase, what's up?" asked Jared.

Everyone stared at the guy who never talked. *This should be interesting. Maybe he's one of those guys who only speaks every once in a while, but when he does it's really earth-shattering.*

"Dunno," he said, shrugging his shoulders.

Or not.

"Come on, you must be thinking something, otherwise you would've raised your hand."

"Just seems like a lot of money for a fitness test."

"That's what I was thinking, too," said Jared, sounding a little bit concerned.

Becky looked at Tony and me. "What about you guys? Are you going to go?"

I looked at Tony and he nodded his head, so I said, "We're going to go check it out, see what's what. It's just an informational meeting - can't hurt just to go hear what they have to say."

Jared looked at his crew to gauge their reactions. Everyone

seemed to be in agreement. "Unless anyone has any objections, I say we all go to the meeting, like Jayne and Tony are, see what's going on with this test and if it's something we want to do."

"Cool!" said Becky excitedly.

"Awesome," said Finn, also looking happy.

"Whatever," said Samantha, getting up to go back outside, probably to go sharpen her knife or something.

Chase nodded his head once.

Spike smiled with those amazing teeth of his, blazing white, right at me. "See you there. I'm gonna catch some Zs now." He got up off the couch, walked over, and leaped onto a mattress. I heard him snoring less than a minute later.

Chapter Six

TONY AND I ATE A quick breakfast of granola bars and juice boxes from his duffle bag in companionable silence, while we sat on the beach listening to the rhythmic sounds of the waves and the seagulls screeching above. I picked up some thick-grained sand, examining it closely. I'd seen sand lots of times, but never paid much attention to it before. I realized I was holding a million or so tiny pieces of rock and seashell in my hand; it made me wonder how many other little details of life I'd missed along the way. I let the sand filter out through the cracks in my fingers while I scanned the shoreline for evidence of beat-up homeless teens, thankfully not finding any. The sun was already soothingly warm on my skin, and the sand sure felt like a more comfortable place to sleep than that concrete floor. Becky's warnings were getting farther and farther away in my mind.

Tony sucked the last of his juice from his juice box. "I think we would have been more comfortable out here on the sand last night than on that concrete."

I just stared at him, a little creeped out by the fact that he'd just read my mind. He really needed to stop doing that.

Tony noticed my look. "What? What'd I say?"

I shook my head, unwilling to speak about it.

"Tell me."

"It's nothing."

Tony stared at me for a few seconds, making me wish I could read *his* mind. He was very busy thinking something that looked important.

"Spike has a nice smile," he said, looking at me intently.

I didn't know what to say at first. *Yes,* Spike did have a nice smile, and really awesome teeth, but why would Tony bring that up now? And why did he say it at all? I'd never mentioned Spike's smile to him, and we weren't talking about Jared's crew at that moment.

Tony kept staring at me, and it was starting to freak me out a little. I realized he was waiting for an answer.

"Yeah, he does."

"See, I already knew that you liked his smile."

"Am I that transparent?" *Shit.* I thought I was being all cool when I was checking him out. I hate when people catch me oogling someone.

"Not to other people, but to me you are."

"Well, you know me better than anyone else in the world, so that's not surprising."

Tony remained silent for a minute, as if he were searching for what he wanted to say - I could see it on his face. I waited patiently for what was coming; it seemed important to him.

"It's more than that."

"More than that? Like how?" I'm not sure I really wanted to know but I asked anyway. Stupid me.

Tony drew shapes in the sand with his finger, avoiding my gaze. "Do you want to know why I had that gun in my bag? Why I had this plan to leave town?"

Uh-oh. We were here now ... talking about stuff I'd rather not be talking about.

"No, but that's okay. I'm sure you had your reasons and I'm here to support you." Maybe he'd go for the distractor.

"Listen, Jayne, we have to talk about this."

I sighed. He wasn't going to let it go. I was feeling sick again. "Whatever." My usual sarcasm wasn't jumping to my lips. All I had left was helplessness, and that just pissed me off.

"I want to tell you something that happened to me a couple weeks ago," said Tony, still swirling his fingers around in the sand.

This sounded safer than talking about me, so I felt a little bit better already. "Okay ... "

"I was in bed, ready to fall asleep ... maybe I was already a little asleep ... and suddenly I heard you yelling. At first I was thinking it was there in my house, the yelling, but then I realized it was in my dream - but I wasn't dreaming. I was in some sort of sleep state, but not totally asleep ... do you know what I mean?" He looked at me for confirmation.

I had to be honest. "No, not really."

"Well, anyway, I couldn't help myself - I fell deeper into this state, whatever it was, and I was suddenly *with* you. I couldn't see anything, but I could hear you and feel your panic, your anger ... your fear."

My face was burning. I knew the night he was talking about. It was the first night that my mother's boyfriend had come into my room.

"I didn't have to see to know what was happening, Jayne. He was there. Your mother's boyfriend."

"I get it! You don't have to say it!" I yelled, standing up and unintentionally spraying sand all over Tony's lap. "I don't want to re-live it, okay?!"

I walked towards the water, leaving my bag behind. I just needed to get away from what he was saying. I'd tried to forget that night and the few others that had happened since. Nightmares. His beer-stinking breath, fumbling hands. I learned after the first night to lock my door. When that didn't work, I had weapons ready. Asshole didn't know what hit him.

Tony was struggling behind me, carrying both of our bags. "Wait! Jayne, wait! I'm sorry!"

I stopped, giving him a chance to catch up.

Tony was practically wheezing by the time he got to me. "I'm sorry. I'm ... " He had to stop to catch his breath. "I didn't mean to ... make you upset. I just wanted ... to try and figure out ... ," he dropped the bags at our feet, " ... why it is that I'm in your head sometimes ... "

I realized what he was trying to say, and the horribleness of my situation became overshadowed by the strange, otherworldly stuff he was describing.

"In my head?" The idea of Tony in my head was both scary and entertaining at the same time.

"Kind of – yeah."

"What's it like in there?" I was smiling now, thinking of all the ways I could torture Tony without lifting a finger. Too bad the kid was as loony as a ... loon.

"Why aren't you taking this seriously?" he asked, frustrated.

"Because, Tony, it's ridiculous. You had some crazy, effed up dream, and now suddenly you're in my head."

"It wasn't a dream, Jayne. I heard you; I felt your feelings. Don't try to tell me something didn't happen with him."

"You're just projecting or something," I said, defensively.

"Oh, yeah? Well how did I know you liked Spike's smile or his teeth or something? And by the way, that's a little crazy, liking someone's teeth, don't you think?"

I didn't know what to say. It probably *was* weird to like

someone's teeth, but how the heck did he know I'd thought that?

I was willing to consider his arguments, but still wasn't convinced. "You just liked his teeth and now you're acting like it's me who liked them. Or, you're trying to do some kind of brainwashing thing."

"I've got one thing to say to you," said Tony, a defiant look on his face.

I hate that look; I usually see it on those rare occasions when Tony finally puts his foot down and I had to let him have his way. *Not this time, buddy,* I was thinking.

He said two words: "*Tom Sawyer*."

My eyes bugged out of my head. *"No!"*

"Yes!"

"Tony, that is just *rude!"*

"What's rude?"

"Getting in my head like that! Those thoughts are *private!"*

Tony nearly exploded. "I *know* that! Do you think I *want* to be in your head? Do you think I want to wander around in that crazy place you call your mind? I don't want to be in there! I care about you, you know that, you're my best friend. But seriously, no offense ... I could never ever go back there again and be *perfectly* happy for the rest of my life. Do you know how *busy* your head is? Like, *all the time* busy. You never stop flooding your brain with thoughts and emotions and ideas and feelings ... it's exhausting!" He stopped to catch his breath, but before I could get a word in edgewise, he was off again. "I would do *anything* to stop it, but I can't control it. One minute I'm drifting off to a nice, quiet, uninteresting sleep and then all of a sudden - *bam* - I'm there in your bedroom ... or I'm in your brain in History class, or Psychology or Health class. Health class! Can you imagine what that's like for me in your head during *Health?!"*

I couldn't help it; I giggled. We had just recently been going over the male genitalia in that class. It was super hilarious, and I did spend an inordinate amount of time running some internal commentary in my head while looking at the pictures we were seeing on the teacher's slideshow.

"It's not funny. It's been torture for me, not saying anything to you. We have to figure out how to turn this thing off." Tony was trying to stay serious, but he couldn't help laughing along with me, particularly since my giggles had turned into hardcore cracking-up at this point.

"What am I thinking ... right now?" I had a hard time saying it because I couldn't stop snorting. I was focusing really hard on recalling the picture of a cross section of a testicle from page fifty of our textbook. Don't ask me why I remember the page number.

"It doesn't work like that, thank God. It only happens sometimes and not when I try to do it."

"When you *try?* Tony, have you *tried* to get into my head?" I looked at him suspiciously, the laughter fading quickly.

He started to squirm a little. "No, not really. Well, okay, I did try a couple times ... but not to invade your privacy!" He could see I was getting cranky, so he tried quickly to calm me down. "I just wanted to see if I could turn it on, because I figured if I could turn it on, I could learn how to turn it off, see?" He looked at me hopefully, a little bit of desperation in his eyes.

"Fine." I sighed. It made sense. I knew for sure I wouldn't want to be floating around in his head. I loved the guy, but I preferred to keep a little mystery in our relationship. "So, you don't know what I'm thinking right now?"

"No. I just get the slight feeling that you're not so mad anymore. You were mad earlier."

"Right. You're right - I *was* mad, but I'm not anymore. I know you wouldn't do anything to hurt me on purpose."

"Never in a million years," said Tony, earnestly.

I grabbed my backpack off the sand. "Well, nobody ever said life with me was going to be dull."

Tony grabbed his bag too. "Nope. Never has been, so I don't expect it will be anytime soon."

We stood on the beach smiling at each other. That lasted a full two seconds before Tony had to go ruin it with his persistence again. I think maybe he learned a little of that from me.

"So, about your mother's boyfriend ... "

"Leave it!" I said forcefully, walking away.

"I just wanted to ask you what you did. I know you did something that made you very happy." He was walking at my elbow now, refusing to be left behind. "You kicked his ass, didn't you?" He was smiling, like he already knew the answer.

"You were there, you tell me," I challenged, still miffed at him that he wouldn't let it drop.

"I told you, it doesn't work like that. I don't *see* anything; I hear and feel ... that's it. I felt ... triumph. That's the only way to describe it."

I smiled in bitter memory of that night. "Yep, you could call it 'triumph'."

"Tell me, Jayne; stop playing with me."

"Fine, you really want to know? I'll tell you. That night, the third night he came - after I found out the bastard could pick my lock - I was waiting for him. I had my softball bat in bed with me. When he came over and tried to touch me, I pulled the bat out and jabbed him in the nuts with it; and then when he was down on the floor, I took my dad's old electric hair razor, and I buzzed off one of his eyebrows and shaved a strip down the side of his head before he got away."

Tony's eyes nearly fell out of his head; he was unable to speak for a full five seconds. Then he whispered, "No?!"

"Yep." I stared straight ahead, no expression on my face. "Why do you think he left town that night, not even saying goodbye to my mom? No way was he going to be able to explain that shit away."

"Holy crap, Jayne." He was smiling. "Remind me never to get on your bad side."

"Yeah, well, don't ever try to put your grubby hands on me in the middle of the night and you won't have anything to worry about."

He looked at me, a little concerned, before he caught my smile. We both laughed at the same time. I was thinking about what that perv had looked like when he hobbled out the door that night minus one eyebrow and a strip from his hair. Tony was probably laughing because he felt sorry for me, but what the hell - it felt good.

"I'm so glad you're my friend, Jayne," said Tony, putting his arm around my shoulders. He still loved me, even though that slimy douche had tried to put his hands on me.

"Me too, Tones, me too. Want to go back to the warehouse? See what everyone else is doing?"

"Nah, let's go to the library ... use their computers to go on the Internet and see what we can find out about that company doing the fitness study."

I nodded in appreciation of his brilliance. "Excellent idea. We can also look up 'psychic phenomenon', see what we can do about this gift of yours - or curse, depending on how you look at it." We reached the seawall that ran the length of the beach, bordered on one side by the sand and the other by a wide sidewalk, now empty. It was still too early for many people to be out. We climbed over the wall and stood there, looking up and down the street that was about ten feet away.

"So where's the library?" I asked.

"I have no idea."

I rolled my eyes. "Tony, Tony, Tony ... what am I going to do with you?"

"What? ... We're not lost ... we have a map, remember?" He smiled at me with a cocky grin.

I wasn't used to seeing that on his face, but I liked it. I liked it a lot. "You'd better be careful, Tones. I think I'm being a bad influence - rubbing off on you."

"Yeah, well, I don't think that's so bad," he said, dropping his bag off his shoulder and bending down to retrieve the map from inside.

I looked out across the distant ocean while he figured out where we needed to go. The same waves were crashing on the shore, over and over. The seagulls were still screeching. I was still surrounded by millions of pieces of crushed up rock and seashell. Everything was the same, and yet, everything had changed, too. Funny how change can sneak up on you when you least expect it.

Chapter Seven

WE FOUND NOTHING OF USE on the Internet. There was no record of a One Eleven company being registered as a business in Florida. After searching around for an hour and then browsing through some books and magazines for another two, we decided to head over to the area where the informational meeting was being held. It was only about five blocks away. The sun wasn't shining as brightly as it had been earlier, and the temperature had dropped a little too, but that wasn't so unusual for this time of year in Florida. In Spring, the weather tended to be a little fickle.

We stopped at a sandwich shop and got a sub and a soda, sharing it on our way to the hotel meeting room. I told the guy making our sandwich to hold the onions, but he'd obviously ignored me. I was hoping to see Spike again soon, but now I was worried that I'd breathe my horrid onion breath on him and he'd never want to talk to me up close again ... or do other stuff. *Hey ... a girl can dream, right?*

"Whatever you're thinking about right now, stop," said Tony, as he pushed on the revolving door at the hotel entrance.

I walked next to him in a slow circle towards the hotel's interior. "What's the matter, getting you nervous?"

"No, you're feeling all warm and stuff, and it makes me feel funny," he said, not meeting my eyes.

"Wow. This does complicate things, doesn't it?" I didn't want to think of all the ramifications. "I thought it only happened when you were going to sleep."

"I think when you're close to me, it's easier to fall into that state of connectedness. When you're far, it has to be a stronger emotion or I have to be in some sort of sleep-like state. That's my theory right now. Don't hold me to it though; it could change."

Our Internet search on psychic reading abilities had spewed out so much garbage, it was hard to filter through it all to come up with something that made sense. There were so many kooks out there claiming to be psychics and vampires and God knows what else. It was frustrating trying to find real information. We decided to go back another time and look again. We'd run out of time and mojo to do it any longer today.

We got directions from someone at the front desk to the meeting room, and arrived at the door to find Chase, Finn, Samantha, and Becky waiting out front.

"Hey, guys!" said Becky, cheerfully. "You made it!"

"Yeah. What's going on? You guys going in?" I asked.

"We're waiting for Jared and Spike," said Finn.

"Anyone else here?" asked Tony.

"Yeah, there's a couple people already in there ... some ol' lady, an ol' guy too. Can't tell if the person runnin' the show is here or not ... don't look like it." Apparently, Finn had been assigned the mission of scoping out the room ahead of time.

"I guess we'll see you guys in there, then," I said, nudging Tony's arm. He was busy acting like he wasn't staring at Samantha again. She was looking in the opposite direction, down the hall, oblivious to his crush.

We went in and took seats in the middle - not all the way in front and not in the back. It wasn't in my nature to be an eager beaver, but I also didn't want to look like a total slacker - there was five hundred bucks on the line, after all. The middle was the best place. I could tell, though, that Tony wanted to be in the front row. He was a front row, note-taking kind of guy. Two years of me still hadn't broken him of that. It was probably for the better.

Soon enough, Jared and Spike arrived. The rest of the crew came in, taking seats in various places. They didn't sit right next to each other, with the exception of Chase and Becky, who sat together on the right side of the room. I wondered about that, assuming they would all want to present a united front. I also wondered if Chase and Becky had something going on. *That would be an odd couple.* I would have expected her to be with Finn before Chase. For some reason, I was pairing Chase and Samantha up in my mind; but what did I know? Tony would say that I suck at matchmaking. He had the scars to prove it, too.

Spike flashed Tony and me a smile as he moved across the room. I tried to keep my blood pressure under control, but it was hard. I kicked Tony under the table in case he was creeping around in my head. I didn't need him knowing I was getting all hot and bothered over a stupid smile. *But damn, Spike has the coolest teeth!*

At one o'clock on the dot, the door opened and a man walked in. He was old. I don't know how old exactly because I'm terrible at guessing ages, but he had silver hair. It was thick and kind of wavy. Not long, but not military short either. He wore a silver-gray suit. It wasn't quite shiny, but I wouldn't say it was dull either. His eyes were the most striking thing about him - they were icy gray and matched his suit really well, actually. I never thought about matching my eyes to my clothes, which was probably a good thing, since they're a mottled combination of mostly green, with brown and gold - a hazel mix that looked a lot like camouflage. I didn't look good in army gear.

When the old guy smiled, I noticed that he had movie star teeth; they were perfectly straight and dazzling white. But they weren't nearly as interesting as Spike's choppers.

"Hello, and welcome to the informational meeting sponsored by One Eleven Group. I assume you have all read the advertisement and know that we are seeking some very special candidates to participate in a study we are conducting. This is a fitness-type study, so it does have some basic physical and mental health requirements. The purpose of today's meeting is to give you information about the study and, for those of you who are interested in participating, a battery of tests to determine your suitability." He looked out over the group of us, resting his eyes on no one in particular. I was waiting to hear clues about the test or about this One Eleven company while also sneaking glances at Spike. I could only see the back of his head and part of his face. *Dammit.*

"The test will commence tomorrow; we are truly sorry about the short notice. We had some scheduling conflicts, so it couldn't be avoided. Hopefully, this will not interfere with your ability to participate." He stopped to share a smile with us. It was very cool and professional, not reaching his eyes.

"The test itself lasts three full days, and then there will be one day after for our ... *ahem* ... focus group." He reached down to take a sip of water from the glass on the table next to him; he seemed to have a bit of a frog in his throat.

He continued, "You will be provided transportation from the Miami Executive Airport to the test location. After the test is complete, you will be brought back to the same airport. For those who finish the test successfully, you will be paid five hundred dollars in cash upon arrival at the airport. For those of you who do not finish the test, but who do complete parts of it, you will receive compensation based on how much of the test you do complete." He clasped his hands together and gave one of those million-dollar smiles again. "Does anyone have any questions?"

I saw the crew look around at each other and then at Jared. He just stared at the guy in gray. Tony leaned in towards me and whispered, "Do we have any questions?"

I decided not to wait for anyone else to break the ice. "Where is your company from and what is the purpose of this test?" *There. That'll get the ball rolling.*

"And your name is, Miss ... ?"

"Jayne."

"Thank you, Jayne, for your question. One Eleven Group is a think tank of sorts, located overseas, mainly in France, but we have branches elsewhere as well. Its purpose is to study humans ... people ... in their environments, and through our tests, we seek to identify those who have certain qualities, so that we can better understand our possible futures."

Well that's about as clear as mud. "Thank you, mister ... sorry, I don't remember your name."

"Oh, no, my apologies, Jayne, I should have introduced myself already. My name is Anton Dardennes." He said it with some kind of accent ... maybe French, I wan't sure. It sounded cool, though. I could never say it the way he did; there was something going on with that 'r' of his. It almost sounded like he said 'Doll-den'.

I noticed Finn and Becky looking over at me. I caught their eyes and they both nodded slightly. Apparently, they approved of my questions. I waited to see who else was going to get to the bottom of this mysterious test.

Chase leaned over to whisper in Becky's ear. As soon as he straightened, she raised her hand.

Mr. Dardennes gestured to her raised hand. "Yes?"

"I ... I mean, *we* ... we were wondering, where is the test location?"

"The test location is confidential. We will bring you there and back, but we cannot reveal its exact location because we do not wish to compromise the validity of our test results."

Another clear as mud answer. Normally when someone doesn't give me information I think I should have, I am instantly on my guard. But for some reason, this particular secret didn't seem like that big of a deal to me. I couldn't see how it would hurt us not knowing where we were going. I decided to let that one slide. I looked at Tony and he gave me a slight nod, as if he agreed. *Maybe this mind reading stuff isn't all bad,* I thought.

"If there are no more questions, we can commence with the battery of tests. For those of you not interested in participating, we ask that you leave now. The next phase of this meeting will take approximately one hour. There will be a written exam and then an interview."

We waited to see if anyone was going to get up, but everyone stayed. Apparently no one else was feeling too concerned about the lack of specific information either.

The door opened and another man came in, carrying a stack of papers. I almost laughed when I saw him because this guy was the last person you'd expect to see being some kind of secretary. He was super buff - even with the suit he was wearing, you could see it. His neck was thick, his hair short. He looked like a combat guy dressed up in his Sunday best. He spoke quietly with Mr. Dardennes for a minute before Mr. Dardennes left the room.

The buff guy walked around he room, giving each of us a packet of papers as he passed by. He didn't look at anyone, keeping his eyes focused on the materials in his hands and where he was walking.

On the top of the papers he handed us was a basic application form, asking for our name, address, phone number and other similar stuff. There were also some health questions like you'd answer on a doctor's office form.

Buff-Guy stood at the front of the room, speaking in a deep, gravelly voice that was slightly accented. He had a different type of accent than Mr. Dardennes did - possibly Slavic or Russian or something.

"Please fill out the forms on top. After you have completed your papers, put them on the table up here. When everyone has finished that part, we will begin the written test. It will be timed and you will have thirty minutes to complete it." He turned and left the room.

Everyone began filling out the forms. I looked at Tony and gestured towards the name and address section. He gave a very slight shake of his head, agreeing with me that we shouldn't put our real information down. I remembered the ad said we had to be eighteen to participate. Tony and I were both still seventeen. I nudged him and pointed to the birthday question on the form, subtracting a year off my date to qualify myself, watching as Tony did the same. For our addresses, we both used a street near our high school. It was more like a fib than an outright lie - I mean, it was in the same neighborhood, at least. If they asked me for identification, I was going to say that I didn't have any. It wasn't that strange to not have a driver's license in Miami ... the public transportation was pretty good. Hopefully, since the One Eleven guys weren't from Florida, they wouldn't know any better about West Palm. Without a driver's license there, you would be stranded most of the time. It wasn't that the city didn't have public transportation, it was just that I normally wouldn't be caught dead on it. There were some serious weirdoes on those buses, which Tony and I found out firsthand when we took the bus to the Tri-Rail station. One guy was sitting in his seat, yelling at no one in particular. He seemed to be hearing an invisible person talking back, too, the way he was one minute shouting and the next minute listening to a response that neither Tony nor I could hear. It seemed like a lot more time than just one day had passed since Tony and I had been on that weird little adventure.

Tony elbowed me out of my daydream. "You done?" he asked, standing to go up to the front with his form.

I signed at the bottom of the form, under some disclaimer I didn't bother reading. "Yep. Here ... " I gave him my paper, and he left to deliver them both to the table in front. My dad is a lawyer and would have flipped his wig over me signing a form before reading the legal stuff. That was part of the reason why I made it a policy not to. My dad was a real dickwad, so it made me happy to do things that got under his skin.

Not long after, everyone else finished their forms and stacked them on the table in the front of the room. I was curious about what Jared's crew was going to use as addresses and birthdays. I'd bet Becky wasn't eighteen yet ... probably not Finn either. The others probably were, though. They looked older, especially Jared.

Mr. Dardennes walked back into the meeting room with Buff-Guy. "Anyone need more time?" he asked, looking around. When no one answered, he continued. "Good, then let's begin with the timed test." He picked up the forms we had just completed from the table and handed them to his assistant, who left the room.

"Please break the seal on your packet. You will find an answer sheet under the first page. Take it out and fill in your names at the top. Don't bother filling out the other information." He waited two minutes while we did that.

I felt like I was getting ready to take the pre-S.A.T. test in school again.

"This test is timed. You will have thirty minutes to complete it. Please read the instructions carefully before answering the questions. Good luck ... you may now begin."

I turned the page on the test to reach the first question. 'How many hours per day do you sleep?' *Hmmm. That's a tough one.* My answer depended on whether there was anything interesting going on. I marked an answer and moved on, not believing for a second that it even mattered.

'Do you ever have a sense of déjà vu?' *Of course, doesn't everyone? Next question ...* 'Do you ever hear voices telling you to do things?' *Oh, come on, who's going to say yes to that? Next ...* 'If you were going to take a vacation of your choice, where would you go? (a) the mountains, (b) the plains, (c) the desert, (d) the ocean.'

Hmmm. That one was harder. Definitely 'no' for the desert and ocean options. I lived in Florida because I was forced to, not because it was my choice. Maybe if I lived somewhere else, I'd pick '(d) ocean', but being a resident of a vacation resort area made the ocean seem like no big deal to me. I chose '(a) Mountains'. I loved the mountains, especially the forest part. I'd only gone to the mountains in North Carolina and Tennessee, but they were magically awesome. It was a long time ago, but I still remembered it fondly. I had to shake my head to get it back into the test.

The next section was similar to one I'd seen in school before. There were a series of shapes and I had to pick the next shape in the sequence. I was good at those.

The last section was weird as hell. I'd never seen anything like it before. The instructions said specifically that we were not to guess answers, and each question had the same letter (d) response: 'I don't know.'

I looked over at Tony who was already on that section. He had a lost look on his face, so I knew he was thinking the same thing as me. The first question was: 'What color are Mr. Dardennes' eyes?'. The answer was '(c) Gray', but what the hell? The next question was even weirder. 'What is the weather like outside right now?'

We were in a windowless room on the inside of a hotel, on the bottom floor. Chances are it was sunny outside - it was Miami after all. But what the heck kind of question was that? The instructions said I wasn't supposed to guess, so I was getting ready to answer with letter (d), but then I thought about it for a second, looking over my answer choices.

(a) It is sunny and dry.

(b) It is rainy and warm.

(c) It is snowing.

(d) I don't know.

Snowing? Ha. That's funny. I was thinking about marking it just for the hell of it, but I stopped, reminding myself that we really needed this money. This wasn't school where I would mark '(c)' without thinking about it. Memories of the warehouse's hard concrete floor trickled through my mind.

I breathed in deeply through my nose, thinking about the outside of the hotel. As I inhaled, I smelled something funny. *What is that smell?* I'd smelled it before, I knew I had. I couldn't put my finger on it, though. *Oh well, no time to ponder.* I wanted to get the test over with, so marked (d) on the weather question. It felt wrong, but I was running out of time.

I continued taking the strange test, answering more crazy questions. The last one was my favorite, though. It wasn't a multiple choice; it was an essay question with ten blank lines under it. The question was:

'If you could be a superhero, which one would you be and why? Fill in the lines below with your answer.'

Superhero? Good guy or bad guy? Do I have to stick to female superheroes or can I pick a male one? So far, their instructions had been pretty specific. I decided there were no limits since they hadn't given any. I looked at the clock; I had five minutes left. I gazed around the room and saw that some people were already filling out their answer and some still hadn't gotten there yet. Tony was already done. He was always faster than me on tests.

My favorite superheroes were of the X-Men variety. I loved the one with the wings, but only because I'd always wondered what it would be like to fly. I wasn't sure that having wings would be very useful or practical in reality, though, so I scratched that one off my mental list. The laser-vision thing would be cool - until you accidentally lasered your house or your best friend. I thought about several other superpowers, and it seemed like most of them had super shitty side effects that I would never want to have to deal with.

What powers would I like? Hmmmm ... I liked the ability to control the minds of others; that would be cool. I think I would like to see through things, like with x-ray vision. Superhuman strength would come in handy, no matter where I was. The problem is, none of these powers added up to one particular superhero, man or woman. Did Superman have x-ray vision? I couldn't remember. He was kind of old-school anyway, plus he had to wear tights and a cape. I sure wasn't going to be any superhero wearing tights or some trampy negligee like Wonderwoman did. Who made those costumes anyway? They were totally impractical for fighting crime.

I looked up at the clock and realized I only had two minutes left.

Dammit, I was running out of time. I really wanted to answer this question and pick a superhero for some reason. I tapped my pencil on the side of my head. *Think, think ... come on, think! Wait ... yes!* I had something. I quickly scribbled it down and gave the accompanying explanation. As I put my last period on the paper, Mr. Dardennes walked in the door.

"Your time is up," he said. "Thank you for passing your tests to the front of the room."

We all passed our booklets up. I wondered which superhero Tony picked. Probably Spiderman. I knew he had some Spiderman comics in his room the last time I was there.

"For those of you interested in continuing, there will now be a brief personal interview, conducted in a separate room. We will take you in alphabetical order by first name. While the interviews are taking place, the rest of you may remain here in this room. Refreshments will be provided."

The door opened and several hotel employees filed in, carrying trays of sandwiches and chips, and wheeling bins of sodas on a cart. Within five minutes they had a whole lunch buffet set up. Tony and I had eaten half a sub before we came, but with our current situation being what it was, I decided I should eat anyway. Neither of us knew when our next good meal was going to be.

"Our first interview will be with Becky."

Becky stood and followed Mr. Dardennes out of the room, glancing back at all of us with her trademark happy smile. The rest of us got up and served ourselves lunch.

Tony came back to the table, his plate piled high with four sandwiches.

"Hungry?" I asked.

"Not really. I'm going to wrap these up in something and put them in my bag for later."

"Brilliant ... me too. Be right back." I made a second trip to the buffet, grabbing three more sandwiches and two bags of chips. I noticed Jared's crew doing the same thing.

Even with all of us grabbing four times what we could eat, there were still plenty of sandwiches left. Dardennes' company must have been expecting more people. There were only about five extra seats, though. *Oh well.* Someone had made an error in calculating the food needed, and I was going to capitalize on it. I grabbed some napkins from the stack for wrapping up our sandwiches.

I got back to the table and all but one of Tony's sandwiches was already gone. He wrapped mine up quickly and shoved them in his bag to join the others. We ate the ones we still had on our plates.

The door opened and Becky stepped through before I was finished. "Chase, you're next. Go down the hall that way, and go in the last door on the left."

Becky went up to the buffet, taking four sandwiches, three bags of chips and two sodas. She was barely five feet tall and surely didn't break one hundred pounds on the scale, so seeing her with that much food was comical. She sat down by Finn and set about wrapping up her sandwiches, just like Tony and I had done. We were naturals at this homeless thing ... a depressing thought.

Jared spoke up first. "So Becky, what'd they say?"

We all stopped chatting and listened for her answer.

"I can't say. They said we can't tell each other until it's all over, or it could compromise the results." She shrugged apologetically. "Sorry, guys. I need the money, so I'm just going to follow the rules. But don't worry," she said brightly, "you'll find out in a minute anyway." She took a big bite of her turkey sandwich and smiled as she chewed.

Everyone went back to eating and chatting, and eventually it was my turn. I got up after being summoned by Jared, who'd been called in before me by a guy who was not part of Jared's crew. I walked down the hall, entering the last room on the left as instructed. There was a round table with three chairs around it at the end of the room. Two of the chairs were already occupied, one by Mr. Dardennes and one by some lady, also with gray hair and gray eyes. They looked like they could be siblings ... twins even. The chair opposite them was empty, so I took it.

"Hello, Jayne," said Mr. Dardennes. "This is my colleague, Céline."

I nodded at her. "Nice to meet you, Céline." I wanted to ask them if they were related, but I couldn't afford to be rude with five hundred bucks on the line.

"We just have a few questions for you, based on answers you gave on your test."

"Okay, shoot." This was like a job interview. I'd gone on a few of those, the last one being at the local frozen yogurt store. I didn't get the job, so I wasn't sure that my interview skills were up to par.

The woman spoke first. "Please, before we begin, may I see your hands?"

It was a strange request but seemed innocent enough. I held my hands up in front of me, palms facing out.

She stretched her hands across the table towards me. "Please place them in my hands."

Now this seemed a little on the creepy side. *What is she going to do? Read my palms?*

I slowly lowered my hands down to the table, putting them palm up in her hands.

"Turn them over, please."

Okay, so she isn't going to read my palms. Are we going to play the slap game? I was pretty good at it. It made Tony crazy that I could flip my hand over and slap the back of his hands before he moved them out of the way. He refused to play with me anymore. Somehow I doubted the sophisticated and controlled Céline was going to let me slap her, but if she decided to slap me, I was probably going to let her. Five hundred bucks was five hundred bucks.

Céline nodded at Mr. Dardennes, signaling him to begin the interview.

"Jayne, you said on your test that you do not hear voices in your head, is that correct?"

"Yes, I did say that, and it's true. But honestly, who would say yes to that question?"

"Different people interpret the questions differently, which sometimes results in them answering differently. Surely you have a conscience?"

"Well, of course I have a conscience ... but it's not a separate *voice* or anything in my head talking to me ... " I stopped for a second to think about that. I did tend to have lots of conversations with myself in my head - but they were with *me*, not some other voice. Then I thought about Tony. *Oopsy.* That boy was hearing *my* voice in his head lately. Did that mean he was crazy? I didn't think so. He'd have to follow my instructions in order to qualify as crazy. Now *that* was an interesting idea ... bossing Tony around telepathically ...

My thoughts were interrupted by Mr. Dardennes who had a very small smile on his face. Or maybe I was imagining that, because suddenly he looked very serious again. "Have you ever physically injured another person?"

Dammit. Did my mother's boyfriend count? He'd totally deserved it. Other than him, I couldn't remember ever hitting anyone. Before I could decide whether to hedge my answer, Céline spoke up.

"Include all instances. Do not make judgments about motivations or whether it would be considered right or wrong from a moral standpoint."

Shiiiiit. Is this woman reading my mind now too? I was going to have to figure out how to keep my thoughts more private real soon. Tony being in there was bad enough.

"I did physically hurt someone once, but he *totally* deserved it and gave me no choice ... and I'm not interested in giving you any details, so if you need them to qualify me for this test, then I'm outta here."

I started pulling my hands away from Céline's grasp, but she closed her fingers and held on. She had a surprisingly strong grip for such an old lady. I guess I assumed she was old because of the gray hair, but her face didn't have any lines on it like it should have ... I mean, for the color of her hair, anyway.

"No, we don't need details; your explanation will suffice," said Mr. Dardennes. "Let's continue. Do you know the ancestry of your great-grandparents or great-great grandparents? Or even further back than that?"

This one was easy. "My mother's family is from Ireland and my father's family is of mixed European heritage." I'd heard my mom say that often enough. She had dark hair and dark eyes, so whenever she said she was pure Irish, I'd make fun of her, saying it wasn't possible since she didn't have red hair or freckles. She claimed she was 'black Irish', whatever that meant.

"What is your mother's maiden name?"

I was wondering if I should tell them, since I was trying to remain somewhat anonymous. But after thinking about it for a few seconds, I figured it wouldn't matter since my mom never used that name anyway. Even after the divorce she kept using Sparks.

"Blackthorn is my mom's maiden name."

My two interviewers exchanged a look. It *was* a super cool last name, I had to admit. When I got older I was going to legally change my name from Sparks to my mother's maiden name. Jayne Blackthorn. It has a cool ring.

Céline continued with the questioning. "When asked what the weather was like outside, you said you didn't know; was that a truthful answer?"

"Yyyeesssss ... ," I said, kind of sure of myself, kind of not.

"You are hesitant in your answer ... why?"

"Well, because it's Miami, so it's probably sunny or rainy, but ... "

"But?"

"Nothing. I just wasn't sure so I picked the 'I don't know' answer."

"I think there is something you are not telling us," said Céline, no expression on her face.

I was starting to get uncomfortable about having my hands in hers. Mine were sweating, and she was being so serious, it made me nervous.

"It's nothing, really."

"Let's try this," said Céline, looking me straight in the eye.

I couldn't help but stare back. Her look wasn't exactly a challenge, but I felt like I needed to let her know I didn't intimidate easily.

"Close your eyes. Think about the weather outside. What do you see, feel, or smell?"

I closed my eyes as instructed, but asked, "Smell?" Her question was weird, but it reminded me that I had detected a funny odor when looking at that weather question on the test.

"Yes ... do you smell something?"

"Yes, I do, actually; but I can't put my finger on it, exactly. I know I've smelled it before."

"Does it smell like rain?"

"No, definitely not rain."

"Sunshine?"

That was funny. Sunshine didn't smell like anything. I laughed.

"What about snow?"

I started to smile at that one too, but hesitated. *Snow ... did it smell like snow?* I inhaled again deeply. *That's it! Snow!* I'd smelled it once when we were in North Carolina. We had taken an RV trip up into the mountains, and when we got near the top of one of the higher peaks, near the border of Tennessee, it had started to snow. I could smell it in the air, and it was amazing.

As crazy as it sounded, I answered her question truthfully. "Yes, I smell snow. I'm not sure where it's coming from, but when I was in the mountains once, when it snowed, this is what it smelled like."

Céline squeezed my hands and then let them go. "I'm done here."

I couldn't tell from her dismissal if I'd answered correctly or confirmed for them that I was a complete moron.

"I have one more question for you," said Mr. Dardennes.

"Alright."

"When the test asked you what superhero you wanted to be ... " He hesitated, as if he weren't sure where to go from here.

"Yes ... ?" It was getting a little uncomfortable, him sitting there saying nothing now, and both of them just staring at me. *Am I supposed to say something? ... What?*

"Your answer was a bit ... unconventional," he finally said.

I shrugged my shoulders. "That's me ... unconventional, I mean."

"Was there any particular reason you chose that ... person?"

"No. I guess it was the one thing I felt like I could identify with the most."

Both Céline and Mr. Dardennes had the same expression on their faces. Confusion? Contemplation? I wasn't sure what it was exactly.

Céline apparently wasn't done anymore. "In what way?"

"In what way do I identify with her, you mean?"

"Yes."

"I don't know ... she's just the most awesomely powerful I guess." I shrugged my shoulders. "It wasn't the easiest question to answer, you know. I'm not a big comics fan and most superheroes are very limited to just one thing. And they wear stupid outfits. I guess I like her because she doesn't have those limits."

"Interesting." Céline and Mr. Dardennes exchanged a silent look. I wouldn't have been surprised to find out they were telepathic. Something about the way they looked and the way they acted seemed very foreign. They were probably French. They both had the same accent.

Mr. Dardennes stood, followed by Céline. "Thank you, Jayne, for your frank answers and cooperation. Could you please go back to the room and tell Samantha that it's her turn?"

I stood to go out. "When will we find out if we're accepted?"

Mr. Dardennes walked me to the door. "We will post a list at the front desk of the hotel tonight by eight o'clock. The candidates will be expected to be at the hotel tomorrow by eight a.m. to take a shuttle to the airport." He stopped in the doorway, and I stepped out into the hall. "And Jayne, please keep the content of this interview confidential. We don't want your answers or advance notice of our questions to taint the other candidates' responses."

"Okay, I won't. See you later, I guess ... thanks."

I went back to the meeting room and told Samantha it was her turn. Spike flashed me a smile as I walked by to sit with Tony, making me feel all warm inside. It was ridiculous how he could affect me like that. I shook it off. I couldn't be all lovesick when I needed to focus on getting through this physical test, or whatever it was. I was never the best rope climber in gym class ... or the best monkeybar climber ... or the best runner. The list went on and on.

"What'd they ask you?" Tony whispered, his eyes darting around to the others. He was about as sneaky as an elephant in a china shop.

"Wait your turn, nosey parker. You'll find out soon enough. I'm not going to blow this five hundred bucks by telling you, if I haven't already with my stupid answers."

Tony immediately dropped the subject, and we speculated about the study itself instead. Samantha came back a few minutes later and then Spike went in. Eventually, Tony had his turn and everyone else got theirs too, so Mr. Dardennes joined us back in the meeting room. It was almost four o'clock.

"Thank you all for coming. We will post a list of the accepted candidates at the front desk of the hotel. It will be available by eight o'clock tonight. If your name appears on the list, you will need to be at the front of the hotel at eight in the morning, tomorrow. A shuttle will be waiting to take you to the Miami Executive Airport. If your name is not on the list, there will be an envelope at the front desk for you with fifty dollars inside, as a thank you for your time today. It was nice meeting all of you, and for those of you who are accepted, I will see you tomorrow."

He left the room as we digested his speech.

"Well, that was interesting," said Becky, coming over to stand by our table, along with the others of Jared's crew.

"Are we allowed to talk 'bout the interviews now?" asked Finn.

"Not now, let's get outta here first," said Jared. He seemed uncomfortable. He looked over at Tony and me. "You guys are welcome to join us."

I looked at Tony and he shrugged, nodding his head. We didn't have anything else to do - might as well go and talk to them about what happened in their interviews. I was curious to see which superheroes they had chosen. I was pretty sure I had answered that one wrong.

We left the meeting room and went towards the front of the hotel, Jared leading the way. He came to a complete stop as he rounded the corner that was just before the glass exterior doors. Samantha was following so close on his heels that she ended up bumping into him. Chase was right behind them, but jumped to the side, missing the pile-up. Tony and I hadn't reached the corner yet, but we couldn't miss the surprise in the voices of those who were there.

"What the hell?" said Jared, obviously surprised about something.

"Is that ... ?" said Samantha, unable to get the rest of her sentence out.

"Wow, I never would have guessed that in a million years!" said Becky, obviously delighted.

Chase just shook his head, saying nothing.

"What? What's up?" said Spike, walking up from the back of our group with Finn. "What's the big deal?"

"Come see for yourself," said Jared, with a deliberately neutral tone.

We all walked around the group at the corner so we could see the front doors too. None of us were expecting to see what was there.

Snow. Snow all over the sidewalks and the bushes ... even in the palm trees.

Chapter Eight

I FELT THE BLOOD RUSHING to my face. My heart was pounding so hard I could feel the pulsing in my neck. How was this even possible? How could it be snowing in Spring in Miami, Florida? How could it be snowing in Miami *at all,* for that matter?

"Anyone mark '(c), snowing' on their test?" asked Jared, looking around.

Everyone but me was shaking their heads. I looked down at the floor, freaking out about the interview, remembering how they were pushing me to answer that weather question with the truth instead of copping out and choosing '(d), I don't know'.

Tony looked at me, nudging me with his elbow. He was probably using that freaky mind-meld thing on me again. I nudged him back, not anxious to have all their eyes on me right now.

I looked up and saw Jared staring at me. He didn't say anything, though; he just turned and went to the front desk, returning in less than a minute to fill us in. "Apparently, some weird-ass storm just went through here, dropping a butt-load of hale and snow all over the city. As you can see, it's mostly gone now. Temperature is going back up. The snow will be gone in less than an hour, probably. It caused a huge accident on I-95." Jared turned, walking towards the doors again.

"Come on, let's go."

We followed him out in twos, walking several blocks back to the warehouse district. The snow was melting, making it look as if a big rainstorm had just hit. Jared took a more roudabout route than I would have taken, but he probably had his reasons. Maybe he was worried about the drug dealer pimp guys seeing us and following. I couldn't figure out why they'd be interested in us, though; we certainly didn't look like we had any money. Beating us up would be a waste of energy, but then again, maybe money wasn't their inspiration.

Once back at the warehouse, we discussed our various interviews and test answers. When they asked me which superhero I picked, I lied and said Wonderwoman. Everyone else had picked a comic book hero, so I felt kinda stupid about the one I chose. That must be why Mr. Dardennes and Céline asked me about it. No one else was asked about the superhero question, but all of them were asked about the weather. No one but me picked snow. I also didn't cop to that at first either, but Jared singled me out, right in front of everyone.

"Jayne, you didn't pick answer 'd', did you?"

I shrugged. What did it matter which one I chose?

"Which one did you pick?"

I sighed. He wasn't going to let it drop. "I picked 'snowing', okay? I don't see what the big deal is."

Everyone stopped chatting to stare at me. Even Tony.

"You picked *snowing?"* asked Samantha, angrily. "How could you possibly have known it was snowing? Did you sneak out and see before the interview?" She looked around at everyone. "Did you guys see her go out?"

That bitch was really pissing me off. Why would my choice on the test make her mad? What was her problem anyway? I stood up, not knowing exactly what I was going to do, but I wasn't going to take her shit sitting down.

"Ease up, Sam," said Jared. To me he said, "Seriously, though ... I'm curious. I know you didn't leave the room or cheat. Why did you pick snow?"

Everyone was waiting quietly for my answer. No one else seemed mad about it, so I felt a little better. I decided to just tell them the truth. It really wasn't a big deal.

"I don't know. I guess I kind of smelled it or something."

"*Pfft.* She *smelled* it. *Right.*" Samantha stalked off, yanking the door open and storming outside.

Spike nodded his head, a look of respect on his face. "She's in tune with the environment. Cool."

Becky laughed. "You're funny, Spike."

"No, I'm serious; don't you guys get it?" He looked around the room, checking each of our faces. All he got were blank looks in return. Chase looked a little pensive, but the rest of us? Lost.

"All the questions they asked, all the things they said in the interviews ... seems to me they were trying to figure out, like, whether we had any special psychic powers or whatever. I'm thinkin' this thing is more like a psychology test. Like X-Men, but minus the finger knives and freeze rays."

"I agree," said Chase, the man of very few words.

"So, what's your power then, Spike?" asked Finn, laughing at him.

"I dunno ... probably something really good, though." He smiled back.

As far as I was concerned, his superpower was that heart-stopping smile. I looked at Tony. "What do you think, Tones?"

He shrugged. "I don't know, I guess he could be right. Maybe they're one of those companies that tries to see if telepathy and stuff like that is real."

"Yeah, but why would they need to do a physical fitness test?" asked Finn.

He was right; that didn't really fit the hypothesis.

"Duh, to see if you can, you know, do psychic things out in the environment." Spike was obviously proud of himself, flashing his Spike smile at everyone.

I felt a little bit of my heart melt. *Man,* I had it bad for that smile. I wondered if his personality was worth getting to know, or if I should just content myself with admiring his smile and fantasizing about what he was really like. So often the reality didn't live up to my fantasies. It was too depressing to even think about right now.

"Maybe they're going to use the stress of physical activity to heighten our senses," suggested Jared.

Everyone thought about that for a second. It sounded a little spooky, actually. I was more excited about the prospect of climbing a rope ladder and crawling under barbed wire or something like that.

"Maybe it'll just be a team building activity, an obstacle course thing," I said. *A girl can dream.*

"You know, Jayne, you bring up a good point. What if this is an obstacle course or group exercise of sorts? Usually the successful groups learn quickly to work together as a team." Jared looked over at Becky. "Becky, will you go get Sam and bring her in here? We need to talk strategy."

Sam and Becky returned, and we all sat down on the couch, chairs, and surrounding floor. At this point, Tony and I had thrown our lot in with the others. We were still free agents; but assuming we would be going through some sort of strategic fitness test, it made sense to work together.

Tony asked the obvious question I probably should have thought of but hadn't. "What if some of us aren't invited back?"

"We'll just work on the assumption that we will, and go from there," said Jared.

"What if working together causes us to *not* be able to complete the test?" I asked. It wasn't that I was against teamwork, but if it were them or Tony and me, I would be Team Tony and Jayne all the way.

"For now, we might as well assume it's not a competition against each other. That wouldn't be fair anyway. Chase would kick all our asses."

Everyone looked at Chase. He just shrugged his shoulders, looking away. He was pretty big with those broad shoulders and thick arms - the strong, silent type. I wondered what was going on inside that big head of his. He didn't say much, but when he did, it was obvious he had been thinking pretty hard about it. He was a mystery. I wondered how he'd done during the interview. It was hard to be a silent interviewee. Maybe he wouldn't be called back because he refused to speak.

*****

We spent the next few hours going over strategy and listening to Spike play the guitar and sing. I've been told I have a pretty good voice, so I joined in with the others, singing the words to songs I knew. After listening to Spike do his thing, I couldn't figure out why he wasn't a rock star standing on a stage in an arena somewhere. He was really talented and sexy as hell, plus he was super nice. But he *looked* dangerous ... perfect rock star material. Another mystery about Jared's crew. It was like everyone here had a secret. Even Tony and I.

We all had extra sandwiches from our lunch meeting, so we had a dinner of subs and chips. The warm sodas went quickly, so Tony busted out his cache of juice boxes and shared with everyone, using up the last of them.

"Hopefully, we'll each have five hundred dollars in a few days and I can buy some more," he said.

I laughed because the last thing I'd buy if I had five hundred bucks right now would be a juice box.

It was nearly eight o'clock, so we left the warehouse to walk back to the hotel. Instead of all of us going in and rushing the reception desk, Jared and I went in, leaving everyone else outside. Sam seemed a little pissed about being left behind, but I wasn't too worried about it. She gave Tony something to stare at while I was gone.

Jared asked for the list and they handed it over to him. He put it in front of us so we could read the names. It was just first names, alphabetically. He read them quietly, under his breath. "Becky, Chase, Finn, Jared, Jayne, Spike, Tony ... *shit.* Sam's not on here. She's gonna be pissed."

"Neither are those other older people either."

He ran his hands through his hair. "I don't feel right about leaving her behind."

"What are you going to do? Not go? It's only for a few days, she'll be fine. I'm sure she wouldn't be mad at you - she knows it's a lot of money. Plus, that means she has fifty bucks here, so it's not like she didn't get anything at all out of the deal."

"I don't know. I'll have to talk to her."

He walked back outside, list in hand. I followed him a few paces back. I didn't want my face to be the first thing Samantha saw when we came out. I tried not to look as happy as I felt. She'd probably take it personally.

Everyone gathered around. Jared waited for me to catch up and handed me the list so I could share it with everyone. He walked over to Samantha, taking her by the arm and pulling her away from the others.

"So, who's on it?"

I held it out for them to see. "All of us but Samantha."

"Oh, bummer!" said Becky.

It was the first time I'd seen a frown on her face.

Spike looked over at Jared and then at me. "What's Jared saying to her?"

I shrugged. "I don't know. Probably trying to figure out if he's going to go without her or not."

We walked slowly back to the warehouse. Jared and Samantha went back into the hotel briefly and then came out, trailing a half-block behind us. I couldn't hear or see her reaction, but I knew it wasn't going to be good.

We arrived at the metal door leading to our temporary home, and everyone but Jared and Samantha went inside. Tony and I decided to go to bed early. I fell asleep before Jared came back in, wondering if he was coming with us, and where this mystery test would be held.

Chapter Nine

TONY AND I ARRIVED AT the hotel five minutes before eight. We didn't stick around the warehouse to see Samantha's goodbye. We figured it would be like rubbing salt in the wound for her, and as much as she'd been a bitch to me, neither Tony nor I wanted to make her more upset.

A shuttle pulled up in the front valet area with a sign in the window that said 'One Eleven Group'.

"That's us," I said.

Tony stood still for a second, concern on his face. "Aren't we going to wait for the others?"

"Nope. They'll be here, and if they aren't, that's their problem." I appreciated their whole 'we are family' thing, but I couldn't let that stop me from getting my five hundred bucks. I kept thinking about that hard concrete floor that had been my bed for two nights now. I needed last night to be the *last* night of that back-aching nonsense.

Tony frowned but followed me to the van. As we took the front row seats, the others came walking across the parking lot. Samantha wasn't with them, but Jared was, and I was happy to see that he'd decided to come.

"Hi, guys!" said Becky, all smiles, climbing into the shuttle.

"What's up?" asked Finn as he got in.

Chase said nothing, choosing a seat in the back row.

Spike was next, flashing me a smile and then sitting down next to me. "Hey, girl, what's up?"

Calm yourself, breathe. "Not much. No guitar?"

"Nah. I wasn't sure what the rules were on bringing music, so I left it hidden in the warehouse."

Jared was the last one in. He didn't say anything, just nodded at Tony and me, choosing a seat in the back next to Chase. I was glad he came. His crew functioned better with him around, and if this test required teamwork, they were going to need his leadership. I could tell, though, that he was bummed, which I could understand. If Tony hadn't been accepted I would have been in the same predicament. I wasn't sure if I would have been on the shuttle without him, so I was glad I didn't have to worry about that.

The van delivered us to the Miami Executive Airport, and we all got out. Mr. Dardennes was there to meet us. He walked us through a reception area to the plane that was sitting out on the tarmac.

I'd never been on a small airplane before, so it was pretty cool. But then again, there was also that issue of us dropping out of the sky. I was worried about this heavy machine's ability to stay up in the air. I'd heard about plane crashes in the news, it was usually a small one involved. I sent a small prayer out into the universe for our safety. I felt a gentle breeze on my face, as if it were answering me back. I didn't know why, but that made me feel just a little bit better.

We climbed up the stairs to the jet. As I entered, the first thing that came to my mind was, 'Holy shit, I'm on an episode of *Criminal Minds*.' The jet was super posh. Cream-colored leather seats in groups of four, with real wood tables in between, filled the spacious interior. The plush carpeting underfoot make our steps soundless, muffling the noises of our boarding. I was willing to bet that those chairs could recline all the way. This is about as far from coach class as I was ever going to get. I grabbed Tony's wrist and squeezed.

"Wow, this is nice," he said, sounding a little in awe. "This One Eleven Group must have a lot of money to be able to afford to fly this thing."

Similar comments came from the others as they entered. We all slowly took our seats. It kinda felt like a dream, the way we were being whisked away from the streets of Miami in a chartered executive jet to ... to ... I had no idea where. I settled into my seat, trying to keep the feelings of uncertainty at bay. I calmed myself by thinking that no one would go to all this trouble and expense just to kidnap a group of homeless teens. Whatever this study was, it must be pretty valuable.

Mr. Dardennes' buff assistant was the last person onboard, entering immediately behind Mr. Dardennes who was standing in the open cockpit door, speaking to pilots I couldn't see. I turned around in my seat as far as I could, but the secretary guy was blocking my view. He stood in the entrance as the stairs were taken away and the door closed. I couldn't see what he was doing exactly, but it sounded like he was securing the big locks. Apparently, he's not only a secretary, he's a flight attendant, too. He also looked like he'd be a pretty good bodyguard, now that I thought about it. *Handy guy to have around.*

The plane rolled away from the hangars. I could hear the jet engines whining higher as they powered up, moving the jet forward. The plane bounced a little as it went over seams in the pavement, making me feel like I was riding across a patchwork cloud.

Mr. Dardennes spoke while walking towards the back of the plane. "Hello, everyone, and thank you for coming." He stopped at the last chair, turning to look at us. "We are very excited about the testing that will be conducted over the next three days. We will be arriving at our destination in no time at all. Mr. Nischa will be with you in just a moment with refreshments. I will answer all of your questions when we touch down, and the test will begin soon after landing." He turned and walked into a room at the back of the plane, closing the door behind him.

I leaned over and whispered in Tony's ear, "Was that the bathroom he just went into?" I giggled. It struck me as funny that someone would do a welcome speech and then make a grand exit into a toilet.

"No, I think it's an office," Tony whispered back. "The bathroom's up front." He twisted around and pointed to a door we had walked by when we came in.

"Ahhhh." I was so friggin' sophisticated sometimes I couldn't stand myself.

Spike raised his eyebrows at me a couple times. "Nice, eh?" He was sitting across from Tony and diagonal to me.

I smiled back. "Yeah, not bad." Especially since I was going to be looking at Spike for the entire trip.

Chase was running his hands back and forth on the leather armrests, of course not saying anything.

"I could get used to this," said Finn, grinning from across the aisle.

Becky was sitting next to him, smiling her face off - nothing unusual there.

Jared was sitting across the aisle from me, an arm's length away, next to Chase. He looked thoughtful. He'd been really quiet ever since we'd left the warehouse and Samantha behind. He wasn't the most talkative guy anyway, but this was too much. When Jared was acting weird, it made everything else feel a little off. Maybe in another time and place, he could have been a pretty influential leader. He had some sort of extra special charisma - like Martin Luther King or Bugs Bunny or something.

My thoughts were interrupted by the guy we now knew as Mr. Nischa, the bodyguard/secretary/flight attendant. He was walking down the center aisle, carrying a tray of amber-colored drinks - one for each of us, plus one extra. After we each took one of the tiny shot glasses - which were heavy crystal and not plastic - he took the last one and stood in front of us, holding it up and clearing his throat.

He spoke in a scratchy voice. "Good morning, ladies and gentlemen. I am Mr. Nischa. Congratulations on being selected for this very important study. In my country, we celebrate honors with a toast and a special drink. It is mildly alcoholic, but do not worry, it will not affect you in that way. It is traditional to say 'Skal' and then drink it in one, quick swallow." He raised his glass in a toast, waiting for us to do the same.

I looked around and saw everyone complying, so I did the same ... but hesitantly. Why was this guy all of a sudden being so friendly? Why wasn't Mr. Dardennes doing the toast with us? Alarm bells were ringing faintly in the back of my mind. Tony looked sideways at me from the neighboring seat, probably picking up on my nervous vibe. He elbowed me gently, telling me to settle down and drink up.

Mr. Nischa gestured his drink towards us. "Skal!" he said, and then quickly put the shot glass to his lips and threw it back, drinking the deep-amber liquid in one gulp.

Everyone else around me was responding in kind. I lifted my glass and said a weak 'Skal' along with the rest of them. They were decidedly more enthusiastic than I was about the whole thing. In my peripheral vision I saw glasses being tipped back and then set back down on tables. My hand was frozen in place, the glass not quite touching my lips yet.

Tony's hand whacked me on the arm. "Ouch, Tones, watch it!" I turned to give him my bitchy look, but what I saw shocked me out of bitch-mode and into scared-shitless-mode, instantaneously. His eyes were shut and his mouth was hanging open; he was out cold. I heard a clank and a crash as someone else's shot glass fell and hit the table. I looked over and realized that everyone but me was unconscious, some of them obviously going into that state before they had even put their glasses down.

I lowered the shot glass away from my face and looked at Mr. Nischa with narrowed eyes. He was standing in place, still in front of the office door, no expression on his face.

"Skal, Miss Jayne," he said, his voice casually menacing.

"Fuck *that,*" was my very firm response. *Skal my ass.* I put my arm across Tony's chest to keep him from falling forward and set the glass down on the table in front of me. "I don't know what the hell you think you're doing here, but I am *not* drinking that shit. And you'd better stay the fuck away from me. I don't care how big you are - I'm not going down and neither is Tony." I could actually feel the adrenaline rushing into my bloodstream, and my heart felt like it had jumped into my throat. I had to swallow hard to make it easier to breathe.

Mr. Nischa reached his arm up and tapped on the door behind him with his knuckle.

Mr. Dardennes stuck his head out. "Yes, Ivar?"

Mr. Nischa said nothing - just gestured at me with a nod of his head.

Mr. Dardennes looked over. "Ah. I see we have a problem." He opened the door the rest of the way and stepped out. "Jayne, you did not participate in the toast with your fellow passengers ... how unfortunate. We really do need you to drink what's in your glass before we go too much farther into our little trip."

I picked up the glass and dumped the contents on the nice, cream-colored carpet. "Whoops, I spilled it. Bummer. Guess I'll have to sit this one out." I figured I might as well go full-on rebel with this. Drugging test subjects never meant anything good, so I knew I was already pretty much dead or sold into slavery anyway ... might as well go down fighting. I unbuckled my seatbelt as casually as I could. I needed to be able to get up and kick some balls if necessary. I wondered if it was a man or woman flying this luxurious kidnapping mobile. If the pilot had testicles, I had a much better chance of getting the hell out of there alive.

Mr. Dardennes smiled - a kind of tired smile. "Jayne, I know how this must look to you, but we find these measures necessary to protect the confidentiality of our operations. All will become clear to you in due time. I ask that you just trust me in the meantime, and take a drink as Mr. Nischa has asked."

I looked at him incredulously. This guy was obviously off his rocker.

"You know, you really had me fooled in the meeting and interview; I had no idea you were a completely insane sex slave trafficker. You can tell your pilot to turn this plane around and go back to Miami because I'm *not* drinking that poison and I will *never* trust you - you can bet your sweet ass on that."

Tony began snoring softly next to me.

"The drink is a sedative so you will sleep until we land. It will not harm you at all. The flight is quite long. You will be much happier to sleep through it, I assure you."

"Yeah, um, no thanks. Just take me back to Miami. I'm not interested in your test anymore."

Mr. Dardennes sighed. "Ivar, bring her another drink. Make sure she drinks it, but don't injure her." He went back into his office and closed the door.

I shook my head. *Boy, does that guy have a lot of nerve.* And Ivar Nischa was gonna be seriously sorry if he even thought about trying that shit on me.

Ivar walked past me, back towards the cockpit. I feverishly looked around, searching for some kind of weapon to use. None of us had brought anything but changes of clothes in our backpacks - I'd watched everyone pack. Tony had left his gun at the warehouse up in the rafters. I reached down and grabbed a shard of Jared's broken shot glass. It wasn't much, but it was better than nothing.

Ivar returned with a crystal carafe of the amber liquid and another little glass. He sat down in the empty seat across from me and set the carafe on the table between us. "You need to take the drink, Miss Jayne." He had no expression on his face and no anger in his voice. Just certainty.

"You need to get the fuck away from me before I make you sorry you ever lived." I lifted my eyebrows for emphasis, my false bravado nearly even fooling me. I was trying like hell to keep the shaking out of my voice. I couldn't let him see me sweat.

"This will be much better for you if you just comply. I do not want you to be hurt. You are very small and I am very big. You will either drink it or I will inject it into you. Come ... let us be adult about this."

"Adult? *Adult?* You want me to be *adult?* How about this: adults don't drug children and kidnap them, at least not high-functioning, sane ones. Why don't *you* be the adult here, and I'll just be the kid."

Ivar reached up and took the glass stopper out of the carafe. He lifted it by its neck, pouring out a shot. "Last chance to do this the easy way," he said quietly, almost sadly, sliding the drink towards me to let it rest a few inches from the edge nearest me.

"Go *fuck* yourself." I quickly swiped my hand across the table, sending the glass and its contents flying onto the carpeted aisle. A little bit splashed onto Jared, but I knew he wouldn't mind.

Ivar jumped up from his seat so fast, I didn't even see it coming. I didn't even have a chance to cut him with my weapon. The last thing I saw was his sad but determined face, less than an inch away from mine, the smell of sweet alcohol on his breath. The last thing I felt was a stinging sensation in my arm.

"You bastard ... you stuck me ... "

And then everything went black.

Chapter Ten

I COULD HEAR VOICES - TONY'S and Spike's. Then I felt someone squeezing my hand.

"Wake up, Jayne, come on." Tony sounded worried. I wanted to squeeze his hand back, but my body was not obeying my mental commands at the moment.

Someone grabbed my foot and shook it gently. "Hey, Jayne, it's me, Spike. Come on, you're gonna miss all the fun, wake up."

Fun? Was he nuts? Since when did sexual slavery sound like fun? The fog was clearing from my brain. I remembered seeing Ivar's face in mine and a sharp, stabbing pain in my arm. *Shit.* He'd gotten the jump on me. He was gonna pay, too, since I now realized that I was still alive. *Bastard should have killed me when he had the chance.*

When my eyes were finally able to open about a minute later, I looked around me, but all I could see was Tony's face, worry etched in the lines above his eyebrows.

"She's awake! Hey, Jayne, I'm so glad you're back. You feel okay?"

I turned my head and saw the crew sitting at and standing around a wood table in the middle of a big room. I was lying on a couch in what looked like a log cabin ski lodge. There was even a big fireplace at the end of the room, not far from me. There was no fire in it now, though – probably a good thing since unless I'd gone into some sort of seven-month-long coma or had changed hemispheres, it was too hot outside.

I sat up slowly, waiting for the dizziness to stop. Whatever they'd stuck me with had really kicked my ass. I didn't remember a thing after my exchange with Ivar, not even any dreams. *And speaking of Ivar* ... "Where is that motherfucker, so I can kick his ass?"

"Which motherfucker would you be referring to?" asked Jared, who had joined Spike at the foot of the couch.

"Ivar first ... then Dardennes."

Spike smiled, but I wasn't in the mood for his beauty, which showed how pissed I was.

"They're not here," said Tony.

"Where is 'here', anyway?" I asked, sitting up and looking around.

"We have no idea. We're in some sort of lodge in the forest. Chase and Finn went outside and looked around a bit, but didn't see anything or anyone."

The dizziness had subsided, so I stood up. Everyone seemed to be waiting for me to speak. "So what the hell happened? Last thing I remember is seeing all of you pass out around me and then getting into it with Ivar, before he stuck me in the arm with some needle."

Everyone looked at Jared for an explanation. "Well, the last thing any of us remember is saying 'Skal'. We all woke up here about a half hour ago. Whatever Ivar got you with must have been stronger than what we drank."

"So, what's the theory? Are we sex slaves now, or what?" I wasn't kidding but everyone laughed anyway.

"Yep, she's back," said Tony, giving me a quick hug. "I was so worried about you, Jayne. You were just so out of it."

"Yeah, well, see what happens to you after you're hit with an elephant tranquilizer ... hey, does anyone know what time it is?"

"No, none of us have our watches or cell phones anymore," said Finn, "but it looks like it's afternoon, if the sun's in the right place."

"Afternoon? What the hell? That means we were on that damn plane and passed out for ... how many hours?"

"There's no way of knowing, since we don't know what time zone we're in right now," said Jared.

I shook my head, not wanting to believe what the facts were telling me. "Where in the hell are we? And am I the only one who's pissed that we've been kidnapped?"

The front door of the lodge opened and Dardennes stepped through, followed by Ivar and Céline.

I saw red. Tony tried to grab my arm, but I slipped through. Spike and Jared noticed the look on my face and both moved to block me. Spike grabbed me in a semi-hug, gripping me across the shoulders with one arm while putting his opposite hand on my shoulder that was under his armpit. "Jayne ... "

I glared at him, angry as hell that he'd stopped me. "I hope you wore a cup today." I wasn't kidding. Anyone with balls was liable to get hurt with the mood I was in. I wasn't sure how I was going to handle Céline ... maybe punch her in the boobs until she begged for mercy.

Spike smiled in response, effectively taking some of the fight out of me.

Dammit. Why does he have to do that?

"Just wait and let's hear what they have to say before you take 'em all down, okay?"

I looked over at the rest of the crew. Everyone was standing stock still, frozen in place. I'd apparently surprised them with my G.I. Jayne act. I caught Chase's eye and he winked. *He winked!* Now I knew he had my back; and he was pretty big too, so that made me feel a tiny bit better. I looked over at Jared, but he was looking at Dardennes and Dardennes was looking back at him. I saw Dardennes give him a very slight nod.

What the hell was that all about? I looked at Spike, but he was still staring at me, so he missed it. No one else said anything - everyone was waiting for me, I guess.

"Well, *shit,* people... are you just going to stand there while our captors come waltzing in to give us another shot of elephant tranquilizer?"

Spike released me, able to tell somehow that I was willing to wait a few minutes before unleashing my wrath on them. He stayed close, though, ready to give me another tough-love hug if necessary. *Man, I so wanted our first physical contact to include kissing. Now he's gone and ruined it. Guys are all jerks.* I glowered at him.

He grinned back at me, flashing those damn fangs again.

Argh. He *had* to know what that was doing to me. There was no other explanation for that much smiling.

I felt Tony come up on my other side and take my hand in his.

I laced our fingers together, glad for his support. I think I was almost ready to fight to protect him, more than myself. It was my fault he was here in the first place. It was his chivalry awakened by my pitiful family problems that had made us runaways. "I'm so sorry I got you into this, Tones," I whispered.

"You didn't get me into anything, Jayne," he whispered back. "We're a team, we stick together. Just don't get yourself knocked out again."

Dardennes cleared his throat.

I couldn't wait to hear what he was going to say – *probably a bunch of lies*.

"Hello, everyone, thank you again for being here. I'm sorry if our methods for keeping our operation confidential were upsetting to you," he gave me a small bow, which made me want to pound him all over again. "But I assure you, it was necessary. All will become clear to you, eventually. But for now, we must commence the test, as we are running out of daylight. Please follow us outside." He and the other two turned, leaving the lodge through the front door.

I looked around at everyone, noticing Becky moving towards the door. I lost my cool again. "Oh, so we're just going to do whatever they say now, is that it? They say jump, we ask, *how high?*"

Becky shrugged her shoulders. "I don't know. What else are we going to do? We have no idea where we are ... ," she finished lamely, looking to Finn for help.

"Them people are our only way outta here that I can see. Chase and I checked the place out. We're out here in the middle of bumfuck Egypt," said Finn.

I looked over at Chase. He shrugged his shoulders and walked towards the front door, which was apparently his way of saying he was going to go see what they had to say. Finn and Becky followed him out.

Jared's eyes were aimed at the floor when I glanced over at him, but he quickly looked up and went to the front door too, not once even acknowledging me. I decided right then and there that there was something fishy going on with him; he was acting very strange. Maybe no one else had seen his little exchange with Dardennes, but I had.

Only Spike and Tony where left with me, and Spike made his move towards the door as it swung shut behind Jared.

"Et tu, Spike?" This was the surest sign I was stressed; now I was quoting from my Lit teacher's favorite Shakespearean tragedy.

He shrugged, his hand on the doorhandle. "Might as well. Beats sitting in here waiting for something to happen."

"Maybe ... maybe not." I turned to Tony. "So, what do we do? Go out there and face the music, or arm up and wait for them to storm the castle?"

Tony sighed. "I appreciate your concern, Jayne, especially since you were basically attacked while we all slept. But I think they're right; we're not going to get anywhere staying in here. At least out there maybe we'll get an explanation, or an opportunity to run away. In here, we're sitting ducks."

"Fine. Let's go, then. Just promise me you'll be ready to kick some serious ass."

"I promise. I'm ready - as ready as I'm going to be, I guess."

We followed Spike out the door, joining the others already standing in front of the lodge.

Chapter Eleven

DARDENNES, CÉLINE, AND IVAR WERE joined by another one of their group. My parents always told me not to stare at people who look different than me, and for the most part I was able to control myself; but this time ... not so much. He was a dwarf. And I'd never seen an armed commando dwarf before, so it totally wasn't my fault that I couldn't look away.

He stood about three and a half feet high, wearing camouflage clothes and combat boots. He even had a black bandana tied around his oversized head, *and* a bowie knife strapped to his tiny thigh. It was only Tony's suddenly very strong grip on my hand that kept me from laughing out loud. I was totally on the edge right now – anything could have set me off; but seriously, no one could blame me for this one.

"This is Niles, your field contact. He will instruct you on the test conditions and supply your provisions."

Céline stepped forward. "We realize that you have arrived here under stressful conditions - some of you more stressful than others." She looked at me, and I gave her my best *screw you* look in return. "Be that as it may, I urge you, *we* urge you, to put that behind you and do your very best on this test. There is not only money at stake here.

Those who complete the challenge, and do so in an exemplary manner, will qualify for additional remuneration."

Additional remuneration? I wasn't sure what the hell remuneration was, but it sounded like more money, and that interested me. Not enough for me to stop being mad, but at least they had my attention now. I looked at Tony, and he nodded his head. We were both willing to listen.

Dardennes was talking again. "The object of this test is to make it through the course to the end."

Obstacle course. I called that one. I looked over at Spike who was already looking at me. He nodded his head in respect.

"There will be four waypoints. At each waypoint, you will indicate your arrival by tying a flag to the waypoint marker. Each of you will have a set of colored flags assigned to you. There is no placing in this test, which means it doesn't matter who comes in first. It only matters that you reach each waypoint and finish the course."

Pfft. Easy as pie.

Tony leaned over and whispered, "What's the catch?"

Exactly what I was thinking.

"This forest is not your typical forest," he continued. "There will be ... obstacles ... in your way; things designed to keep you from reaching your goals. You are permitted to use whatever is at your disposal to ... eliminate or incapacitate those obstacles."

Incapacitate? What kind of obstacles needed to be incapacitated? That sounded a little too ominous to me. I looked sideways at Tony and saw confusion on his face too. *Okay, so I'm not the only one lost here.* Chase looked like he always does, totally in control. Spike had a big question mark floating above his head. Finn and Becky were standing side by side, looking nervous, Becky hopping from one foot to the other like a little bird. I looked at Jared and he just stared straight ahead, his expression revealing nothing. *Sneaky bastard. He's up to something.*

"The rules you are used to, the rules of our day-to-day society, do not apply here. You are very far from home. Consider this place to be ... a rule-free zone. The only rule is: there are no rules." He smiled, coolly.

Now, normally, I was a 'rules are made to be broken' kind of girl, but I was pretty sure he was talking about something more serious than curfews and smoking sections here.

Tony was whispering in my ear again. "Does he mean what I think he means?"

God, I hope not.

"Be mindful that this 'no rules' policy applies across the entire forest. Anyone in the forest will be aware of this rule and will also be following it. Your goal is to survive to the end."

I couldn't keep quiet any longer. "Survive? What is this? Some kind of tacky reality TV show?"

Tony squeezed my hand. I was taking that as his approval.

Céline answered me. "This *is* all about survival, but it's not a TV show and nothing is being filmed. What happens in the forest, stays in the forest."

That never meant anything good when it was used in Las Vegas, so it gave me a bad feeling to hear it said in relation to a forest I was about to spend the next couple of days in. And I wasn't fooling myself anymore - into this forest I was going ... if not to complete this test, then to find another way out of here. These guys were fucking nutballs, and I knew they weren't going to just let me walk away.

"Does anyone have any questions?" Dardennes looked out over our group, waiting for a response.

Finn raised his hand. "How long do we have to complete the

course?"

"As long as you need."

Finn looked as confused as I felt. "Well, what if it takes us a whole week?" he asked.

"It won't," was the mysterious and very unhelpful answer.

Not surprisingly, no one had any more questions. If the answers were going to be this ridiculous, there really wasn't any point.

"Okay, I will now turn you over to Niles. The sun will be going down soon, and he needs to have you outfitted before sunset."

Dardennes and Céline went back to the lodge, stepping inside and closing the door behind them. Ivar stood next to our commando mini-man who was now speaking.

"Follow me to get your provisions and further directions." He turned and disappeared between the trees, Ivar closely behind him.

Jared went first. Tony let go of my hand so we could walk single-file. Behind us were Finn, Becky, Spike, and Chase. I found myself wishing Samantha were here. Her take-no-shit, badass attitude would have made me feel a little bit better being out here with these crazy fucks in no man's land. I'd bet she would have spoken up. They probably would have had to stick her with the tranquilizer needle, too. It was a sad thing, really, this nostalgia I was having for a girl who probably considered me her enemy.

A couple of minutes later, we ended up in a clearing. In the center were a few tables made of huge slabs of sliced tree trunk propped up by thick stumps. The trees around us were so dense they nearly blocked out the remaining daylight. Our feet made no sound on the carpet of needles and long-dead leaves. My feet sprung up with every step, telling me the layers of decomposing forest went very deep. I turned around, realizing that I had already lost my bearings. I had no idea which way the lodge was from here because everything looked the same.

Tony stayed close, not saying anything. The others remained quiet as well, their heads swiveling in all directions, taking in the incredible majesty of the forest around us. I wasn't so angry that I couldn't appreciate this kind of beauty. It was truly breathtaking.

"Everyone please take one pack from the far table."

I looked over and saw that one of the tables was covered in small, camouflage backpacks. Tony went and got two, one for each of us. I stayed where I was, keeping my eye on Niles, commando dwarf. He didn't waste a second looking back at me. He was all business and a little bit scary. I'd bet he knew how to use that knife strapped to his leg.

"Inside each of these sacks you will find waypoint flags, a map of the forest with waypoints indicated, food, water, flint, a small flashlight, and a rescue flare. If you don't know how to use a flint, please raise your hand."

I was glad Becky raised hers. Even though I didn't know how to use one, I didn't want to admit it for some reason. As the seriousness of this situation sank in, the less I wanted to expose any weaknesses I had.

I watched out of the corner of my eye as Ivar demonstrated the flint for her. It seemed easy enough. I noticed I wasn't the only one watching, too. The only ones who didn't seem to care much were Chase and Jared. Maybe Chase was in on whatever Jared had going on. I was going to keep an eye on both of them.

"Step over to the middle table."

I followed Tony to the table in front of Niles. I hadn't paid much attention to it before, but now I sure was - now that I realized it was covered in weapons. *Weapons?*

"What the hell do we need weapons for?" I asked angrily.

Niles just looked at me, not answering. He had no expression on his face - just like Ivar. Two cold, heartless bastards they were. I had a mind to use one of those weapons on them.

"The biggest will pick first. You ... ," he gestured towards Chase, " ... choose your weapon."

We studied the table. Laid out in nice even rows were a gun, a bowie knife, a compound bow with arrows, a double-bladed axe, a spear, a slingshot with pellets, and a sharpened stick. *A sharp stick? What the hell good is a sharp stick? No way am I getting stuck with that shit.*

Chase walked over to the table and picked up the gun, shoving it in his bag.

"You ... next."

Jared walked up to the table and took the spear.

"You ... your turn."

Spike stood in front of the table for a few seconds, eventually selecting the slingshot. He turned away and stretched the rubber bands out, pretending to play them like a guitar.

I had to smile at that. At least someone was having fun out here.

Spike caught me staring and smiled back, but even his sexy self couldn't make me happy right now.

"You, freckles ... "

Finn looked pissed, but walked up to the table quickly. He picked up the compound bow and arrows without hesitating. I hoped he knew how to use that thing - I'm afraid I'd shoot my own foot if I had to try to work it.

"You ... " Now it was Tony's turn.

"What do you think?" he asked me quietly.

"I don't know ... axe?"

"Yeah, that's what I was thinking too." He walked up and took the weapon off the table.

"Little girl ... you ... " He was gesturing to Becky.

"Hey, wait a minute! I'm bigger than her!" I was pissed. I knew what was going on here. I was being punished for giving Ivar a hard time. The big oaf looked at me, and I could have sworn he smiled. It might not have reached his mouth, but it was definitely in his eyes. *Bastard.*

"You can go ahead, Jayne, I don't mind."

Damn her for being so nice. "No, Becky, you go. I don't give a shit which weapon I have."

Becky's no dummy; she walked up to the table and took the knife.

That left me with the sharp stick. *Yay, me.* Now I'd be able to use my mom's favorite saying – *That's better than a sharp stick in the eye!* – and have a prop too. I walked up to the table and took the stick. I tapped it in the air in Ivar's direction; then I kissed the tip of it, keeping my eyes on him. *Asshole.* A little piece of me wished I were going to see him in the forest later. Of course, I'd have to sneak up on him since he was three times my size. And I'd have to borrow Tony's axe and whack Ivar with the flat side of it on his head, since I really couldn't see myself stabbing him with my stick or actually chopping any of his body parts off ... but still ...

"Your instructions are simple. You are to leave this clearing and head to waypoint number one. Once there, you tie your flag to the waypoint itself. Then you head to waypoint two and repeat the process. Continue until you reach the fourth and last waypoint. Once you have tied your flag there, follow the instructions that will be provided to proceed to the debriefing. Are there any questions?"

It didn't matter if we had any, because he didn't wait. "If, at any point in the test you decide to surrender, light your flare. Someone will come and take you back to the lodge. For each waypoint you have reached and tied a flag to, you will receive one hundred and twenty-five dollars. If you have not yet reached any waypoints when you surrender, you will receive only fifty dollars. Any questions?"

He continued once again without waiting. "There is no way to cheat during this test. In fact, there is no such thing as cheating on this test. Anything goes. Do whatever it takes to get to the waypoints. There are no rules here ... there are no laws. Not even the laws you remember from home. Do you understand?"

I looked around at everyone's faces in the clearing. It was getting darker and it was harder to see them. Finn, Spike, and Becky were nodding. Chase and Jared had no reaction.

Tony raised his hand.

"What?!" asked the impatient dwarf.

"Um, I just want to be sure I understand ... when you say 'no laws' do you mean, like *no laws*, like, *at all*?"

Niles sighed loudly, obviously frustrated with the apparently incapable idiots in front of him. "No laws. I can't be any clearer than that."

"Okay, so if Jared wants to throw his spear through Chase's head, that's okay with you guys?" I asked, flippantly. This was totally stupid. They had to specify what they meant by 'no laws'. They couldn't just leave it out there for us to figure out.

"That's exactly what I mean. Thank you, Jayne, for that excellent clarification."

I choked, having swallowed some drool down the wrong tube. Tony had to whack me on the back a few times to get me breathing again.

I heard Becky squeak in alarm.

Finn let out a, "What in the sam hill?!"

Chase just shook his head slowly from side to side.

Jared looked down at the ground.

Tony grabbed my upper arm and squeezed like hell.

"Ouch, Tones, lemme go!"

"Oh, shoot, sorry. But holy crap, Jayne! I think they expect us to *kill* people out here!"

"Don't worry about it," I muttered. It wasn't every day people were let loose in a forest of homicidal maniacs. Something was going to fix this. Something had to happen. This was too fucked up to be real. I refused to panic over something this outer-limits messed up. In fact, it was highly possible I was just having a really bad trip from the drug they injected me with. Of course, I had just felt Tony pinching my arm. *Dammit.*

"It's seven o'clock. I suggest you get started. Nightfall comes quickly here and the forest is very dark. You have enough food in your packs for two nights if you're careful. Good luck. I'll see you at the flare or waypoint four, whichever comes first." He grinned then, and it was very disturbing. He looked almost happy about setting us loose in this lawless land - me with a stupid sharpened stick to protect myself.

Niles and Ivar walked away, leaving us alone in the clearing.

"Hey! Wait a minute! You can't just leave us out here!" I shouted at their retreating forms.

They ignored me and kept going.

"Should we go after them?" asked Tony.

I didn't know what to say. I had a feeling they'd be zero help if we did. And I had this sharp stick in my hand and was itching to use it on Ivar, so it was probably better if we didn't.

"No, let's just try to figure out where the hell we are and where we're going."

Tony put his sack on the ground and bent down to open it up. "Well, the good news is, we're not lost."

I laughed bitterly. "Of course we're lost. What the hell are you talking about?"

"Nope. We're not." He looked up at me and grinned, pulling a map out of his bag. "See? We have a map."

I bent down and gathered Tony in the biggest, strongest bear hug I could muster. No matter what happened in these fucked up woods, I had my map-toting best friend Tony Green with me.

Chapter Twelve

WE ALL MOVED TO THE center of the clearing, gathering around the weapons table that was now bare. I emptied out my backpack to see what was inside. My flags were purple. *Cool* ... my favorite color. Everyone else dumped their bags out too. Tony's flags were green, which was both hilarious and spooky since there was no way Tony Green could have known which bag had those flags in it. This forest situation just got creepier and creepier every minute. Chase had blue flags, Jared yellow, Finn red, Spike black, and Becky orange. We also had the supplies Niles had mentioned: flint, map, army-style food packets, two bottles of water each, a mini-flashlight, and a big candle. I guessed that was the flare.

"How are we supposed to light these damn flares, anyway?" I asked.

"The flint," answered Jared.

"Yeah ... the flint ... now why didn't I *know* that?" I looked at Jared suspiciously. I guess I wasn't hiding my feelings very well, because I felt Tony nudge me in the back.

Jared brushed my comment off. "So, we have an obstacle course to get through," he looked over at me but I refused to be flattered, "and I suggest we stick together, like we discussed."

I turned, pulling Tony a little off to the side. "Are we going to do this with them or are we going it alone?"

"This is a pretty big forest, Jayne. Maybe we'd be better off if we stuck together."

I sighed. He was right. Still, I wasn't all that excited about hanging out with Jared and now maybe Chase either. I just wasn't sure that I trusted them. They seemed pretty unaffected by all of this. Anyone who wasn't freaking out right now, in my opinion, was either a stone-cold badass or in on this scheme somehow; and I didn't think Jared was all that badass - maybe Chase, but not him.

Tony and I went back to the table, and I said, "We're in for now. We'll take it as it comes; I can't guarantee we'll stay with the group for the entire test, though."

"Fair enough," said Jared. "What about the rest of you guys?"

Everyone nodded, so Jared pulled out his map and laid it on the table. Niles had been nice enough to mark a red spot on it, a type of 'you are here' marker. The first waypoint was to the northeast. There was no scale or legend, so it was impossible to know how far away our first stop was. I was no map expert, but even I knew that this one sucked.

"We're here, at this red dot. We need to get *here,* to the first waypoint. That means we have to go that way." Jared pointed off in the distance.

Tony and I quickly agreed. The final rays of the setting sun that I had noticed earlier gave us a good reference for the compass points. "Man, do I wish I had a compass right now," I said to no one in particular.

Spike happened to be walking by me at the time. "Well, you kind of have one."

"Oh yeah? Where?"

"On the trees; rumor has it that moss grows more on the north side of the tree than the south side." He winked before walking ahead of Tony and me.

"Is that true, Tony?"

Tony shrugged his shoulders. "I've heard that before, but I'm not sure if it's true. We need to find the North Star for our night walking. We can use the sun during the day."

"I think we should sleep at night - it's pretty friggin' dark in here." It wasn't even totally nightfall yet and I could barely see ten feet in front of me.

Jared left the clearing, the rest of us gathering up our stuff and following not far behind.

I hurried to catch up to Chase, since his form was quickly disappearing into the thick trees ahead. I could hear Becky struggling behind us. Finn was staying close by her, I think to make sure she didn't get left behind. I could hear him encouraging her along.

There were fallen trees and low-hanging branches everywhere. I had thought this was going to be a leisurely stroll through the forest, but I soon learned differently. Everywhere we stepped it was tough going. *Where are all the damn paths in this place, anyway?*

A breeze moved through the trees, pushing some branches aside. I thought I caught a glimpse of ... *Yes!* It was a path of some sort.

"Hey, guys! I think there's a path over here!" I pointed through the trees.

Tony looked around the branch that was in our way. "Yeah, she's right - there is a path here. This would be a lot easier to follow, I think. It seems to be going in the same direction."

Jared came back to where we were standing and looked for himself. He smiled absently, confusion momentarily flitting across his face before he nodded at me. "Good job, Jayne." He looked over his shoulder, encouraging us to follow. "Come on, everyone, let's go this way. Tony's right; it's going in the direction we want."

Spike and Chase easily kept up with his pace, but the rest of us fell behind. Tony was looking at the ground as we walked. He didn't see some branches in front of him and so they hit him in the face. As they swung back, they barely missed whipping into me.

"Pay attention to where you're walking, Tony," I said, irritated.

"Sorry ... I'm just ... do you notice anything weird about this path?" he asked.

"Weird? No, what do you mean?"

"I mean, it's not really a path. There's no trail on the ground. It's just some branches that have been shoved aside. But look down ... "

I looked at the ground to see what he was talking about. Sure enough, there was no trail under our feet. We were still walking over fallen branches, rocks, and other things - not what you would expect to see on a path that was well-traveled. But the way the branches were well away from the area, it seemed as though it could have been used quite a bit.

"Weird," was all I could think to say. Maybe whatever used the path didn't have feet. Or legs. I laughed nervously with the direction my mind was going. "Is it my imagination, or is this place glowing green?" I was feeling like I was going to see some fairies jump out at us at any second.

Tony laughed. "No, the only things glowing green right now are my teeth. I feel like I haven't brushed them in three days."

"I know, right? My teeth totally have fur on them right now."

"What're you guys talkin' 'bout?" asked Finn, coming up behind us.

"Oh nothing - just furry teeth and enchanted pathways. What's up with you?"

"Nothin'. Just tryin' not to trip and fall on my keester."

"Hey, guys! Wait up!" said Becky from behind us.

The three of us stopped to wait for her. She was short, so it was hard for her to climb over the bigger branches - unlike me, graceful gazelle that I was. Okay, maybe not so graceful or so much like a gazelle, but I had at least four inches on Becky, and I wasn't tall by any means. Everything about her was tiny. Even her tiny head had tiny ears attached to it. She wasn't a dwarf - more like a miniature person. Perfectly proportioned, but extra, extra, *extra* small. She probably had to shop in the little kids' department.

She finally caught up after scrambling over a particularly large log. "Where are we? Are we almost there yet?"

"I have no idea," I answered. I hadn't even taken my map out yet. "Let's go ask Jared."

"Where'd he go?" asked Finn.

We looked up ahead at the path in front of us. It was dark now, and I couldn't see anything but some trees and then blackness.

"*Shit,* we've lost them," I said, pissed that those turds had left us behind. "Dammit, this isn't a race! Why didn't they wait?"

"Maybe they didn't realize they'd lost us," offered Tony.

I made a very inelegant sound in response. Tony was always giving people the benefit of the doubt. I knew if *I* were in front, I would make sure the people behind me were still behind me, *especially* in a dark creepy forest filled with friggin 'obstacles', whatever those were going to be.

"Let's just keep moving ahead on the path and see if we can catch up to them," suggested Tony.

Tony took the lead, turning on his flashlight, and we followed - first me, then Becky, then Finn. We didn't want to risk losing Becky the way we'd been lost already, so we kept her between us.

We were walking along for several minutes, with no sign of Jared, Chase, or Spike, when we heard shouting and screaming up ahead. The shouting was human; the screaming ... not so much. We all stopped dead in our tracks.

Tony shut off his flashlight.

My heart quit beating for a second and then rushed to catch up to its now accelerated rhythm. "What the *fuck* was *that*?" I asked, whispering loudly, totally freaking out.

Becky's eyes were practically the size of saucers. I could see them easily in the dark, glowing beacons coming from her face. She opened her mouth to speak, but nothing came out.

Tony grabbed my arm, squeezing as hard as he could.

I slapped his hand away and shot him a dirty look.

He apologized silently, just moving his lips.

Finn was staring ahead of us into the darkness, probably wishing he could see like a cat so he could figure out what was waiting for us up ahead.

I was seeing okay here in the dark, more so than I did back home - probably the moonlight was helping. It was brighter here or something.

We heard another shout then and a scream. I recognized the voice. "It's Chase!" I whispered loudly, desperation in my voice. We couldn't just sit here while Chase, Spike, and Jared were getting their asses kicked. "Come on, we have to go see what's going on." I gestured for them to follow me, but Finn and Tony rushed to get in front. Frustrated with their uncoordinated chivalry that inadvertently knocked me to the side, I grabbed Becky's hand to drag her along and make sure she didn't get left behind.

We rushed up the path as quickly as we could, not worrying about the sounds we might be making as we crashed through the undergrowth. Chase and whoever else was up there were creating enough noise to cover the evidence of our arrival. I could tell we were getting closer now because we could hear grunts too - the sounds of men fighting in close contact.

Suddenly, a shot rang out.

Chase! The vision of his gun sitting on that weapons table and him putting it in his backpack rushed through my mind. I never considered that he'd actually use the stupid thing. My next thought nearly stopped me cold: *What the fuck am I gonna do with a sharp stick?!* I had no time to worry about that now, though. We had arrived at the scene.

None of us were prepared for what we saw.

Chapter Thirteen

WE HAD REACHED A SMALL opening in the trees. It was dark, but the moon was nearly full and shining brightly across the clearing, making it seem like there was a streetlight above our heads. It was enough for us to make out the form of Chase lying on his back, Spike's dark figure hunched over him.

"Chase!" I yelled, rushing to get to him, shoving Tony and Finn out of my way. I was anxious to bend down next to Spike and see if he was okay.

"Jayne, *stop!*" yelled Tony, panic in his voice. It didn't register with me for a split second, but by the time it did, it was too late. The dark figure that was crouching over Chase straightened up, and I immediately understood why Tony had called out anxiously to me.

It wasn't Spike. And whoever it was, he wasn't checking to see if Chase was okay. He was a little too close to Chase's bloody neck to be doing that.

I froze in my tracks, five feet away from the creature. He turned around to face me, wiping his mouth with the back of his hand. I saw the glistening streak of crimson left behind as he slowly lowered his arm down to his side.

"Well, hello there, you sweet, ferocious thing. Nice of you to stop by. Are you here to rescue me?" He simpered when he talked, exactly like my flamingly gay music teacher from tenth grade who used to wear red pants and pink shirts to school. The creature smiled at me, and I could see blood on his teeth. Chase's blood.

So this is what a so-called 'obstacle' looks like. Shiiiiiit.

I was torn between the desire to jump on him and smash that smile off his face, and the urge to run away as fast as I could while screaming like a girl on fire. The look in his eyes reminded me of the big wildcats Tony and I would watch on Animal Planet ... crouched down and waiting, totally still, for the perfect moment to pounce on their prey and tear it to itty bitty bloody pieces.

A more subdued form of self-preservation won out - I walked backwards slowly, trying not to get him too excited about chasing me.

I heard Finn speaking quietly off to my left, a little behind me. "Jayne, take a step to your right ... slowly ... "

He didn't have to tell me twice. I stepped to my right and back, hoping it would put me between Tony and Mr. Tall, Dark, and Bloody. One more step and I was even with Finn on my left.

He had his bow up, arrow notched and ready to go.

Now that I was out of the way, our mystery man ... creature ... whatever he was, saw Finn too.

"Oooh, scary. A bow and arrow." He put his hand up to his mouth in mock fear. "Whatever am I going to do?"

Before the word 'do' was completely out of his mouth, he was standing three feet in front of Finn. I didn't even see him begin to move and then suddenly he was just *there*. "Hello, sweetheart. I ... " The rest of the cruel taunt he was in the process of lisping at Finn was suddenly cut off when Finn let the arrow fly, embedding it in the creature's chest cavity.

Finn slowly lowered the bow to his side as we all stared, stunned, at the arrow now protruding halfway out of the creature's chest and partway out of its back.

"Take that, shit-fer-brains," said Finn.

The creature was breathing heavily, the simpering smile wiped from his face. "Dammit ... a *wooden* arrow? Who gave that dangerous toy to you, little boy?"

And then he was gone ... *poof* ... like he'd never even been there in the first place.

Finn let out the breath he'd been holding in one big whoosh, bending over and holding his hand over his heart.

I totally understood what he was going through. I was having a small heart attack myself, and I hadn't just stuck a blood-sucking creature from my worst nightmares through the chest with a stupid arrow, unlike Finn.

Tony looked over at our hero, his own face so white it looked nearly blue. "Where'd you learn to shoot like that?"

Finn stood up and shrugged his shoulders. "I come from a long line o' rednecks; we bowhunt all kinda crazy shit in Central Florida. Nothin' like that, though."

I decided right then and there that I was never going to mock or disrespect a redneck ever again, for as long as I lived. He'd just saved all our bacon.

I put my hand on his shoulder. "Finn, my friend, you have nerves of absolute steel. I almost peed my pants when that gargoyle just appeared in front of you like that. I didn't even see him move."

"He reminded me of a rattler. Just waitin' to strike. We got lots of rattlers out where I'm from."

My newfound admiration for Finn's redneckery was interrupted by the sound of Chase's moaning. In all the excitement I had kind of forgotten the poor guy. Thank God he was still alive. My brain was not ready to accept death yet. Anyone's. Not even that freaky deaky monstrosity that had just vanished into thin air. It's not that I minded him being dead, so much as I just didn't want to have to look at him anymore; and if he had died, he'd still be here with us, as a reminder of how the deep the shit was that we were in right now. *I don't think they make wading boots tall enough.*

Becky was the first to reach Chase. She knelt down, peering at his face, careful not to touch him. "Hey, Chase. You okay?"

I wasn't so worried about the touching part. I bent down and tapped his cheek a couple times. "Hey, Chase ... you in there?" I figured he'd appreciate the tough love approach more than the fawning and sniveling stuff.

His dry lips parted a little and he said weakly, "Yeah ... barely."

"Can you open your eyes?"

He opened them, and I couldn't help but gasp in surprise. The light of the moon was shining down onto his face, almost as bright as a flashlight. What were once the brightest cornflower-blue eyes I'd ever seen, were now a dark and dull ... I don't know ... *blah.* If 'empty' could be a color, this is what it would look like. "Holy shit, Chase ... your eyes."

"I can't see anything in this light," said Becky, pulling her flashlight out of her bag and shining it in Chase's face. As soon as she saw what I was talking about, her eyes got even buggier than they already were, welling up with tears. She snapped off her flashlight and turned her head to quickly brush them away.

Chase struggled to sit up, blinking the remnants of the brightness away. "I can see fine, but it is a little dark."

Tony and Finn came up to see what the big deal was. They both got on either side of Chase to help him stand. He swayed a little on his feet at first, but then he seemed to get his equilibrium back.

"Dizzy ... "

"Still a man of few words, I see," I said, jokingly. It was time to get some positive vibes back into this group, so I was determined not to start shrieking and having a total mental breakdown, even though that seemed like the natural thing to be doing.

Becky choked, laughing and crying at the same time. "Sorry," she said, embarrassed about her tears. I thought she was the only one having a normal reaction right now though, so I patted her on the shoulder to make her feel better.

Tony and Finn leaned in and got a closer look at Chase's eyes. Finn shined his flashlight on Chase's face. "Dude, what color are your eyes s'posed to be?"

"Blue."

Finn let out a low whistle. "Well, they ain't blue no more."

"Yeah, they're a kind of, I don't know ... gray? Is that gray, Jayne?" asked Tony, concern marring his features.

"That's what I'd call it," I answered. That was better than saying 'lifeless' or 'empty'. I changed the subject to something more pressing. "So, where the hell are Jared and Spike, and what the *fuck* was that monster doing to Chase?"

"Looked like it was eatin' him, to me," said Finn, matter-of-factly.

"I don't think it was eating me," said Chase.

The teeth marks and blood streaks on his neck said differently. "What was it doing then?" I asked. Maybe it had injected him with a poison that was making him stupid.

"It was draining my life force away, I think, not just blood. After it got the drop on me and nailed me to the ground, I tried to fight it; but almost right away, I got tired. Then stuff just stopped mattering to me and I kinda zoned out. I quit fighting on purpose."

"Stuff? What stuff stopped mattering?" asked Tony.

"Life. Living."

A life-sucking creature. Here in this forest. With us. "Sonofa*bitch*!"

"*Shhh,* Jayne, not so loud," said Tony, sounding panicked.

"What?! Those assholes put us in this forest with humanoid creepers that like to suck the life outta people! You know what that means, Tony? *Vampires!* And not the hot, *Twilight* kind either. How am I supposed to remain calm about *that?*"

Becky spoke up. "He's right. We have to be quiet. That thing might not be the only one out here. Maybe he has ... friends."

I looked at Chase. "How do you feel now ... about life, I mean?"

He shrugged his shoulders. "Better. Tired."

"I've read a lot of vampire books, and I've never read one that said they suck the will to live out of you," said Tony, keeping his voice down.

"What's the difference? Blood ... life ... the end result is the same," I said, pissed off all over again. When I got my hands on that Dardennes guy, he was gonna be *so* friggin' sorry.

The thought of lighting my flare and giving up entered my mind, but the reality of knowing it would do no good quickly chased that thought right out again. The assholes who gave us the flares were the same assholes who knew that vampire was in here. The chances of them coming to rescue us, I was quickly realizing, were probably nil. Our only hope was to press on and get to the end.

"Where are Spike and Jared?" asked Tony, looking around.

"Maybe they ran off," said Finn.

"Maybe the creature got them and they're on the ground around here somewhere," said Becky, looking around fearfully, stepping over to hold onto Finn's arm.

Smart girl, going with the guy who has the poison arrows and knows how to use 'em. I took a step closer to Finn too and immediately felt emboldened. "Or maybe," I suggested, "they're hanging out with Niles having a nice little laugh at our expense."

Tony frowned at me. "Jayne, how can you say that? They wouldn't do that." He was getting mad, thinking I was joking at an inappropriate time. And to be fair, I have been known to do that before, but not this time.

"I'm not kidding, Tony. Something was going on with Jared. I saw him giving goo-goo eyes to Dardennes earlier. After I caught him, he wouldn't look at me anymore."

That made Becky cranky, if the tone of her voice was any indication. "Jayne, you're wrong. Jared's been nothing but kind and helpful to all of us. If it wasn't for him, we'd all still be out on the street, fending for ourselves."

"Yeah," I scoffed, "instead, you're here in the haunted forest, about to have the life sucked out of you by a flamingly gay vampire."

"Nah. I ain't buyin' it," said Finn. "Jared's a good guy." He was shaking his head, refusing to listen to anything negative about his absentee leader.

"I agree with Jayne," said Chase.

No one was more stunned than I was at this. "You do? Why?"

"I saw the same thing. And once that life-sucker guy appeared, Jared went AWOL. Spike stuck around for a bit, but then he left, too. At least Spike tried to help. Jared ... " His shrug said it all.

"Ha! I *told* you, Tony."

Tony shook his head. "I still don't believe it. Just because someone gives someone a look and runs away when a blood-sucking demon jumps out of the trees - like any smart person who wants to live would do - it doesn't make him an accomplice. I'm withholding judgment until I have more proof."

"Ugh, you sound like a lawyer, Tony." I hated lawyers. I knew they served a purpose, but my dad was one and that was all I needed to know.

He shrugged an apology at me, but I knew Tony well enough to know that when he puts his foot down, it's down. He'd have to see Jared sucking the life out of someone with his own eyes before he agreed to my theory.

"It don't matter," said Finn. "We hafta get outta here and find that first waypoint."

"Does anyone have any idea where we are?" I asked, bending down to open my bag and get my map out. My hand brushed up against the sharp stick in there at the same time we heard a crashing in the trees nearby. I grabbed it and yanked it out, ready to jab anyone who came too close.

I had pretty decent eyesight here in this forest, but when I pulled my weapon out, it looked blacker than black. It seemed to meld into the shadows, almost impossible to see. I had no time to contemplate this phenomenon, though, because someone or some*thing* was coming right for us. And fast.

Becky was pointing her flashlight in the direction of the noise, her knife held in her other hand.

The rest of us kept our weapons at the ready.

Blood pressures were rising.

Anxiety was at maximum capacity.

This thing needed to come out and give us a damn good explanation for why it was scaring the shit out of us, and *quick,* or it was gonna get stabbed, arrowed, sliced, axed, and shot.

The branches parted and out stepped Spike, his slingshot dangling from one fist. "Hey, guys ... whoa, easy there ... don't shoot." He held his hands up in front of him in a gesture of surrender, the rubber bands of his slingshot dangling limply. He flashed his trademark smile at us.

Instead of turning me on this time, though, it creeped me out, looking all too familiar. I could still picture the blood smeared on a very similar set of teeth not too long ago. Everyone but me lowered their weapons.

"Not so fast, there, *Spike,* if that's your real name ... " I stepped around Finn and Chase, advancing on him slowly. "Lift up your shirt."

"What?" Spike looked lost.

"You heard me. Lift it." I gestured with my stick, point first.

Spike looked at all our faces, one by one. "Guys? Help me out here. Why the striptease?"

"Oh Gawd, Jayne! Not again!" said a frustrated Finn. "He ain't the bad guy here!"

"You heard her," said Chase. "Lift it."

"You too?" Finn asked Chase, but Chase ignored him.

"Listen, guys, I don't know what's going on here, but I was lost for a little while and now I'm just glad I found you."

"Save it. Lift up your shirt, or taste my pointy stick, *Spike*." I was so sad right then, thinking I was going to have to stab the hottest guy I'd seen in a long, long time. Maybe ever. *Those fucking teeth.* I should have *known* they were too good to be true.

I heard a noise behind me. It was the sound of Finn's arrow being notched and drawn back. He sounded tired when he said, "You heard her, Spike. Show us the goods."

Spike swallowed loudly. I could see his Adams apple move up and down with the effort. He dropped his slingshot on the ground in front of him and slowly reached for the bottom of his shirt.

"Okay, guys. I don't know what the hell is going on here, but if you want to see my chest that bad, go right ahead. Get your fill, cuz this show is available for a limited time only." He slowly lifted his shirt to reveal the body beneath.

Chapter Fourteen

SPIKE BROUGHT HIS SHIRT UP and over his head to reveal a very heavily-tattooed torso. The multi-colored tapestry ended at his wrists and neck, exactly where his shirt would be when it was on.

We saw plenty of ink, but no injury. No scar. No marks. So unless Spike was able to spontaneously heal himself of an arrow wound to the heart in five minutes, leaving no trace and perfectly formed tattoos behind, well, he wasn't our man ... or our vampire ... or whatever that thing was.

I wagged my stick at him. "Go ahead, put it down. We've seen enough." *More than enough actually. Yummers.*

Spike put his shirt back on, pulling his sleeves down to cover his tattoos. "Well, that was fun. Now it's your turn, Jayne." He smiled at me, nearly downing me with his combination magic smile and now, as I'd just discovered, gorgeously tattooed self. He was like my hottest bad boy fantasy fused with the niceness of Tony.

Why, oh why, was I meeting him right before I was going to die? Where is the justice in life?

"Where's Jared?" asked Chase.

I turned, walking back to join the others, catching Becky's eye. She was fanning herself, and not because it was hot in the forest. She gave me a look and I knew exactly what she was thinking. *Holy hotness.* Spike was something else. He could suck on my neck any day of the week and twice on Sundays - so long as he didn't drain the life out of me, of course.

I closed my eyes for a second and gave myself a mental shake. I had to get my head back in the game. There was no use fantasizing about Spike while sitting on death's doorstep. There would hopefully be plenty of time for that later.

Spike walked over to us, answering Chase's question while tucking his slingshot into his back pocket. "I have no idea where Jared went. One minute the three of us were walking down the path, the next minute that ... thing ... was on me. I got one good punch in before he knocked me on my ass. I was about to get jumped on again when Chase shot him in the back - by the way, thanks for that, Chase - and then I got the hell outta there. I figured Chase had done the same thing. I just ran until I couldn't hear anything anymore. I waited a bit, got a little lost, and then found my way back."

"Did you see which direction Jared went?" I asked.

"Nope. I don't even remember seeing him when that guy was around."

"Uh-*huh* ... he wasn't even around, eh? Interesting ... ," I said knowingly, looking at Tony and then Finn. They both shook their heads at me.

Spike noticed. "What? What'd I miss?"

Finn sighed. "Jayne and Chase think Jared may be in on this thing with Dardennes and them."

Spike considered it a second. "Nah. Not Jared ... he's a good guy."

I just raised my eyebrows. I'd already said my piece on this. We'd find out soon enough which side Jared was on. He could run, but eventually, we'd catch up.

"Well, I vote we stay here and wait until morning. I can't see a damn thing out here. With my luck, we'll just get farther and farther away from the waypoint," said Becky, sinking down to sit on the forest floor.

I looked around. It didn't seem all that dark to me, but everyone else agreed with Becky. I didn't argue because I'd had enough excitement for one night and this seemed as good a place as any to spend the night - except for the fact that it was the very spot where Chase had been attacked. I decided that if he didn't have a problem with it, I shouldn't either. "You cool with this, Chase?"

He shrugged, which apparently meant he was okay with it.

We all gathered around the flattest spot we could find, and even though the night wasn't that cold, we huddled close together.

"Should we build a fire?" asked Becky.

"I dunno if we should or not," said Finn, looking to the rest of us for our votes.

I yawned. "I'm tired enough to just fall asleep right now, fire or not." I had fished out one of my meal packets and was getting ready to tear it open.

"You might wanna conserve as much of that as you can," said Finn.

I thought about it, looking over at Tony for his input.

He nodded.

I dumped out the bag's contents - something in foil, something else in foil, and something else in foil. *Stupid. Who packs rations without labels on them?* I opened up one of the smaller ones and some crackers fell out. I picked them up and ate them slowly, savoring the familiar taste. They reminded me of Townhouse crackers, which I usually ate with thin slices of mild cheddar cheese. I sighed, wishing I had some.

I'd bet my mom had a big block of it in our fridge ... at home.

The thought of her and our house made me sad. I wondered what she was doing right now, while I was traipsing around in a nightmare forest a million miles away. Maybe worrying about me a little. But then again, maybe not. She probably wasn't as concerned about me as she should be, which was a small comfort; I wasn't not sure why. I was just glad she wasn't thinking about me being mauled by vampires and crap like that. I had never texted her to tell her I had left. I sighed. Things were definitely complicated between us right now, but I still felt bad about not telling her where I was going.

Tony nudged me with his foot. "Whatcha thinkin' about?"

"Nothin'," I said. I didn't want to talk about my problems in front of everyone.

Tony let it go. He just put his arm around my shoulders and squeezed.

I was so glad he was here with me. Then again, a part of me wished he were really, really far away - far away from this seriously next-level, screwed-up shit.

"I'll take the first watch," said Chase, sitting with his back to us, looking out into the center of the clearing.

"How're we gonna work this?" asked Finn, kneeling and sitting back on his heels, his bow leaning up against his thighs.

"I'll do two hours, then we switch; each of us does two hours 'til the sun comes up. If you hear or see anything questionable, wake everybody up."

"Anybody know what time it is?" asked Spike.

"Prob'ly about eight or nine, I'd guess," said Finn.

"Someone's gonna get lucky and miss out on guard duty," said Spike, winking at Becky and me.

"I don't expect to miss out, guys," I said.

"Me neither," said Becky.

"Don't worry, girls, you'll get your chance," assured Finn. "You can go first tomorrow night."

"Maybe we can finish the whole thing tomorrow," said Becky.

"That's not very likely," came a voice from the trees behind us - Jared's voice.

I grabbed my stick and stood up. I saw Chase reach behind his back and slowly pull his gun out of the waistband of his pants, keeping it hidden down by his side. None of the other sitting ducks did anything.

"Hey, Jared, where've you been?" asked Becky, jumping up to run and give him a hug.

He didn't stab her with his spear, so that was a good sign. He also didn't bite her neck - another point in his favor; but he'd be stupid to do that while everyone was watching, so I still wasn't convinced.

I walked over with the point of my stick facing out. "Lift up your shirt, Jared." I wanted to see if he had a little boo-boo over his heart.

He just looked at me, no expression on his face, moving to the side, as if to step around me and get closer to the group. Becky was hanging onto his arm, giving me a worried look.

"Don't go any farther, or you and me are gonna have a problem," I said, menacingly. Everything he was doing right now was only making me feel more secure in my suspicions. The time for playing nice was over.

"What?" he half-laughed. "Are you gonna stab me with your stick?" He smiled at me, as if trying to disarm me with his niceness, but I wasn't having any of it.

"Lift up the shirt, or feel the pain of my stick in your stupid guts, Jared. It's that simple."

Tony's voice came out two octaves higher than normal, "Jayne, stop! It's Jared!"

Chase showed up at my side. "Do what she says, Jared."

I glanced sideways at Chase and then looked quickly back at Jared. I was grateful for the support, but I didn't want to take my eyes off him for even a second. I saw how fast that vampire thing had moved. Actually, technically speaking, I had *not* seen how fast it had moved because it moved too fast to *be* seen.

Without lowering my weapon or dropping my watch I said, "Thanks for speaking up, Chase. I thought I was going to have to do this on my own."

Spike strolled up and stood at my other elbow. "Well, what the hell. I had to do the striptease, Jared. It's only fair if you have to do it too." He didn't cock his slingshot, but it's not like it would have been very scary even if he had.

"Striptease? Are you guys drinking out here or something?" Jared laughed, looking from person to person while giving all of us his most charming, innocent smile.

Mr. Innocent, my ass.

Chase pulled his gun out of hiding. "Just do it, Jared, then we can move on to other things."

"Let me get this straight. You want me ... to pull up my *shirt?"*

I nodded silently.

Jared sighed. "Whatever ... " He let his spear drop to the ground next to him, and reached down to pick up the bottom of his shirt. "This is ridiculous, you know."

We all watched as more and more of his torso was revealed.

I don't think I've ever seen anyone that white before. He was glowing like the moonlight out here. "Holy shit, man, does anyone have any sunglasses?" I asked. I could already see that his chest was a smooth as a baby's butt - no stab wounds anywhere.

Jared's face was still under the lifted shirt. "Can I get dressed now?"

Chase put his gun back in his waistband, walking away.

"Yes, please," said Spike. "I'm getting snow blind from looking at you."

Everyone giggled. Then we were all laughing. Hard. Apparently, trying to stay quiet when you laugh, while also worrying about being killed by a vampire, is impossible. Pretty soon we were all grabbing our stomachs and moaning.

"Stop ... stop laughing ... my stomach ... ," said Becky.

Even Chase was smiling. His eyes were looking bluer too.

"Chase, your eye color is coming back," I said.

Tony squinted in the darkness, trying to see Chase's eyes.

Finn tried to do the same. "How can you see that from here?" he asked.

I shrugged. "It's as plain as day. The moon is lighting him up like a candle."

Tony looked around and up into the sky. "No, it's not. It's pitch black out here ... now that Jared's pulled his shirt back down."

"Oh-ho! *Zingah!!"* I shouted, laughing my ass off all over again, before eventually collapsing in near exhaustion.

Eventually we all quieted down, once the adrenaline had left our systems. I knew now that Jared wasn't the vampire. I still wasn't totally convinced he wasn't somehow in on it, though. His lame excuse for where he'd been mirrored Spike's, but it was less believable since he had been gone for so damn long *and* neither Spike nor Chase remembered seeing him there in the clearing during the attack. Still, it was a good feeling to have everyone together again, to see Chase's eyes returning back to their usual blue, and to have some kind of a plan.

We decided we were going to sleep under the trees at the edge of the clearing tonight and get up bright and early to kick this test's ass tomorrow. Then we were going home.

I fell asleep wondering just where home was for me.

Chapter Fifteen

WE GOT UP AS THE first rays of sun were penetrating into the clearing where we'd spent the night. I didn't see how bright the morning light was at first because there were so many damn leaves on me; the trees around here had a serious shedding problem. No wonder the ground was so soft everywhere.

I threw the green leaves off of me as I sat up, pulling several of the more tenacious ones out of my hair. Once they were gone, I realized just how low the temperature was. Apparently, leaves made good insulation. I shivered from the cold and my still sleepy metabolism. I wasn't much of a coffee person, but I sure wouldn't have turned down a cup of it just then. I stood up and stomped my feet a little, getting the circulation going and my body warmed up.

Chase was still sleeping, snoring lightly. He had stayed up for the first watch and had wrestled with a vampire and lost, so I didn't blame him for being extra tired.

Jared had taken the map out of his backpack and was looking it over with Finn and Tony.

Spike was staring off into the trees, eating crackers out of one of his meal bags. It was easy to see he was more of a night owl than a morning person. I'm not sure his brain was totally functioning yet.

His hair stuck out in all directions, making me wonder if he was called Spike because of this particular style. Even unkempt and unwashed, I loved it. Now if only he'd take his shirt off again ...

Becky stepped up next to me and nudged my hip with hers. "Wanna go pee with me?"

"Sure. I'm glad you said something; I've had to go all night."

We made our way out into the trees.

"Me too. I guess I'm glad we have limited food and water right now."

"You said it."

Once we were out of earshot, Becky asked, "So, do you feel better about Jared now?"

"Enough to let him sleep with us, so long as we have a guard - but no, not totally. Becky, you missed it. He seriously was giving Dardennes some kind of look, and Dardennes was returning it."

Becky shrugged. "Well, I think he seemed good last night, right?"

"Yeah, but his explanation of where he'd been didn't really make much sense, did it?"

Becky sighed. "Maybe not. But I have to believe he's with us, Jayne, on our side. He's been really good to everyone, including Sam. He really helped her out. He almost didn't come without her; she insisted, though."

That really didn't work with my theory so well, but I wasn't going to give up that easily. "Let's just agree to disagree on this for now. I'm sure it will work itself out in the end."

Becky smiled. "Deal. Now the question is: what are we going to use as toilet paper?"

"Leaves?" I suggested.

"Just don't use any poison oak or poison ivy ones."

I hesitated, instantly picturing an itchy red rash on my hoo-hah.

Yikes. "I have no idea what poison anything looks like unless it's in a container marked with a skull and crossbones."

"We'll be okay if we take a leaf off a tree - I think the poison stuff is on the ground."

"Yeah, but did you notice how high up those branches are? How are we going to reach a leaf?" I pouted for effect. "Dammit, I want a leaf."

Suddenly, a giant, long tree limb that was above our heads moved, slowly lowering itself down to stop next to my shoulder. The sound of its huge body of wood straining and cracking to move in such an unnatural way was eerie as hell. I stood stock still, unable to make my feet go.

"What the fuck?" I whispered desperately to Becky, looking for some kind of guidance. The panic from last night was back. Was the *tree* going to kill me? Was it in league with the flamboyant, Chase-nibbling vampire?

Becky's eyes were nearly bugging out of her head. She whispered loudly, *"I think it wants you to take a leaf!"* She grabbed my hand, squeezing the crap out of it. I was glad for the contact, though, and squeezed back.

Please don't let this tree kill me, please don't let this tree kill me. I wasn't sure who or what I was praying to, but I hoped he, she, or it was listening.

I slowly reached up to the branch sitting next to my shoulder and gingerly plucked two leaves off. As soon as I pulled my hand away, the branch sprang back up, making a mighty groaning sound, the branch and leaves creating a whooshing sound as they rocketed from my shoulder back towards the sky. Tons of leaves, loosened by the branch's unnatural movement, flew off and floated down around us.

Becky held her hands up, catching some as they fell. She looked at me, her hands now grasping a bunch of leaves to her chest, whispering, "Holy crap, Jayne. What just happened?"

"I have no friggin' idea." I looked up at the tree. There was a crack in the limb that had moved for me. And there was no doubt in my mind that this branch had moved *for me*. I said I wanted a leaf, and it gave me a thousand of them - from its own ... *body*. Sap was coming out of the crack in the branch near the place where it connected to the tree, and I was suddenly overwhelmed with sadness. Tears sprang to my eyes and my heart started aching a little bit.

"Jayne, what's wrong? Why are you crying?" Becky giggled a little bit, confused about my seemingly incongruous emotions.

I pointed. "Look at the sap coming out of that crack. The tree is bleeding. It's *bleeding* because I asked for a stupid leaf to wipe my ass! I caused that to happen. I don't know why, but it's making me really sad." My explanation was nuts and my feelings being so over-the-top made no sense, but it was what it was.

Leaves rained down on my head, the tree shuddering, loosening them and causing them to fall. It just made me even more unhappy. I stood there being showered with leaves while crying like a baby.

Becky rubbed my back, and in an understanding, soothing voice said, "PMS sucks."

I frowned through my sadness, screwing up my eyebrows in concentration. I'd just finished my period, so according to my calculations, this wasn't PMS; but I didn't say anything to Becky. Let her think I had a chemical reason for being so wacky right now. It was probably the stress. I was going to figure this out with Tony later ... on second thought, as soon as I got back.

I wiped the tears off my cheeks and took a deep breath. "I still have to pee."

Becky laughed. "Me too." She looked around and then up at the tree, apprehension written all over her face. "Where should we go?" she whispered.

I looked up at the tree too. It had stopped sending leaves down on me, which was a good thing, because pretty soon I was going to be completely covered in a mound of them, and the tree was going to be naked. I seemed to recall from biology class that trees needed their leaves to absorb the sun's energy and feed themselves. Why I decided at that moment to remember some random fact from one of my science classes, I don't know, but it managed to make me feel guilty all over again. *Shit! Focus. Move on.*

"Well," I said, getting back to the business at hand, "I don't really want to pee with this tree watching me."

No sooner had the words left my lips, than I felt the ground under our feet start to tremble. The tree groaned again, twisting its trunk.

It hit me then that the tree was actually *pulling* itself up *out* of the ground. "No! *Wait!* Tree, don't move!" It stopped moving, so I continued my begging. "You can watch me pee! It's okay! Here look, I'm peeing! I'm peeing! You can stop uprooting yourself." I looked in desperation at Becky, nearly yelling, *"Start peeing for chrissake, Becky!"*

She yanked her pants down and peed on the spot, not saying a word.

The ground had stopped moving and the tree had ceased its groaning and shuddering. The only thing I could hear was my heart beating in my throat and our pee splattering on the leaves beneath us.

After we were finished and had stepped to the side, we stood there, looking at each other, at the tree, and at all the leaves around us - completely weirded out, not knowing what to say. Both of us had seen it, so there was no denying it had happened. I was *pretty* sure I wasn't crazy. But then a thought came to me.

"Maybe this is one of those mass hysteria things, you know? Where stress causes people to have the same psychotic episodes."

Becky thought about it for a second, still not moving, and said, "Yeah, but what about all of this?" She gestured to the pile of leaves and the crack in the branch above us.

"Maybe it was already here and we just made up situations to fit the scene?"

Becky shrugged, not looking very convinced. "Maybe."

"Come on, let's go back," I said, turning towards our camp, with Becky anxiously following and then quickly overtaking me in her hurry to get to the clearing. I glanced over my shoulder at the tree and stopped. I spun around to go back.

"What are you doing?" asked Becky, now ten paces farther down the path we'd followed coming in.

Without answering, I went up to the tree and stood at the base of its trunk. After all that it had done for me, even if it was just a psychotic episode in my mind, I couldn't just *take* from it and then leave without doing something in return.

I didn't think about what I was going to do too much; I just did it. I put my arms around the trunk and squeezed, turning myself into the type of person I had mocked many times in the past - the proverbial tree hugger.

It was impossible for me to describe the feeling that came through that tree and into my arms at that moment. There just weren't any words for it in my vocabulary. But if I took everything I loved - like cotton candy and the smile on my best friend's face and a tiny, fuzzy-wuzzy kitten - and wrapped it all up into one sensation, this was what hugging that tree felt like. I couldn't stop the smile from bursting across my face.

I felt joy from the tree too. I didn't know what trees liked -

probably not cotton candy and kittens - but whatever ... I was sure that my tree was feeling those things when we connected.

Don't get me wrong; the tree didn't hug me back, not with its branches anyway. But I felt an energy coming *to* me *from* it, so I was calling it a hug. If someone wanted to put a scientific label on what was happening with our touch, they could probably say it was an exchange of life forces - human and plant - and be not too far off.

Whatever it was, whatever it was called, it was fucking *awesome.* I wondered if I'd get the same sensation from every tree in this forest or just this one.

"Um, Jayne? ... What are you doing?" Becky had crept back over and was standing a few feet away from me, staring.

"Come over here and do this with me. You're not going to believe this shit." I didn't want to let go just yet, so I spoke with my face resting against the tree's rough bark.

Becky walked over hesitantly, looking at me with a worried expression. "Are you okay?" She was obviously concerned for my mental health.

"Shut up and hug the damn tree, Becky."

Becky sighed. "Oh, screw it, I might as well. I've done stranger things." She went to the other side of the tree, wrapped her arms around its wide trunk, and squeezed.

"Do you feel it?" I asked, excitedly. Now Becky was going to see firsthand how awesome this was.

"Feel what?"

"*It.* The awesomeness."

"Uh, no. All I feel is hard and pokey tree bark."

"Maybe you're not doing it right."

"I wasn't aware there was a technique to tree hugging." She started to pull away.

"No, wait! I'm coming over there. Stay put."

I released the tree and lost my connection. *Bummer.* Back to regular life - no cotton candy, no kittens. I walked around to the other side of the tree to look at what Becky was doing. She seemed to be hugging the tree properly; not that I was an expert, but I seemed to have a knack for it.

"Maybe put more of your body on it ... not just hug with your arms, but with your whole body."

"I'm not going to hump the tree, Jayne."

"Shit, Beck, I'm not talking about humping. This is hugging only - Rated G, like a Disney movie."

She sighed, but moved closer so her whole body was touching the tree.

"Well?"

"Sorry, I've got nothing."

"Let me help you."

I stepped forward and got next to her at the tree. I leaned in to hug it again, this time putting my arms above hers on the trunk, so I was touching the tree and her at the same time. I instantly felt the rush of good vibrations again.

Becky yelped. "Holy *crap*, Jayne! What the heck *is* that?!"

I shouted, my cheek against the tree again, "*A-ha!* You feel it now too, don't you?!"

I let go in my excitement and saw Becky's expression go from joy to disappointment in a flash.

"Get your butt back on the tree, Jayne, I just lost the mojo."

I jumped back into hugging position, and as soon as I was hugging the tree and touching Becky at the same time again, her face lit up.

"It's like ... it's like ... falling into sunshine on a cool day ... ," she said dreamily.

"I know." I had the biggest grin on my face. "I could hug this tree all damn day."

"We need to get the guys in on this," said Becky.

I stepped back away from the tree, severing our connection to it and each other.

Becky's face fell. "What's wrong?" She stood up straight, looking at me questioningly.

"I don't think we should say anything just yet."

"Why?"

I didn't answer her right away, and she got a sad look on her face. "It's because you don't trust Jared, isn't it?"

I shrugged. "I just want to feel more comfortable with him first, okay? I mean, it's my call, right?"

Becky nodded. "Yeah, it's your call. You're the tree whisperer, not me." She looked up at the tree wistfully. "That was amazing, though. I wish the others could feel what we were feeling. Even just one time would be worth it. I don't think I could ever forget that."

"Yeah, me neither." I got a mischievous look on my face. "Wanna try another one? See if it's just this tree or if it's all the trees?"

Becky jumped up and down excitedly, her smile back in full force. "Yes! Which one?" She looked around eagerly, seeking out a candidate.

"Let's move closer to the camp. Maybe it's just this area that has the special mojo."

"Good idea."

We walked about thirty feet back towards the clearing. We were still out of sight, but we could hear the others, their voices a low murmur.

"How about this one?" I suggested.

I pointed to a skinnier tree - one that had different bark and leaves too. Our experiment required a change in variables like the age, species, and location of the subject. I knew my science lab teacher would be so proud right now with the integrity of my study variables, or whatever the hell he always called it.

I went up to the new tree but didn't start hugging right away. I felt like it might be kind of presumptuous of me to just walk up and do that, so I started talking first.

Becky was standing next to me, and I saw her eyebrows go up a little, but she was letting me run the show. She remained quiet, listening patiently.

"Um, hello, Tree. I'm Jayne ... and this is Becky. We wanted to hug you, so here we are. You're ... um ... a really nice-looking tree, so that's why we picked you. I mean, all the trees here are nice looking and all ... "

Becky sighed, her patience running thin. "Just hug the tree already, would ya?"

"Fine. Don't rush me." I turned back to the tree. "So I'm going to hug you now, and I hope you give me one of those tree-hugs back."

I reached my hands out and put them on the trunk. My arms easily went all the way around. I instantly felt the energy coming back to me; this time it was more vibrant, more green, if a color can be used to describe a feeling. I didn't think about cotton candy this time. I thought about a cool breeze on a hot day, fireworks on the fourth of July, the excitement of being chased by someone who I hoped would catch me. Above all, I felt love. Just plain love. There was a connection here that went much deeper than flesh and bone, bark and wood.

"Can I join you now?" asked Becky, smiling at the look of happiness on my face.

"Yep. You're gonna love this."

Becky stepped up quickly, obviously anxious to feel the sensation again. She wrapped her arms around the tree, making sure to touch my arms as well. Her face radiated joy as soon as we were linked. "Oh my *goodness*, this is nice - different, but nice. This is a younger tree, I can tell."

She was right. The feelings were younger somehow. The bigger, older tree had given us something just as wonderful, but more ancient, more mature. It was impossible to describe with words - I couldn't even think about it properly in my own head.

"What the hell are you guys doing?" Spike's smiling voice penetrated our euphoria. "Are you hugging that tree? What ... did I take a wrong turn somewhere? Am I in Berkeley?"

We broke away from the tree, smiling nervously as if we'd been caught doing something we shouldn't have been doing.

"Yep, just thanking the tree for some toilet paper is all," I said, trying to brush him and his suspicions off with an overly casual tone.

Spike nodded his head in appreciation. "Well, that's just the polite thing to do, isn't it?" He smiled right at me with those damn teeth of his, and I was glad to feel the familiar sparks warming my insides. This time I didn't see the blood smear image generated by memories of that awful vampire creature thing.

I smiled back, still feeling the tree's energy and now basking in Spike's sexual vibe.

He moved a little closer to me than he normally did.

I forgot Becky was there entirely.

"I never took you for a tree hugger." He was still smiling, only now it was down at me; we were so close I was practically under him. I had never realized before that he was this much taller than me.

I could feel my face starting to burn. "You are going to set me on fire one of these days, you know that?" *Holy shit, did that just come out of my mouth?* What the hell was wrong with me? I looked back at the tree for a second. That damn thing had loosened my tongue or something. *Shitshitshit.*

Spike looked amused. "Is that so? I think I'd like to see that - so long as it isn't actual flames you're talking about."

I stepped back to get some breathing room, suddenly very nervous. "Um, yeah ... I mean, no ... not actual flames. Not a fire. Not ... *shit,* never mind. We need to get back." I stepped around him and walked briskly towards the camp. I didn't look back to see if he was following.

Becky, who had observed the whole embarrassing interaction, ran to catch up to me. She had a sly grin on her giddy little face. "What was *that* all about?"

I hit her arm with the back of my hand. "Nothing, shut up."

She chanted in a singsong voice, very quietly, "Somebody likes Spiiiiike, somebody likes Spiiiiike."

"Seriously, Becky, what? Are you in second grade? Shut up before someone hears you."

"Don't worry, Jayne, your secret is safe with me ... I mean, your *secrets* are safe with me." She smiled at me conspiratorially and winked.

I couldn't help but smile back. She was the first girl friend I'd had in a long time. Hopefully we wouldn't die in this forest before we could go shopping, talk about boys, or do whatever it is that girl friends do together.

Chapter Sixteen

BY THE TIME WE REACHED the others, they were standing there with backpacks on, waiting impatiently for us to leave for the first waypoint.

"That has to be the longest pee break in history," said Finn, shaking his head as he walked towards Jared. "Women ... "

"Come on, everyone, let's get going," said Jared, going with Finn back towards the path leading out of the clearing. Chase followed them. Spike came from behind, jogging to catch up to the guys. Becky was just in front of Tony and me.

"Did you all come up with a plan of action?" I asked, coming up next to Tony.

"Yep. Jared thinks he knows where we are in relation to the first waypoint. He found a river last night, and it's not far from here. All we have to do is follow it and we'll come to the waypoint."

I walked and pulled my map out at the same time. "Did you look at the map yourself?"

Tony shrugged. "Nope, I just watched Jared do it."

"Were you looking over his shoulder?"

"No, should I have?"

I frowned at him, scolding him silently. "Yes. Don't you think we should know where we're going instead of just blindly following *him*?"

Tony sighed loudly. "Not really."

"Tony, are we still a team here or what?" It was time for him to stop messing around and man-up. I wasn't just going to start going somewhere in these spooky woods without knowing where.

"Yes, Jayne, we're still a team."

"Then help me figure this stupid map out while we walk."

I folded it down, with Tony's help, into a manageable size, but I gave up trying to figure out where we were within thirty seconds. Tony took over, since he was much better at directions than me. I watched as a frown spread across his face.

"What?" I asked.

"I don't know, it's just ... "

"Just what?"

"It's just ... well, it seems like Jared's not going in the most efficient direction."

"Not efficient? In what way?"

"Well, he's headed towards this water, see?"

He tried to show me, but I tripped over his big feet and almost went down. Walking and reading a map is just a recipe for disaster as far as I was concerned. "Don't show me, just tell me."

"Well, he's headed towards the water, but that's kind of a roundabout way of doing it. We could cut off over here to the right and save ourselves at least an hour - probably more."

"Let's do it, then."

Tony folded the map down smaller, intending to put it away. "No, that's okay. This way's fine, too."

I put my hand on Tony's shoulder stopping him. "Tony, just because Jared says it's the way to go, doesn't mean it is the way *we're* going to go. We need to get to those waypoints and get the hell outta here, know what I mean?"

Tony was quiet for a minute, thinking.

The others continued walking, oblivious to our conversation.

"Just tell me what your problem is with Jared, before I decide what to do."

"It's just a feeling I have, based on looks he exchanged with Dardennes. And his disappearing act last night, and his basic attitude. Don't you think it's a little suspicious that Jared's the one who somehow got all of us together? And then all of a sudden we're in this study together, and magically the few other people in that meeting room, the ones he didn't pick up somewhere, were not accepted? It just makes me uncomfortable, that's all. And I'd rather just depend on you and me to get out of here. There's no one I trust more to have my back than you, Tones."

He pursed his lips a few seconds before nodding and saying, "Jayne, I know you can be kinda crazy sometimes, but I also know you're pretty perceptive. You see and sense things that I don't. And there's no one I trust more to have my back than you, so if you want to split off from these guys, then I'll do it. I just keep thinking about that vampire thing from last night. We might have a better chance of surviving something like that if we're in a group."

"I thought about that, too; but I also know that as a big group, we'll attract more attention. It's impossible for seven people to move through the forest quietly. Maybe with it being just two or three of us, it wouldn't be so loud."

"Three?"

I shrugged. "I thought maybe Becky might go with us, I don't know."

"Fine, come on. Let's at least tell them we're going a different way. She can choose to come or not. Maybe Spike will want to come with us, too," Tony said that a little too casually.

"What's that supposed to mean?"

"Oh, nothin'."

"Nothin', my ass. What was that supposed to mean?"

Tony smiled. "I see how you nearly pass out every time he smiles at you. You think I can't sense that heart attack you get every time he's around? And now that we're on the subject, what the heck happened with you and Becky in the woods? If I didn't know you any better I'd say you had some sort of bi-awakening moment out there. You were feeling just too ... I don't know ... dreamy or something."

I whacked him on the arm. "I didn't have a 'bi-awakening moment' at all, don't be an idiot. I just so happened to have discovered the joy of tree-hugging, and it made me happy. And Spike has ... well, let's just say he has a nice smile. It makes me feel tingly all over."

Tony rolled his eyes. "Spare me. And what do you mean 'tree hugging'?"

"I'll show you later. Let's go tell those guys we're going the other direction."

*****

Not surprisingly, the group was less than thrilled about our decision to go a different way. Becky gave me a stern look, but kept my secrets. Chase just stared at us for a second and then looked back in the direction they had been heading before we stopped them. Spike just looked at the ground, not saying anything.

"Now why in the sam hill would you wanna split up like that?" asked Finn.

"The way we're going is shorter," I explained. "Anyone who wants to join us is welcome. Becky?"

She shook her head. "No thanks, guys. I appreciate the offer, but I'm gonna stick with Jared and them."

"Suit yourselves. Guess we'll see you at the finish line," I said, not surprised that Becky had turned us down. She was totally Team Jared.

Tony stayed silent; he didn't like conflict.

"Just be careful, guys," said Jared, seemingly resigned to the fact that he was losing members of his crew.

"Yeah, Jayne, be careful," said Spike, for once not smiling.

"You too." Of all of them, he was the one I hated leaving behind the most. We parted ways, them continuing their roundabout towards the water, Tony and I angling off to the right, and all of us quickly losing sight of each other.

Tony took the lead, and neither of us said anything for a while. Now that we were alone, I was able to fully appreciate the immensity of the forest and it made me question the folly of my plan to be alone. It was probably too late, though, to admit I wished we had more people around us. Tony would kill me.

"It's kinda beautiful and spooky out here, all at the same time," said Tony softly.

I could see what he meant. The sunlight filtered through the treetops, narrow beams shooting like white lasers to the forest floor, lighting up dust motes that floated lazily, aimless in the air around us. The beating wings of a bird moving from tree to tree and the occasional falling leaf added to the whispering of the breeze that brushed past us on its way through to somewhere else.

The whispering sound got louder ... and louder still. I soon realized that it was actual whispering and not the metaphorical stuff I was hearing.

"*Psst. Hello there! You there! Hello!*"

"Tony ... did you hear that?"

"Wasn't that you?"

"No, it wasn't me, you dope. Where's it coming from?"

We stopped and listened intently. The forest was denser ahead. I moved closer to Tony as he stepped back, getting nearer to me. I slowly eased my backpack off my shoulder and unzipped it, pulling my sharpened stick from inside.

I whispered as softly as I could, my lips pressed against Tony's ear, *"Get your fucking axe out and be ready to chop off some vampire heads."*

Before Tony could move, we heard the voice again - this time not whispering, but talking softly.

"Hello! Hello ... you there."

It was coming from behind some bushes off to our right now. There, a fallen tree had created a fertile place for smaller trees and ivy to grow up over it, making a nice shelter for whoever or whatever was calling to us.

"Can you see who it is?" asked Tony out of the side of his mouth.

"No, can you?"

"No."

"Who are ye talkin' aboot?" said the voice, just at my elbow.

"HOLY SHIT ON A FUCKING STICK!" I yelled, jumping as far to my left as I could, brandishing my weapon out in front of me.

Tony yelped like a girl, simultaneously wrestling with his backpack, trying to get it open, and high-step running about five feet ahead, before spinning around to face whatever was there next to us.

I crouched down in a fighting stance, or the closest approximation of a fighting stance that I could come up with, ready to slay the vampire demon I imagined coming for us, its teeth dripping with blood - probably Becky's blood because she was the slowest, weakest one of the herd.

But boy was I surprised when it finally made its appearance.

"What the hell?" I stood up, my head tilting to the side in confusion.

Tony straightened up, looking at me and then back at our visitor - our two-foot-tall visitor with bubbly, lumpy-looking skin, wearing a plaid kilt-looking thing and brown moccasins.

"Who are you?" Tony asked.

"Who?"

"What do you mean, 'who'? You."

"Me?"

"Yes."

"Ye want to know who I be?"

I'd had enough of this *Who's on First* crap. "Listen, little troll ... who are you and what the hell are you doing scaring the shit out of us like that?"

"I beg yer pardon, human girl, but I'm *not* a *troll* and I doan appreciate the insult, I can tell ye that, oh righty. Ye know, in me day, we had respect. Simple respect. A body could walk through the forest, mindin' his own business, and if he happened to cross paths with someone, well, ye could be sure that the least they would do is say hello and exchange some pleasantries. But nooo ... "

And the creature carried on, and on, and on in its Scottish or Irish accent, I couldn't tell which, until I was ready to knock it over the head with my stick. I sidled over to Tony who was standing there, his backpack hanging forgotten by his side, staring at the creature with his mouth open. I nudged him just to be sure he wasn't in some sort of trance.

"What the heck *is* it?" he asked me, his eyes not leaving the spectacle before us.

The creature continued, oblivious to our conversation, "What's so hard about saying hello I'd like ta know? ... "

"Well, not a troll, apparently. Let's just walk away, real slow. I don't want to get it angry. But get your axe out just in case."

Tony looked down at his bag and reached in to get the axe, taking his eyes off the thing in front of us.

I saw the creature's eyes sparkle as the axe made its appearance from the bag. That seemed to finally get it to shut up for a second.

"Well, well, *well* ... what have we here? The axe of the Hawthorne if I not be mistaken ... " The lumpy dwarf moved toward us, eyes on the axe, hand reaching out as if to touch it.

"Not so fast, little non-troll," I said, holding my stick out at it, point forward.

The little thing stopped, eyes growing wide as it stared at my scary little stick.

"And the Dark of Blackthorn too. Oh me goodness, this is a verra interesting day in the Green Forest fer sure, a verra interesting day, indeed." Its eyes were glittering with excitement, and it hopped from one foot to the other like it had ants in its pants - except that it wasn't wearing pants.

Oh please, God, let that thing be wearing underwear under that kilt. I wasn't sure if the creature's enthusiasm was a very good thing, or a very, very bad thing, so I decided to err on the side of caution.

"Yes, it is! The ... um ... Dark pointy stick ... of Blackthorn, or whatever. And the axe of Hawthorne too! So stand back, trolly non-troll, or feel their sharp edges!" I brandished my stick a little to give my threat more oomph, nudging Tony with my elbow.

He held the axe up a little, but not very enthusiastically.

I was going to have to talk to him about that later. First impressions were everything, after all. Regardless, it seemed to do the trick.

The creature held up its hands in surrender. "Oh, goodness me, no, *please* ... I mean ye no harm - absolutely no harm atall, I can assure ye of that. Lucky for ye I've stumbled upon ye here, in the middle of nowhere, totally by happenstance. Yes, very lucky for ye, indeedy do!"

She, or he - I wasn't sure whether the thing was a male or female, even with the skirt, since it could possibly be a man-kilt - was all smiles now.

"Yer lost, I can see that. And I will help ye find yer way." It put its little lumpy hands together in front of its chest, as if in prayer. "So tell me, where would ye like to go?"

Tony and I stood together in silence for a moment, letting our brains process what we were seeing. Not a vampire, for sure. But not a dwarf or a midget either. Something smaller and lumpier. And not a troll. I didn't trust it, and I was sure Tony didn't either, even though we hadn't yet said a word to each other. *Damn,* how I wished that vibe reader thing Tony possessed was a two-way connection.

Tony was the first one to get a grip. "Let's start with you. Who and what are you?"

"Oh, human boy, I'm so verra sorry for not having introduced meself to ye earlier. How incredibly rude that were of me. And there I be, berating ye for yer lack of manners when I so clearly could use a few of me own. Ye know, that's the problem with the world today, so many fa ... people, just runnin' about their business, so self-centered, not worryin' about anyone but therselves. No time fer even the most basic pleasantries, the most basic manners, like a proper introduction ... "

My brain was spinning and I could feel a headache coming on. This was why I hated babysitting. This thing reminded me of a little kid - talking, talking, talking, blah, blah, blah ...

Tony cleared his throat loudly, interrupting the creature. "You were telling us your name and what you are ... ?"

"Ah, yes, sorry, got away from meself there. Me name, young boy, is Gilly, and I be a gnome of the Gar." It took a deep bow, lowering its head almost to the forest floor. It really didn't have that far to go, but it was still impressive.

I was glad we weren't behind the gnome at that moment because I was pretty sure its dress or kilt went right up in the back, revealing a lot more gnome than I was ready to see today. Or ever.

"Hi, Gilly," said Tony politely.

Sometimes that kid scared me with his innocence. "Gilly, why aren't you wearing a pointed red hat and red boots?" I asked.

Gilly frowned at me. "Ya know, stereotyping be a sign of limited intelligence. I might have asked ye where yer lower back tattoo be or yer lip piercing, but I didna." It folded its short little arms and cocked out one funky-shaped hip in a defiant stance.

You've got to be fucking kidding me. I decided after that move that Gilly must be a girl gnome. Only chicks and seriously bitchy gay guys had that particular brand of sass. *Is there such a thing as a gay gnome? Hmmm ...*

"Jaaayne. I know what you're thinking, but don't," said Tony.

"Fine," I said, frustrated that I couldn't mess with the gnome. I don't know a lot about these creatures, other than the fact that they are usually ceramic and hanging out in gardens, but I was pretty sure a gnome in a dress was hilarious in any social circle, human or otherwise.

I sighed. "Okay, Gilly the gnome, we are trying to reach a waypoint and you probably don't even know what that is, so I'm wasting my time here, but ... "

"Well, of course I be knowin' what a waypoint be. There be many of them here in the Green Forest. Four in fact." Gilly was looking at her fingernails, which I now noticed were disgustingly dirty. She started chewing on one of them, which was totally gag-worthy.

I was glad I'd only had a cracker for breakfast. *Oh shit, do not think about how nails are like crackers, do not think about how nails are like crackers ...* Now I was feeling sick to my stomach.

Tony nudged me, getting me back on track.

Holy bat balls, the little lumpy chick knows where to go! "Well, we'd like directions to the first waypoint," I said.

"And which one would that be?" asked Gilly.

"The one on my map." I struggled to pull it out of my bag. "Right here, at this spot." I held the map out to her, stretching my arm as far as it would go, a little worried about the dirty gnome coming too near.

Gilly arched her eyebrows, widening her eyes, but she didn't come any closer. Her eyes kept darting to my stick.

I put it behind my back, tucking it in my waistband, realizing it worried her. I didn't know why. The worst it could do was scratch her, and her skin looked so lumpy, I doubted it would even penetrate. *Ugh,* it was like looking at flesh-colored toad skin.

After the stick was out of sight, Gilly moved forward cautiously, snatching the map from my hand and stepping back.

"Hey, that's my map!" I said.

A voice came from behind us. "Doan give 'er that map! She'll ruin it fer certain!"

Tony spun around to see who it was.

I glanced back but then returned my gaze to Gilly. I didn't want her taking off with my map. "What the hell is it now, Tony?"

"It's another gnome. I think this one is a guy."

"Eh? What'd ye say there, human boy?"

I could hear the leaves rustle as the second gnome approached. "Ye humans are all the same. Ye come in here, tramping around, making all kinds o' noise, disturbing the peace - doan even have the common decency to introduce yerselves. And now look - ye've gone and given yer map to Gilly here. I hope it wasn't important to ye, because she'll surely never get it back to ye in one piece."

"Shut yer yap, ye old turkey waddle. I'm just takin' a look to see which waypoint they want."

"Well, I'd think that'd be obvious. They'd be wantin' the one by the High River of course, it be the closest one."

"How do ye know they didna want to go to the one in the Dell, eh? That one's the best one by me reckonin'. I'd go to that one if it be me."

"Well it's not ye, is it then? It's these two young humans." The second gnome turned to us now. "And what would two humans be wantin' with the waypoints, anyway, eh? And how did ye get here then? Who sent ye?"

The first gnome chimed in. "There ye go again, giving orders, expectin' people to just jump when ye haven't even bothered to introduce yerself. You know, that's the problem with fa...forest dwellers these days, don't even bother with the niceties anymore ... "

The headache was coming back. "Holy horseshit-on-a-stick, Tony, these gnomes are nuts." They couldn't even hear me, they were arguing back and forth so much about common courtesy and manners. *What was it with these gnomes and their manners, anyway?*

"Excuse me, sir and ma'am!" said Tony loudly, immediately causing the gnomes to stop talking and give him their full attention.

He started with a small, awkward bow, hurriedly tucking his axe back in his bag. "My friend Jayne and I - I am Tony by the way, it's nice to meet you - would like to humbly beg you for directions to the waypoint by the High River. And if it wouldn't be too much trouble, further directions to the waypoint in the Dell. Please accept my humblest apologies for my late and hasty introduction." He bowed again when he finished.

I stared at him, incredulous. He sounded like he was reading out of a book for the Knights of the Round Table or something.

He nudged me in the side and said, *"Bow!"* out of the corner of his mouth.

I dropped down into the stupidest looking curtsy imaginable.

Both gnomes instantly reacted. Huge smiles broke out across their faces. I tried not to grimace at the dirt between their disgusting, pointy teeth. They seemed so happy, almost to the point of embarrassment. I saw a faint pink color rising up on their lumpy facial skin, visible even beneath the dirt streaks.

The second gnome was the first to speak. "Sir Tony, it would be our pleasure to direct ye as ye wish. I, Gander, and me mate Gilly, will happily tell ye which way to go. First, ye must know that the waypoints are located equally distant from one t'other in the Green Forest, in the four different territories of the fae folk. Ye and yer lady friend Jayne, of course, be in the territory of the Gar. Welcome to our home." They both bowed. Once again, I was damn glad I wasn't standing behind Gilly and her short skirt.

"The best way to get to the waypoint of the Gar, located at the High River, be to go that direction for seventy-two oaks and fifteen maples, making certain to continue in a south-westerly direction." He finished with a self-satisfied grin and a sharp nod of affirmation.

"Please allow me to correct me mate Gander's directions just a wee bit so that ye will successfully reach yer destination. Ye must, in fact, go only *sixty-one* oaks, and *fourteen* maples, followed by six birch saplings, of course in a south-south west direction. Then fer certain, ye will be at the waypoint of the Gar."

Gander got a grumpy look on his face and turned to look crossly at Gilly. "Dear Gilly, ye know ye be hopelessly incorrect, as usual. Ye know direction is not yer strong suit. Now, if one needs to find a hidden tulip bulb, lost in the Spring frost, or the bones of a woodchuck, then yer the one to call fer certain. But when it comes to finding one's way in the Green Forest, I'm the gnome all the Gar can depend on." He jabbed himself in the chest with his tiny, stubby thumb.

Gilly rounded on Gander with her next volley of arguments against his sense of direction, raising her finger to wag it in his face.

Deciding we didn't need to stick around for this lover's quarrel, I said, "Tony, I think it's time we got the hell out of here."

"I agree. Can you get your map?"

Gilly, in her excitement, had dropped it. It was lying on the ground a few feet away from her. I sidestepped over, bending down slowly to pick it up. I walked backwards towards Tony once I had it in hand, and he took my arm to guide me slowly away from the gnomes. They looked harmless enough, but their teeth were sharp and dirty, and I knew for sure I'd want to vomit if either one of them touched me with their creepy, lumpy hands. As soon as we were out of sight of the gnomes, we took off jogging.

"Are we following their directions?" I asked, breathlessly.

"Yes. They both said southwest-ish, so that's the way I'm going."

"How do you know?"

"I don't. I'm going the way they pointed."

I didn't count, but I was willing to bet that as we arrived at the waypoint of the Gar, we had passed about sixty-one oaks and a couple of maples. Those two gnomes made a good couple.

Chapter Seventeen

THE WAYPOINT OF THE GAR rose up out of the ground in front of us. It was an obelisk landmark of granite or some other heavy-looking gray stone, topped with a metal spike that looked like it was made of brass. It couldn't be brass though, I decided, because it was so shiny. Real brass would have been dark and weathered, being exposed to the elements like this one was. At my dad's house, the one he lived in with my stepmother, he had a brass bell outside the front door. My anal, OCD stepmother would polish it every Sunday to keep it looking perfect, because if she missed a week it would start to turn a funky, mottled brown.

The waypoint was in the center of a small clearing. Where the forest had been full of the sounds of birdcalls, and bird flight, leaves rustling and wind blowing - the space surrounding the waypoint was totally silent. It didn't feel right talking out loud when we arrived, so I whispered.

"We made it, Tones!"

"Yes, we did." He grabbed my shoulder in a side hug.

"Give me one of your flags," I said, reaching into my bag to grab one of mine.

Tony handed me a strip of green cloth.

We walked up to the obelisk together, looking for a place to tie our flags - one green and one purple. The entire surface was smooth and shiny. There was nothing to tie the flags to that I could see.

"Where are we supposed to put these friggin' things?" I asked, looking around.

Tony didn't say anything; he just pointed.

Above my head and on the side of the obelisk facing away from me was a thick iron ring sticking out. It was rusted, and some of the mottled orange color had moved to the stone where the ring was embedded. It looked really, really old. Attached to the ring were the tattered remains of two flags - one yellow and one pink. Pink wasn't assigned to anyone in our group, but yellow was. Yellow was Jared's color. But these flags looked like they'd been there for a while, faded from the sun and shaggy, their woven threads beginning to unravel.

"Tony," I asked in hushed tones, "do you see what I see?"

"Two flags. Old ones from the looks of it."

"Yeah, but did you notice the colors?"

"Pink and yellow. So?"

"So yellow is Jared's color. And these have been here a while."

"Just because it's yellow doesn't mean Jared put it there."

"But what if Jared *has* been here before? And this is from another test he did ...earlier?"

"Jayne, you're being paranoid. We went over to that table with Niles and picked up bags randomly. I could have just as easily grabbed the yellow flags as the green ones."

"Yeah, but isn't it strange that you, Tony *Green*, got green flags, and I got my favorite color, purple? Don't you find that pretty coincidental? Plus with all of Jared's weirdness going on and ... "

"Enough, Jayne! You're starting to scare me with your conspiracy theories. And I don't mean 'scare me' as in I'm starting to believe you -

I mean 'scare me' as in I'm starting to doubt your sanity. Just let it go, okay?"

I could tell he was irritated with me, so I dropped it. But only for now. I was still going to be figuring this out and watching for signs of Jared's previous participation.

I slowly reached up and tied our flags to the pole, touching the others gently with my fingertips as my hand came back down. I wondered who had put the pink flag there, and where he or she was now. I sent up a silent prayer that this mystery person was still alive and happily drinking hot chocolate in front of a crackling fire at home with a mom, dad, and a family pet.

Tony interrupted my nonsensical daydream with, "I guess at the very least, this means we're not the first ones here. This isn't the first test they've had, I mean."

"I guess not."

"I wonder where the flag owners are now."

"Stop reading my mind, Tony."

"I wasn't!" he said, a little guiltily.

I shot him a look.

"Okay, fine, I was feeling you a little."

"Feeling me sounds kinda creepy, don't you think?"

"Okay, I was vibing you then."

"Vibing me? Okay, well, stop *vibing* me, then."

"I would if I could, believe me."

"Yes, I know, you've already told me how nutty it is in there - in my head."

"Not nutty, that's not the right word. It's just ... intense. Sometimes I just can't keep up and I get a little lost. Anyone watching me would probably think I was having a major brain fart or something."

I laughed, reaching over to hug him tight. "Tony, thank you for saying brain fart. That really brought me down to Earth."

He smiled. "Down here on Earth where there are vampires and gnomes, you mean?"

"Shit, don't remind me." I pulled my map out of my bag again. "Tell me where we need to go next, would ya?"

We looked over the map together. The next waypoint was directly south of this one. The color on the map was a slightly darker green through the area where we had to travel, so we assumed that meant the forest would be thicker, which seemed hardly possible. I wondered if the trees there gave hugs.

"What?" asked Tony.

"*What,* what?"

"What were you just thinking about?"

"Why?"

"I was accidentally vibing you ... sorry. It's just that I was feeling something like when you and Becky were messing around in the forest earlier."

I smacked Tony on the back of the head.

"Ow! What was that for?"

"For saying I was messing around with Becky. We were peeing, that's all."

"Well, then you get way too much pleasure out of peeing with another girl." He ducked, moving his head out of my reach and wagging his finger at me. "No hitting!"

"If you keep hinting around that I'm hot for Becky, I'm gonna do more than hit you, brain fart boy."

"Well, tell me what that vibe was all about, then. You seemed so happy and excited."

I gave him a warning look.

"Not excited in a sexual way - just really happy."

I sighed. I didn't like keeping secrets from Tony, and it wasn't like I was intentionally not telling him. It just seemed too weird to talk about. I decided that it would just be better to show him.

"Come on, follow me."

"Why won't you tell me?"

"I'm going to show you, not tell you. It'll be better that way."

Tony got a gleam in his eye. "Are we going to play doctor?" He jumped out of the way before I could smack him again, yelling, "Missed me!"

I shook my head. "What's gotten into you, Tony? You're not normally this hyper."

"I don't know. The joy of being alive, I guess. Where are we going, anyway?"

"Just farther into the trees."

We went away from the clearing, over to an area where the trees were bigger. They were close together too, blocking out most of the sun. A little light filtered through, but not much.

I stopped, surveying the area around us. "Pick a tree."

"Pick a tree? What, are we going to pee together?"

I sighed. "Just say that one more time and see what happens."

"Okay, okay, fine." Tony looked around. "Should I pick something special, like a certain kind of tree?"

"I don't think so. Just pick one and we'll see."

"That one." Tony was pointing to a giant reddish-brown tree. It was nearly twice as big as the first one Becky and I had touched.

I looked at its base and then slowly ran my eyes up to the top of it. I actually couldn't see it very well, since it was so obscured by its own branches and those of the nearby trees. I walked over, urging Tony to follow. "Come on, we have to touch the tree."

I arrived at the trunk and put my feet on either side of a huge root that was running from the tree quite a distance across the forest floor. "Stand here next to me and put your arms out, towards the tree."

Tony didn't say anything, he just stepped up to the tree and stood where I told him to, stretching his arms out. I loved that he just followed my directions without question. It showed me how much he trusted me, even when I was being weird. That said a lot about our friendship.

"Now, put your arms out to the side, like this. We're going to hug the tree."

Tony looked at me like I was crazy. "Hug the tree? That's what this is all about?"

"Shut up and hug the damn tree, Tony. Maybe in a second it will all make sense."

He shrugged his shoulders. "Here goes nothin'." He leaned towards the tree, steadying himself with his hands and then stretching his arms out to lay them horizontally against the bark. "Now what?"

"Just wait a second." I put my hands out to steady myself against the trunk, getting ready to lay my body against it. Already I could feel the energy, with only my hands touching. "Yeah, I think this is going to work."

"What's going to work? Come on, Jayne, I feel stupid standing here like this."

I leaned into the tree, moving my arms out laterally into hugging position. I stretched out my right arm so it rested on top of Tony's while also touching the tree. I turned towards Tony's so I could see his reaction.

His face instantly lit up as soon as we connected. "What the heck ... ?"

I smiled. "This is what Becky and I were doing in the forest."

Tony closed his eyes, inhaling deeply. "My god, the feelings ... Can you feel that? It's ... it's ... *unbelievable.*"

"I know." There was nothing else to say. This tree was ancient. I didn't have to see its size to know this. It had been here a very, very long time. There was a sense of peace, a deep understanding, flowing through our connection. Strength. A certain knowledge that whatever was happening right now was just a moment of time in an infinite amount of time. Years, centuries, eons would come and go, and this tree would still be here, standing sentinel. Wars would be fought and won or lost, and this tree would still be here. Silently. Waiting and watching.

Through this connection, I was able to realize for the first time that everything in this forest was linked. The trees were connected to each other, to the land, to the things that walked the forest floor and flew through the air. The memories were all still here. I couldn't see them like pictures; I only got the sense that anything that happened here, stayed here as shadows. And there were lots of shadows in this forest.

Something was niggling the back of my mind. Something was there, wanting me to pay attention. But then Tony began speaking, and I lost it.

"I feel like I'm being rocked in a rocking chair by a grandma I never had. This is just ... so incredible. No wonder you were vibing all that happiness. I'm, like, on cloud nine right now." He smiled contentedly at me, and for the first time, I realized how truly beautiful my friend Tony was on the outside. I've always known about his inner beauty, but with the clothes and the glasses and everything, his outer gorgeousness was sometimes too easily hidden.

"You're really beautiful, you know that, Tones?"

"I was just thinking the same thing about you."

We both smiled.

"What are two gorgeous bombshells like us doing out here in this fucked up forest full of messed up creatures, anyway?" I asked.

"I don't know. But as much as I'd like to stay here and hug this tree all day, I think we really need to get going to that other waypoint." Tony broke the connection, pulling away from the tree and standing up straight. The light on his face faded out and he became regular old, serious Tony again.

I sent a big thank you up to the tree as best I could, hoping it could read my mind and feel the gratitude I was trying to transfer through my arms, before standing to join Tony.

"When do you think the others will get to the first waypoint?" I asked. I had half expected them to show up while we were there.

"I don't know. From the look of the map, it seems like maybe an hour or two after us. We were just lucky to have met those gnome things."

"Yeah, well at least *they* didn't try to eat us."

"Did you see their teeth?" Tony asked, shivering at the memory. He was walking through the forest again, glancing back to make sure I was following.

"Yeah, disgusting. I've never seen anything like that before. Makes me want to keep Mister Biggles out of the garden forever." Mister Biggles is my old cat who loves to go and lay right smack in the middle of my mom's flowers. It made her crazy because his fat butt always squashed them, but it made me laugh. Thinking about one of those lumpy gnomes with their dirty, sharp teeth coming up from behind and ... *ew. Poor Mister Biggles.* "Should I call my mom and tell her to keep Mister Biggles in the house?" I was only half-joking. I had to believe that as much of a pain in the ass as I was to my mom, she was worrying about me now.

"No. First of all, you don't have a cell phone, so you can't; and second, all you'd do is freak her out. This forest isn't normal. There are no gnomes in Florida or we would have seen them or signs of them - or someone would have. This is some ... enchanted place or something. Once we're out of here, life will go back to normal."

"Enchanted forest, eh?" I'd bet old Walt Disney had never envisioned this kind of shit going on in *his* enchanted forests. Maybe a few dwarves, sure. But nasty-toothed gnomes? Vampires? *No, I think not.* "Face it, Tones. Life is never going to go back to normal after this. We've seen something we shouldn't have. This forest. The Green ... this connection with the trees. It's alive, and I don't mean alive like just living. It's alive like *aware* alive. I don't know if I'll ever be able to look at the world the same way again." *The Green* seemed like the perfect name for this weirdness around us and the energy that I was able to connect to.

"You're probably right. I'm not sure that we fully appreciate what's going on here right now, but I'm not in the best frame of mind to figure it all out. I just want to focus on finishing this thing and getting out of here. Must be my survival instincts." He took his axe out of his bag as he walked along.

"Why do you have your axe out?"

"I think it's a good idea to keep it handy. When those gnomes showed up, I was totally unprepared. We're just lucky they weren't killer gnomes, otherwise I would have been dead meat."

"Well, you would have had some nasty bites on your ankles for sure, but I'm not so sure about the dead part."

"I'll bet even an ankle bite from those little things would be deadly. Those teeth ... " Tony shuddered.

"Yeah, you're right. It would be like being bitten by that dragon thing. What was it called? We saw it on *Animal Planet* one time."

"The Komodo Dragon - bites its prey and then leaves it, tracking it for days until the bacteria poison in its saliva destroys the prey's blood and eventually kills it. Then the dragon moves in and ... "

" ... munches on the easy prey."

"Exactly. Easy prey." Tony held up his axe. "I'm not going to be easy prey for the rest of this trip. Anyone who gets in my way ... " *SWOOSH!*

Tony swung the axe in the air. I was glad I was far behind him at that particular moment, because the axe was all messed up. A sound filled the space around us, like a humming, and a blue shadow hung in the air where the axe had just been. It was like a laser light show or something, only with less defined lights and more afterglow.

"What the fuck was *that*, Tony?"

Tony was staring in amazement at the blue streak that was slowly dissipating. "I have no idea."

"Do it again!" I urged, unable to keep the glee out of my voice.

Tony swung the axe again, but nothing happened. He lifted it up towards his face, staring at it curiously. "Did I imagine something happening last time?"

"Not unless it was mass hysteria and I'm imagining crazy shit too. Try again."

Tony swung it a third time. Nothing happened.

"What did you do different?"

"Nothing I'm aware of."

"Look at your feet. Are they in a different position?"

"No, I haven't moved."

"Did you swing it softer? Or harder?"

"Nope."

"What were we talking about before you swung it last time?"

"I was saying that I wasn't going to be easy prey anymore."

"Okay, say that again and then swing it. Maybe there's a magic word in there."

Tony held the axe above his shoulder and to the right. "I'm not going to be easy prey anymore." He swung the axe, and I thought I heard a very slight hum.

"Did you see that?!" asked Tony, excitedly.

"Was that some blue there?" I asked.

"I think I saw some. Not as much or as bright, but some."

"That is *so* cool." I pulled my stick out of my bag. "Maybe I have a lightsaber too." I swung mine around, but nothing happened. I gave Tony's magic words a try. "I'm not gonna be easy prey!" I swished the stick out in front of me, back and forth, giving some high-quality forward jabs too for good measure.

Nothing happened.

"Oh well ... figures. Finn gets vampire killer arrows, you get a lightsaber axe, and I get a stick. That Dardennes guy had it in for me from the start."

"Jayne ... "

"Come on, Tony, you know it's true. When it was time to pick weapons Niles put Becky in front of me. *Becky*. She's, like, half my size."

"Well, that's a bit of an exaggeration."

"You know what I mean."

"No, you're right. She's definitely smaller than you, and we were supposed to be picking by size." He shrugged. "Your weapon will be valuable for something, I'm sure."

"Yeah, for what? Digging up mushrooms?"

Tony laughed at my disgust. "Just keep it handy. I don't think we'll be lucky enough to get through to the fourth waypoint without meeting anything else along the way. A sharp stick is better than nothing."

He was right. I took his advice and kept my stick out. I continued to wave it around as we walked towards our next destination, trying different techniques to see if I could wake it up, but nothing worked. *Stupid stick.* Those gnomes had called it Dark Blackthorn or something, though, so I held out some hope for my little friend, the sharp stick. It did look like a giant thorn - a really giant one. I decided to call it Blackie. It was black - a weird color for wood - plus I had a little black Pomeranian once, creatively named Blackie. He was tiny but he was badass. The postman refused to come onto our property because of old badass Blackie. Best dog ever. He died when I was twelve, but I still remembered him fondly.

After walking for about an hour my stomach began growling. "I'm hungry. Can we stop for lunch?"

"Sure."

Tony stepped off the trail to go sit on a fallen tree.

I sat down next to him, and we opened up our bags, deciding to eat an actual meal this time since we were starving. We'd gotten one quarter of the way through this test and still had another full meal and most of the side bits remaining. I had one bottle of water left; Tony had one and a half. We could afford to splurge on the calories.

We had finished eating and were packing up our wrappers when we heard a sound. Tony grabbed my arm to stop me from moving. We both listened carefully to see if we could hear anything else.

The noise came again. It sounded like voices.

"Quick!" whispered Tony. *"Get behind that root!"*

The end of the fallen tree that we'd been sitting on was a huge root, taller than me. Piles of leaves and other branches had collected around it, making a small mountain of debris to hide behind.

Tony and I hunkered down, looking out between a crack in the cover, towards the direction of the voices. They were coming from the path we had been following.

Two figures appeared out of the dark tree shadows. One of them was Niles, wearing full cammo gear and carrying an axe very much like Tony's - only much bigger. Walking next to him was another dwarf, similarly dressed, but younger-looking. He was also carrying an axe, holding it in a deceptively casual way that told me he knew how to use it.

I looked at Tony and nodded at his axe. Tony glanced down and then nodded back at me. Apparently, Tony had the weapon of choice for commando dwarves around here.

Niles was talking. "They came this way for sure. They couldn't broadcast their trail any louder. *Idiots.* We'll make quick work of them if the others don't get to them first."

"What about the other humans?" asked the younger dwarf, practically running to keep up with Niles' longer stride. Even thinking that made me want to laugh, because I realized I had never seen truly funny until I saw that long dwarf stride.

Tony shot me a stern look, probably vibing my humor. He was right; the last thing we needed was two axe-wielding army dwarves up our asses. Even though they were little, they probably had low centers of gravity, and I didn't think Blackie would be any match against their weapons. I quickly choked down my hysteria, amazed at how quickly it went from inner laughter to abject fear.

They were soon gone from our immediate vicinity, but Tony and I stayed put, whispering so we wouldn't bring them back with further ineptitudes.

"*Fuck!* What should we do now?" I asked. This test had gone horribly, horribly wrong. We weren't being tested ... we were being *hunted*. And that was a whole other deal altogether. I was going to have to survive just so I could kill Dardennes when this was all over. The concept of life or death was way, *way* too far into the land of the unthinkable for me to even remotely consider right now, even though my rational mind knew it was my current reality. I tamped it down, shoving any distress I was feeling to the back of my head to panic about later.

"I'm not sure what we should do. I guess we can't keep going in that direction. They could stop and we'd come right up on them. And from what Niles said, it sounds like they're tracking us and so are other ... people, or dwarves, or whatever. Who the hell knows? *Dammit!"*

"Easy, Tony. Now's not the time to take up swearing. Your mother would be so *very* disappointed in you." I wiggled my eyebrows at him.

Tony shook his head impatiently. "Shush. We need a plan. Help me make one."

I put my hand on the root of the downed tree that we were hiding behind. I don't know what I was expecting, but I was a little surprised to feel something there - an energy. I grabbed Tony's hand to link him up with me.

"What's that?" he whispered.

"It's that tree energy, I think."

Tony frowned. "But this tree is dead."

"I don't think anything in this place is completely dead." The energy was faint and it didn't bring to mind anything in particular, but it was definitely sending something out to me - something I could feel. I looked around by my feet. *What is the connection? Are they linking with me through the trees themselves? Or is the ground under my feet and my hands on the tree making some sort of circuit?* I wished I had paid better attention in science class last year. We had made a circuit in our lab. Tony kicked ass with that stuff, but if I asked him about it now he'd probably get cranky. I should probably stop worrying about it so much and start figuring out how to get the hell out of here. I let the tree go so I could focus.

Tony had his map out and was trying to get an idea of where we were. He pointed to a spot that was about two inches from the second waypoint.

"I calculated, roughly, about how long it took us to get from the camp where we spent the night to where the gnomes were and where the first waypoint was. Based on that, I'd say we're *here*." He pointed to a spot in the middle of the darker green area.

I looked around me. It sure was green here. And dark. "Seems like it could be right." I wasn't good with directions, so that was the most help I could be; but Tony understood. He'd been lost with me at the wheel enough times back home.

Home. Mom. Mister Biggles. School. Safety. I'd never appreciated that stuff before. I had hated it all - well, except for Mister Biggles - but now I didn't have it anymore. Regret, I found, had a very bitter taste.

"Stop worrying about that crap. Just help me figure out how to get out of here," said Tony, frustrated.

I pushed him, silently admonishing him for vibing me.

"Come on," he prompted, folding the map up and putting it back in his bag. "We should go this way." He gestured behind us, into the darker areas of the forest.

"Are you sure? It looks really dark in there." No lie, I was pretty scared at this point. All the tree love had left me and now I was just feeling cold and alone - very alone, in a big place that had mean little bastards with bad attitudes running all around and carrying deadly sharp things. My grip on Blackie tightened as I followed behind Tony.

"So what's the plan, then?"

"We're going to circle around a bit to the west and then angle back in when we think we're perpendicular to the waypoint."

"Do you think the others are okay?"

"Well, it doesn't look like Niles found them yet, based on what that other dwarfy guy said, so maybe they're fine."

I had to hope so. As much as I didn't trust Jared, I didn't want the others to be harmed just because they'd decided to stay with him and ditch us. It was better anyway - with all of them we would have been like a herd of elephants crashing through the trees. I was glad it was just Tony and me, although I was hoping really hard that I was going to see Spike again, and under better circumstances.

We walked for another hour, picking our way carefully across logs and branches and through brambles and other sharp pokey things. I had scratches all over my wrists, neck, and face. I was glad I had jeans on to protect my legs. My hoodie protected my arms for the most part, but I had pushed up the sleeves a bit because I was so hot. All this walking and climbing over shit was making me sweat.

"Are we there yet? How much longer?" I whined. This was like road trips I had taken with my parents when I was younger that seemed to go on forever.

"I think we should turn back east soon. Not yet, though. I'm not sure. I wish I could see above the trees."

I thought about this for a minute then came to an abrupt halt, grabbing Tony's sleeve. "Why don't we climb one?" Looking up, I could see that some of the trees would be good candidates. They had lots of branches.

Tony looked up too. "I was never much good at climbing trees. I panic when I get above ten feet."

"*Shit.* Me too. But I think we should try anyway."

Tony cinched up his backpack, making it tighter. "Fine. Let's do this. Which tree?"

I picked the one that had the most branches. It wasn't nearly as big as the one we'd hugged earlier. I walked over and put one hand on the trunk.

"Hello, Tree. We need to climb you to see above the forest. I don't want to hurt you or be disrespectful, but it's important." I tried to send my thoughts into the tree. I got only an answering glow back. I wasn't sure if it was a response, permission, or what - but it didn't feel angry or anything, so I figured we were good to go.

Tony just watched me, not saying anything. As soon as he saw me start climbing, he walked over to the tree too, putting his hands on its bark. "Hi, Tree. What she said. I'm ... uh ... gonna climb you too."

I was already a couple of levels up. "Did you feel it?"

He shook his head. "Nope." He grabbed the lowest branch and came up behind me.

I was touching the tree with various parts of my body, and I could feel its welcoming green glow going all through me. I'd never felt this as a kid, climbing trees. If I had, I probably never would have come down.

Tony was a few feet below me, his pace slowing.

"You okay down there?" I asked.

"Um ... getting a little nervous, actually." He looked up at me, sweat glistening on his upper lip and forehead.

"Just stay there. I'm fine. I'll go the rest of the way alone."

I was now up higher in this tree than I'd ever climbed in my life, which was kind of ironic, because as I've grown up, I've learned to have a greater appreciation for my mortality. When I was a kid, I never worried about falling and hurting myself or possibly dying - it never even crossed my mind. But now that I was older, I didn't climb trees anymore because I *did* worry about that kind of stuff. I fully appreciated at this moment what a bummer that is - how limiting it makes your life when you walk around always afraid something tragic could happen.

I reached a spot that didn't have any handy branches I could use to help me get to the next level. I stopped and looked around, trying to figure out what to do. I could see Tony's small form still below me but much farther away. I just needed to go another ten feet or so...

"What are you doing?" asked Tony.

"Trying to get higher. But I can't."

"Why not?"

"There aren't any branches nearby." *Shitshitshit.*

Then I remembered the leafy toilet paper incident. I bit my lip, looking around at the nearby trees. The one I was on didn't have any branches that could help me, but the tree next to mine had some really big ones up here - branches that, if they moved, could get me as high as I needed to go. *Should I do it?*

"Come on, hurry up!" said Tony as loudly as he dared.

I made my decision. I placed my arms around the tree trunk. The energy that had been tingling through my hands as I climbed was amplified a bit, now that more of me was making contact.

So, how does this work? I wondered. *Do I ask in English?* "Tree, move a branch for me so I can see higher."

Some branches nearby moved a bit, but it could have been from a breeze, it was so slight.

Okay, not English. French? No, that isn't going to work. All I could remember how to say was *Je vais à la plage* - I'm going to the beach. Not helpful.

Okay, how about pictures? I closed my eyes and imagined in my head what I wanted the tree to do. My mind's eye saw one of the big nearby branches swinging over to where I was standing, positioning itself to hoist me up to the highest level of the tree I was latched onto. Then I pictured myself looking out over the treetops off to the east.

I was so busy picturing every little detail, I wasn't paying attention to what I was actually physically doing on the tree.

Tony's voice cut through my daydream. "Holy crap, Jayne, what are you doing?"

I opened my eyes. The branch that had been fifteen feet away from me had moved. The tree it belonged to was groaning, but the branch remained still, extended out directly in front of me. I tentatively put my foot out, left one first, onto the big branch of the larger tree, keeping my hands on the trunk of the smaller one. I realized then that I hadn't thought this out very well. I had nothing to grab hold of. I swallowed the panic that rose up and quickly closed my eyes again, imagining a second branch being there for my hands to hold onto. I opened my eyes in time to see it swinging over to join the first. As soon as it came close enough, I let go of the trunk and swiftly grabbed hold with a death grip, telling myself not to look down, no matter what.

"Jayne, don't do that! You're going to fall!"

"Shush, Tony! Don't upset the tree. I won't fall."

I could hear him muttering below me. "Upset the tree. Upset the tree? She's nuts, upset the tree ... "

Please lift me up, I asked the tree, showing it in my head what I wanted it to do.

It was like being on an elevator in the forest. The tree strained, lifting its two branches as high as they would go. I heard the groaning of the wood and then a cracking. *Okay, stop! Hold me here for just a moment.* It made it difficult to concentrate on anything else, this picturing stuff to communicate instead of talking. I kept closing my eyes to make it easier.

I quickly opened them to look around. I was now above most of the trees in the forest. The sun was barely shining, the clouds covering most of its brilliance. *No wonder it's so dark down there.* The forest seemed to stretch out forever in all directions. I couldn't see an end to it no matter which way I turned. "Fucking A," I said to no one in particular.

To the east and a bit south, I saw a break in the trees and what looked like a small sliver of something shiny peaking out. *It must be the second waypoint.* I strained my neck to see farther, hoping to see the third waypoint, but I couldn't. *We must be too far away.*

"Okay, tree, down we go." I pictured the big tree putting me back where I had been on the other one. Within seconds, the groaning and creaking began again, and I was transported over to the smaller tree. As the branch started to move to its original position, I reached out and touched it again briefly with my hand. *Thank you, Tree.*

I felt a burst of energy in return. *Love.*

I was definitely going to plant some trees when I got home. I'd make a mini forest right in my mom's back yard. Front yard too.

I looked down to report my observations to Tony but I couldn't see him anymore. "Tony?"

No answer.

I was worried, thinking he might have fallen. We were out here in the middle of nowhere - now I'd seen just how out in the middle of nowhere we really were - and if he were hurt, I wasn't sure how I was going to get him out of the forest or even to the next waypoint.

I scrambled down the tree as fast as I could. When I got to the last branch, I dropped to the ground and stood, anxiously looking around the base of the tree, trying to locate Tony. He wasn't there, but his backpack was. And his axe was lying on top.

"Holy shit ... *Tony!*" I whisper-yelled because I was afraid Niles and his little buddy were still close by. *"Tony!"*

I heard the sound of a voice - a female voice - coming from around the other side of the tree.

That's weird. I walked around in time to see Tony standing in front of a crooked old hag, getting ready to plunge into what looked like a heavy-duty makeout session. His hands were on the hag's waist and his head was tilted, angled to the side in expectation of a real juicy liplock.

"Oh, shit, Tony, that's *disgusting!* Get away from her!" I ran over to break up the love fest.

She saw me coming and pulled back a few inches from Tony, anger brightening her beady eyes.

"SSSStaaaay awaaaay human giiirrrrl," she hiss-screeched, foamy spittle collecting at the corners of her mouth.

I nearly gagged, thinking of my Tony getting his first kiss from that ugly-ass woman. She looked about two hundred years old with stringy, greasy gray hair hanging down past her shoulders. One of her eyes was a cloudy light blue, the other one black; I couldn't see any iris - just one big, inky pupil, sunk within a wrinkly, mottled skeletal face. She was wearing a shapeless, dingy-gray cloak, stained and ragged. I looked with disgust at her rotted and crooked yellowish-brown teeth.

"No fucking way are you kissing my Tony with that mouth," I declared, stepping towards her with my stick in one hand and Tony's axe in the other.

She took a step back, releasing his arm.

Tony stood still for a second as I approached and then looked up, turning his head to face me. His eyes were open, but I saw no recognition in them when he looked me. Tony turned and moved towards the hag again, his arms reaching for her waist in a bid to finish their disgusting business together.

"*Huh-uh,* Tony Baloney, not so fast." I reached out and gripped his shoulder, pulling him back away from her.

He put up little resistance.

The hag backed farther away from me, her eyes not on the axe but on Blackie.

She seemed to be worried about it, so I held it up. "You want a taste of Blackie? Well then, *bring it,* bitch."

The hag raised her chin, staring at me malevolently, growling out in her rusty, acidic voice, "You know nothing of what you do, of what you have. I can see it in your eyes."

"Look again, hag." I brandished Blackie in front of me. "Come on, put your money where your mouth is, old lady. Don't think for one second that I won't stab this motherfucker right in your ugly, cloudy, beady-ass eye. Or maybe I should go for the good one!" I adjusted the point of my stick a smidge to the right.

The hag considered me for a moment and then looked at Tony.

"Darling," she simpered, "please ... help me. She's going to hurt me." She turned back to me, grinning maliciously.

I looked at her with disgust. Like Tony was going to fall for that shit. She was about as far from a kindly cookie-baking grandma as someone could possibly be.

I felt Tony's hand on my shoulder.

"Tony ... "

I never got the rest of my sentence out. Tony pushed me to the ground, quickly grabbing the axe that fell from my hand. He stood over me, a rage like I've never seen before, blazing in his eyes.

"Leave her alone, Jayne. She's *mine."*

I felt the vomit rise up in my throat. I had to swallow hard to make it go down and stay there. My ears were hot and ringing. What the hell was going on? Tony was hypnotized or something. She'd put a spell on his stupid ass. *For chrissake ... as if I didn't have enough problems already.*

"Tony! She's an old hag! She's hypnotized you or something! Come on, it's me ... Jayne, your best friend!" I searched his face desperately, but there was nothing there. Tony was somewhere far, far away. And this guy in front of me? I had no idea who he was. Some necrophiliac apparently, because that hag looked like a walking corpse, and I'm pretty sure it was lust I had seen in his eyes earlier.

"Hag?" he said, confused. He shook his head, smiling condescendingly. "Those who are blind cannot see." He gestured to the woman. "She's the most beautiful girl who ever walked this earth. You remember her, Jayne, don't you? She was with us at the warehouse." He turned to the old woman. "Samantha, come over here and say hello to Jayne."

Chapter Eighteen

"SAMANTHA? NO FRIGGIN' WAY, TONY, that is *not* Samantha." I stood up, shaking my head from side to side, backing away from both of them. I wasn't sure exactly what was going on here, other than the fact that Tony had been mind-fucked, but there was no way in hell Samantha, or whoever that was, was gonna suck face with my best friend. Over my dead body.

Tony stood in front of me, his axe hanging at his side. "Jayne, you're just confused. Samantha came back for us." He turned his head to look at the hag again. "She came back for *me."* His face was shining with deranged happiness.

The hag walked up to resume her place next to Tony, putting her hand on his arm. He rubbed her forearm and leaned down, preparing to kiss her again.

I couldn't take it. Maybe I was going to be cursed or whatever by the hag, but I was not going to let that kiss happen. I just hoped that when this was over, I'd get my Tony back - the real Tony, not the bewitched, necrophiliac Tony. I ran as fast as I could at the hag, ready to knock her antiquated ass to the ground.

She saw me coming and readied herself for my attack.

Tony was still slightly mesmerized, looking down at his new

girlfriend, so at least for this brief moment I only had one battle to fight.

I had Blackie in my fist, held out in front of me, as I rushed forward. The point wasn't out because it was too awkward to carry like that when I was running, plus I wasn't totally comfortable with stabbing her. She was disgusting and she had cursed my friend, but she *was* an old lady after all.

The hag raised her left hand, her palm facing in my direction. As we collided, the fist holding Blackie was the first thing that came into contact with her body. The side of the stick's tip grazed her shoulder, emitting a hissing sound and the acrid smell of sulfur. A split second later, a blast of some horrible black energy erupted from her hand and hit me smack in the chest, sending me flying backwards.

I should have landed on my ass in the middle of some brambles, but instead I found myself in a pile of leafy limbs. Three trees standing witness to our battle had interlocked their branches, creating a net of sorts. I was caught inside it, but was released as soon as it had stopped my backward movement.

I sent out a vibe of gratitude. It felt good to know that at least The Green was on my side. I had a feeling I was going to need some allies, after having seen and felt that black powerful whatever-it-was coming out of her hand. My chest felt cold and *bleak* where it had made contact. That was one unhappy dose of magic she had going on there.

Tony watched what was happening, confusion marring his features. He looked from the hag, to me, and back again. "Jayne?"

"Don't look at her! Look at me! *Samantha*. Remember, darling?"

Tony's face broke out in smiles again. "Hello, Samantha. What are you doing to Jayne?" He didn't seem mad about the fact that she'd just blasted me with some sick-ass black lightning - just confused.

"Jayne is bad, Tony. She's trying to hurt me. You need to stop her."

"Jayne, is that true?"

"STOP HER!" the hag yelled, raising her hand again.

Tony lifted his axe and came towards me, a very determined look on his face.

Trees, don't fail me now, was all I could think. I played pictures through my mind as I grabbed hold of the nearest branches. I prayed that the connection I had with one tree could somehow be communicated to the others. All I had without them was that fucking black stick.

Tony was swinging his horrible axe, blue glowing pathways cutting through the air, and the humming sound rising to a crescendo that could only mean one thing: that axe was one bad motherfucker of a weapon, and if it hit me, it was going to be lights out.

Everything happened so fast, it took me a few moments to remember exactly how it had gone down. As Tony approached, the tree that had branches above his head bent down, wood popping and snapping with the effort. A wall of pine needles and leaves smashed into Tony's face, loosening his grip on the axe. The weapon fell to the ground and a vine of ivy raced across the forest floor, wrapping its tendrils around the axe and pulling it away, deep into the woods. I lost sight of it within seconds.

Luckily, so did Tony.

While Tony was wrapped up in battling leaves and branches, I slipped around the side and faced off with the hag.

"You think you're so clever, girl, with your tree friends. We'll see how badly they want to help you when they feel my fire!"

She held her palm up and blasted the tree next to me, the one interfering in Tony's struggle to get untangled. The potent stench of sulfur filled the air again, immediately followed by the smell of burning wood. I felt the pain of the tree - not as my own pain, but as echoes of sadness and disintegration. It was one of the most horrible sensations I'd ever experienced. I just wanted it to stop.

"Don't!" I yelled, desperation and anger coloring my voice.

The hag laughed maniacally and sent another cruel blast to the tree.

I could feel its strength waning. The ache of unshed tears jumped to my throat. If the tree continued to help me, she was going to destroy it - demolish its soul. I realized then that this is what she did; this is what made her happy, her reason for being. She thrived on the pain of others. As the tree suffered, she grew stronger.

This shit had to stop. *Now.*

I charged her, Blackie held out in front of me, point first – *fuck the old lady pity card.* She wanted to play rough, so she was going to have to deal with my new take-no-prisoners plan.

She raised her palm to stop me, but a quick thought-message from me asking a nearby vine to wrap itself around the hag's wrist and pull, sent her blast wide. I flinched as it hit a tree behind me, but it was the last minute distraction that I needed.

I didn't stop, even when I was upon her. I ran as hard as I could, ramming my pointed stick into her chest, refusing to let go even as I felt it sink into her bag of decrepit, brittle bones. She screamed, the unholy shriek rising higher and higher, hurting my ears with its ugliness.

A deep green glow burst from her chest where my stick had penetrated her flesh, blazing up and down to fully consume her. It touched my hand, the one that was still gripping the stick, but I felt nothing.

No blood came from her wound; instead, a blackness seeped out and spread slowly across the forest floor, causing whatever it touched to quickly move out of its way or shrivel up, turn gray, and die.

I danced my feet out of the way to keep the molten evil from touching my Converse sneakers.

The hag sank down, grabbing hold of my wrist and staring at me with her one good eye. "Youuuu ... giiiirrrlllll ... Motherrrr ... " A single tear welled up in each of her eyes, and for a brief moment - so quickly I thought I was probably imagining it - I saw another face there ... a younger one ... a beautiful one. But then the hag was there again. A smoking blackness, reeking of rotten chemicals.

I let go of the stick, and the defeated hag crumpled to the ground. The pitch-blackness that had seeped out of her, returned quickly, covering her body and boiling up over it.

I stepped back, grabbing my sweet Tony and pulling him along with me. He stumbled behind, saying nothing. When we were a few safe feet away, we stopped and stared at the mass of writhing blackness. I heard what sounded like the beating of wings and a chorus of deep, otherworldly evil screams that I knew I would experience in my nightmares for the rest of my life.

And then there was a flash of bright green light and a loud *POP!* ... and it was all over.

The hag was gone and my stick lay on the ground, small and black, still pointed on the end, and no longer glowing green or covered in the hag's heinous awfulness. It was as if the battle had never happened, except that in the place where the hag had been swallowed up by the blackness, a piece of scorched earth remained. I thought about covering it up with dirt, but then something made me decide not to.

Something terrible had happened here. As awful as she had been, she'd had some sort of life in her - and I had taken it. The bitch had to die; I knew that, rationally speaking. But when I thought back to that momentary vision of her, the one that had appeared just before her evil light was finally snuffed out, I thought maybe she hadn't always been a hag. Maybe, a long time ago, she had been a different person. Maybe even somebody Tony could have loved - someone I'd even let him make out with.

I looked at Tony. He was staring at the black spot on the ground, not saying anything.

"Tony? You okay?" I wasn't sure if my old Tony was back, or if I was going to be stuck with Zombie Tony for the rest of my life.

He shook his head slowly from side to side.

My guts clenched and I felt sick again. *Please God, let me have my Tony back.*

"I'm not really sure what just happened, Jayne. I came down from the tree, and I saw this beautiful girl. She looked like Samantha. She was here ... and then ... I don't know. I don't remember what happened after that." He looked up at me with tears glistening in his eyes. "But I remember being really angry at you and coming after you with that axe. And I don't know why I would ever do that, Jayne. It's killing me!"

He was crying for real now, not just tears but girly sobbing too.

I went to him and hugged him fiercely for a moment before pulling away and grabbing him firmly by the shoulders. The kid needed some tough love right now, and he'd caught me at a good time. I'd just kicked a crone's ass and burned her to smithereens. I wasn't feeling overly tenderhearted right at that moment.

"Listen, ya big baby ... you fell in love with an enchanted hag who tricked you and convinced you I was the bad guy. Luckily, you suck at hurting people and I easily kicked both your asses with the help of my friends, the trees and vines." I sent them a silent message of gratitude through my feet on the forest floor and was rewarded with a shower of leaves and evergreen needles.

Tony grabbed me and hugged me hard enough to squeeze my breath away. "I love you so much, Jayne. I never want to hurt you. *Ever.*"

"I know that, Tony, I know," I mumbled into his shoulder. "Just promise me that if I ever get mesmerized by some ugly-ass, evil old wizard guy, you won't let me make out with him either, 'kay?"

"Um, okay." Tony thought about what I said for a second and took a step back, keeping his hands on my shoulders. "Do you mean that ... did I? ... Oh, God, please tell me I didn't ... " His eyes searched my face for answers I could tell he wasn't sure he wanted.

I reached up and patted him on the cheek. "Thanks to me and Blackie, you're still a virgin and you didn't make out with old One-Eye." I gestured meaningfully with my eyes at the black spot on the ground.

Tony dropped his hands from my shoulders and rubbed his stomach absently. "I feel sick." He wiped his mouth with the back of his hand, looking highly distressed. In a way, he'd been violated, so his reaction was totally understandable. But I hated to see him dwell on it.

"Come on, let's grab our bags and go. I know the right direction. I saw the second waypoint from up in the tree. It shouldn't take us long to get there."

I asked the trees for Tony's axe back. It came sliding out from under some brambles and stopped at Tony's feet. He stared at it for a minute, not immediately retrieving it.

"Come on, Tony, let's go. We don't have a ton of daylight left, you know."

"Maybe I shouldn't have a weapon."

"Listen, I know you're afraid you're going to try and use it on me again, and to be honest, I am a little pissed that you almost did, because apparently you've figured out the secret code that gets this fucker working like a freaky-ass lightsaber. But I know it wasn't your choice, and you kinda sucked at it anyway, so it doesn't matter. Pick it up and let's go. Stop feeling sorry for yourself."

Tony gave me a dirty look and then picked it up, walking over to stand next to me. "You have a terrible bedside manner, you know that?"

I smiled. "I know."

Tony put his arm around me as we walked. "That's one of the many qualities I love about you."

"I know that, too."

We made our way through the forest in the direction of the waypoint, reaching it in less than an hour. I went up to the obelisk and tied our flags to the iron ring. There was only one flag on this one - a yellow one.

Tony and I stared at it for a while. He was the first to comment.

"Do you think the hag got to the person who had the pink flags?"

"I don't know, Tones. Maybe."

It was a sobering thought. Dardennes had the nerve to call vampires, gnomes, killer dwarves and a wicked corpse-like hag 'obstacles'. We'd only made it to the second waypoint and we'd already encountered this much. What would be next? And would we survive it?

Chapter Nineteen

I GOT DOWN FROM THE tree I had climbed in search of the third waypoint, caressing its trunk as I stepped away, sending thank yous out through my mind.

"The next waypoint is way the hell over that way," I said, gesturing to the west. "I could barely see it. It's next to a lake, on its far side."

Tony looked up at the treetops. "Well, it's probably about five o'clock. We can either keep walking or find a place to camp for the night. It's up to you."

"I think I'd like to stop for now. I'm a little tired after having defeated Evil and all, so maybe we can walk until we find a good spot and then quit for the night. Maybe even make a fire this time?"

"Sounds like a plan," agreed Tony, his voice telling me he was tired too.

We walked for close to an hour and then came to a very small clearing in the midst of the dark woods. "How about this spot?" asked Tony.

"Fine with me." I dropped my backpack on the ground and sunk down to my knees. The pine needles and old leaves were like a carpeted floor, soft and a little bit bouncy. "You know, before coming here, I'd never really spent much time in the woods, other than that trip to North Carolina I took with my parents."

"Yeah, me neither."

"Except for the evil creature part, I really like it here." I knew I must be going crazy to feel this way, but it was true.

"Well, I think you belong in the woods," said Tony, getting food out of his backpack.

"Belong here? How so?" I was trying to decide if I should be insulted, seeing as how this forest's inhabitants were not only bloodthirsty but also pretty damn ugly.

Tony looked at me like I was missing something. "Well, duh. You talk to trees. Hello."

"Yeah, well there's that. I'm sure it's just this forest, though - there's magic here, obviously. I don't talk to trees at home." I wasn't sure if it was a good thing or a bad thing that I was accepting the presence of magic in my life so readily now. Seemed like it should have been a tougher pill to swallow.

"I wouldn't be too sure about that," said Tony, mysteriously.

"What do you mean?"

"Don't you remember? That day with Brad Powers?"

"Of course, I remember the day; how could I forget? But I guess I missed the part where I talked to a tree."

"When Brad pushed you, all those leaves just fell down all over. You looked like you'd jumped into a pile of freshly-raked leaves, but they weren't there to start with. They only fell after you did; the tree shook them off. At the time I thought it was the wind or something like that, but after having seen you here, I think it was you talking to that tree and just not realizing it."

I thought back to that moment, which seemed like it had happened last year but actually had taken place less than a week ago.

My, how time flies when you're fighting repulsive, supernatural creatures in an enchanted forest.

Tony could be right, but I didn't want to consider that possibility right now. I had been thinking all along that as soon as this test or hunt was over, we would be able to go back to our normal, mundane lives. To imagine that I might still be talking to trees when we were back in Florida was more than a little unsettling.

Yes, life had been boring in high school. I sat around every day in class, waiting for the world to come to me and offer me something more. Now, here I was, getting exactly what I had wished for - something a lot, lot more than just geometry and homecoming dances. But I was, in a way, regretting the fact that I hadn't appreciated before how easy my life was. How uncomplicated it was. So, I had a molester in my house? Nothing a swift shot of my softball bat couldn't fix. Now instead, I had ... *this.* Whatever *this* was. I had wished for a more interesting life, and now I had it - in spades. I had only myself to blame for what was happening to me right now. *Dammit,* I hated being adult about things, and that was what this felt like. It was all so serious and gut-wrenching and annoying. *What a drag.*

While I bemoaned the direction my life had taken, Tony got a fire started. He'd found plenty of dry pieces of wood lying around the forest near us. Even the rotten wood still had a vibration to it, although it was more like echoes and shadows than the electric energy I usually felt from a living tree. My green friends didn't seem to mind the burning of their already dead parts. The night air was getting cooler, so the warmth they generated felt awesome. *Thank you, Green Forest.*

Tony and I finished our dinners and then laid down by the fire, using our backpacks as pillows. We were head to head, keeping our bodies parallel to the flames.

"Jayne?"

"Yes?"

"Did I kiss that ... thing back there? You can tell me. I won't freak out."

"No, Tony, you didn't. You wanted to, but I wouldn't let you."

"That is just so disgusting. I can't stop thinking about it."

"Yes, well, now you know how I feel about that asshat boyfriend of my mom's."

"Now I'm sorry I didn't shoot him."

I laughed out loud. "You're awesome, Tony. Thanks for being my friend."

"Thanks for forcing me to be yours."

"You're welcome." I was smiling when I said it. I had good taste in friends, Tony was proof of that.

A few minutes passed in companionable silence before Tony said, "Do you think we should sleep in shifts?"

"No need."

"Well, if I were a blood-thirsty creature, I'd probably wait until we were sleeping to come in for a snack."

"Yeah, but we have guards on our side, and I'm too tired to stay awake all night or even part of the night."

"Yeah, too tired from fighting Evil, I know."

"Yeah, and don't forget, I'm tired also from battling *you,* trying to keep you from making out with Her Hagginess or chopping me into little pieces with your axe."

Tony groaned. "Please, don't remind me!"

I snorted. "Sorry. I'll stop. We will never speak of your cadaverous girlfriend or murderous ways ever again."

"Thank you. And so who are these so-called guards that are going to protect us from the night creatures, anyway?"

I gestured above our heads. "They are."

"Oh. Cool. Good idea." Ten seconds later, Tony was snoring. Poor kid was exhausted.

I couldn't help but feel flattered that he trusted in my abilities and ideas so completely. It was a heavy responsibility, though. *Dammit,* but this hunt was causing me to come to all sorts of annoying and rationally mature realizations, *perish the thought.* I wondered briefly if it was it too late to wish for my old life back.

But then I knew - the truth was that I didn't really want things to go back to the way they were. The life I had right now was seriously fucked up, yes; but there was no denying it was different than anything I'd ever experienced before, and no one could ever call it boring. And something told me there were going to be some other things to discover tomorrow and the day after. At least I wasn't sitting in a classroom drawing on my hand and doing the same old thing over and over again, wishing life could be different.

I put my hands on the ground, digging my palms and fingers into the leaves, pine needles, and soil beneath me. I stared up into the treetops, deeply inhaling the forest air and then letting my breath leave my lungs with a slow, controlled exhale. The serenity came to me softly but surely. I could smell the trees and the earth, feel the breeze and the pulsating energy that surrounded us. I sent my message to the living things growing in the Dell or wherever we were in the Green Forest, knowing now that my link to them was with the earth and even in the air around us. I was wired and wifi, and it was fucking *awesome.*

Protect us from those who wish to hurt us.

I received an answering feeling of shelter and security. *Love.* I knew the trees would let us know if the bad guys were coming. I wasn't sure exactly how that would happen, but I trusted that it would.

I realized later that I probably should have been more specific and maybe included a wider range of potential issues in my request - but I was new to this tree-whispering stuff and could never have known what was going to happen while we slept.

Chapter Twenty

WE WOKE TO A COLD, dewy morning, the fire having long gone out. I stretched my arms above me, yawning without opening my eyes. My hand made contact with Tony's head, waking him up. I slid my leg to the side, intending to sit up, and it made contact with something hard. Not a tree. Something warm. Another body. For a second, it didn't compute. Tony was behind me, not on the side of me. *What the ...*

I jerked upright into a sitting position, yelling, "Tony! Get up!" I scooted as far away from the lump of clothed somebody as I could and rammed right into Tony's still half-asleep form.

"Ow! What?"

"Get up. Something's here."

Tony sat up quickly, pushing his knotted hair to the side and scrubbing his eyes and face to wake himself up more fully. He squinted at the lump, trying to focus. "Who or what is that?" he asked, cautiously.

I stared at it but didn't notice any distinguishing characteristics. We couldn't see its face the way it was lying there. And out here, it was possible the thing didn't even *have* a face. I stood slowly, backing away as quietly as I could.

Tony did the same.

After we were a few feet away, I felt more comfortable. "I'm gonna poke it with my stick. You get ready with your axe."

"I'm not so sure that's a good idea, Jayne."

"Do you have a better one?"

"Yeah. Let's leave it alone and go."

I thought about the communication with the trees I'd had, before I went to sleep last night. I was sure they wouldn't have let something malicious get through to us; so that had to mean that this thing, whatever it was, wasn't planning to cause any trouble. At least, it wasn't planning to last night.

"I'm just gonna try to wake it up. I won't hurt it."

I took Blackie in hand and tiptoed over to the pile of clothes. I gingerly touched it with the blunt end of my stick, nudging it just a little.

"Hey. You. *Get up."*

Nothing. No response.

I poked a little harder.

"Yo! Wake up!"

"Uhhhhnnnmmm ... "

I looked at Tony. That groan sounded suspiciously human. It sounded a little bit like ...

Tony walked over, crouching over the figure on the ground. "Becky?"

"Uhhhnnmm ... "

"Holy shit!" he said, his face going white.

I jumped to Becky's other side, pulling on her shoulder to turn her over.

Her face was covered in bruises and scratches, and she had dried blood caked around her mouth and nose. Both of her eyes were blackened and swollen.

"Shit, Becky, what the hell *happened* to you?" I wanted to help but I was afraid to even touch her. If her face was this bad, I could only imagine what the rest of her was like. She looked like she'd been run over by a truck.

"Jayne?" she asked weakly, not opening her eyes.

"Yeah, it's Jayne and Tony." I looked up at Tony. "Get her some water."

Tony ran over to our packs and brought back a bottle.

"Here, Becky, drink this water." I tipped the container up to her mouth, forcing her to take small sips.

Her eyes fluttered a little as she tried to open them, but she was mostly unsuccessful, only able to get them open a slit. The whites of her eyes were bloody-looking too. Someone had really done a number on her.

I had a million questions, and they all started pouring out of me at once. "Can you tell us what happened? And where are the others? Are they okay? How did you find us?" I stopped when I felt Tony's hand on my arm, telling me to shut the hell up.

"Sit me up," groaned Becky. "I want to get up - please."

Tony and I helped her upright. She sat there, hunched over for a minute, either gathering her strength or just unable to move anymore, I couldn't tell which. I was amazed she was even able to do that much. If someone had kicked my ass that bad, I'd be on my back for at least a week, demanding ice cream and cookies every half hour. Even out here I'd do that.

"We were attacked when it got dark," she said softly. "Jared got away. I saw him run before I got hit the first time. Finn ... " She couldn't finish because she was crying too much. The tears slid down her cheeks, silently, making salty paths on her dirty red and purple skin.

I looked at Tony. I was afraid from her reaction that Finn hadn't made it - that he'd been killed. I couldn't believe someone we came here with might not be going back. It was too ridiculously awful to even consider.

"Did you see Chase or Spike?" I asked gently. I didn't want to push her, but I needed to know.

"I ran away. I saw Finn go down, but when I left, Spike and Chase were still there, fighting. They were back to back." The sobs shook her body now.

I rubbed her shoulder gently, making whatever comforting noises I could come up with.

"I feel so guilty that I left them there. And Finn ... "

Tony tried to make her feel better. "You had to leave. It sounds like you were outnumbered. You have to take care of yourself in this place."

She snorted, sounding both bewildered and angry. "Outnumbered? Ha! That's a *joke*. It was the five of us against *one*."

"One *what?"* I asked. Tony and I already knew that a single certain type of creature could be like ten normal people.

"I don't even know what it was. It was there and then not there, too fast to watch. You never knew where it was going to show up next. It kept appearing, hitting me, tripping me, slapping me down. I had my knife, but I don't think I even got a single nick on the thing."

"Did you see what it looked like?" I asked. I wanted a description, thinking maybe there was a way the trees could help us.

"Not really. It was a man. Maybe just a boy. He was small, not much bigger than me. I saw him standing in front of me for barely a second. He, or it, looked angry. I'm not sure why - it's not like we challenged it or did anything. One minute we were setting up camp, the next minute we were getting our butts kicked."

"What happened with Finn?" I asked softly, waiting for more tears.

She took a deep, shaky breath and exhaled strongly. "He had his bow and arrows out. The thing was attacking Spike, and Finn let one of the arrows go. The thing turned around fast, and actually caught the arrow in its hand, in mid-flight. Then, in a flash it appeared in front of Finn and jabbed the arrow into his chest." She stopped talking and dropped her face into her hands, hissing at the pain she caused herself. "Ow, that frigging hurts," she said, before crying again.

Tony rubbed her back while I stood, pacing in front of them.

"What do we do now? Go find them? Or continue our search for the next waypoint? This is so messed up; I don't have *any* idea what we should be doing right now. *Doublefuck!"* My pacing was helping, clearing my mind of the worst bits of panic. "I think we need to go back. If they're as messed up as Becky is, they're going to need help."

"We could be walking into a minefield."

"Yeah," I agreed, "a minefield of seriously fucked up shit. You remember how to use that axe, Romeo?"

Tony blushed. "I'm sure I could, if given the right circumstances."

"Well, if I recall correctly, those circumstances include you getting very pissed."

"I'm sure if we see our friends in trouble, I'll be pissed enough."

"Good. Becky, can you remember how you got here?"

"No, I don't think so. I fell down after that thing hit me for about the tenth time, and when I looked up, a path in the trees opened in front of me. I crawled in and the trees closed behind me. I followed the path that kept appearing, hoping it was you and your tree-hugging stuff. Eventually I ended up here. I saw your fire and sat down next to it, and that's the last thing I remember."

Tony looked at me, frowning in confusion. "Jayne? What's she talking about?"

"Wellll, I did ask the trees to protect us from harm. It's possible I was picturing Becky's face at the time when I said 'us'."

"I thought you said the trees would let us know if someone came around? If she were a bad guy she could have slit our throats while we slept." Tony scowled at the trees around us, as if they could see him scolding them for their shoddy guard-duty work.

"Actually, I think I only asked for protection from those who would do us harm. Becky doesn't fit that profile. I guess next time I should be more specific."

Tony narrowed his eyes, still looking at the trees. I could tell he wasn't totally ready to swallow the whole idea of the tree-love, even though he'd felt it himself. He'd missed all the really good stuff when he was mooning over Her Ugliness, the hag, so I couldn't blame him for the doubt. It was still hard for me to believe sometimes.

"I think the trees helped me last night. I know they did, and I'm so grateful. Thank you, Jayne. You and the trees saved my life. Will you tell them thank you for me?"

I walked over and sat down next to her, taking her hands in one of mine. I put my other hand into the earth next to me. "Thank them yourself."

I connected to the trees, allowing them to feel Becky's gratitude. She closed her eyes, tears coming out of the corners to track down her face one after the other. She smiled, though, and sighed with a happy tone. "Gosh this feels good."

Tony was looking at Becky with a funny expression on his face. "Becky, do you feel okay?"

She laughed. "Well, everything considered, I guess so. At least I'm alive."

"I'm asking because your eyes aren't as swollen as they were, like, five minutes ago."

She opened them, now actually able to expose both of her eyeballs. And they weren't bloody-looking anymore. "Hey, I can see you guys now." She smiled and turned her head back and forth. "And my face and neck don't hurt as much."

I could feel a vibration in our connection - an energy thrumming through my body, going from the trees, through me, to Becky.

"Guys, I think the trees are doing some kind of healing thing on the Beckster."

"Okay, stop now," said Becky, a little breathless, severing her connection to me by pulling her hands away. "Wow. That's some pretty powerful stuff." She put her hand up on her chest.

"What happened?" asked Tony.

"I don't know. The feeling got too intense. It started out as a fluttering, then grew into a humming and then the vibrations started getting, I don't know, more vibratie ... too vibratie. My heart is still racing."

"Vibratie? I'm pretty sure that's not a word," said Tony.

"It's the only way I can describe it. The vibrations were too vibratie."

I hadn't felt what she was talking about. The vibrations just hummed along quietly for me. But I was glad that she was able to heal at least a little. I had been afraid she wouldn't even be able to walk, and that would have caused us a ton of problems to add to our already mountain-sized pile.

I stood and brushed myself off. "So, what's it going to be? Going back to Becky's camp or getting to waypoint number three?"

"Becky, did you guys get to waypoint two yet?"

"Yes. We saw your flags on one and two, so we knew you were ahead of us."

"How did Jared take it?" I asked.

Tony shot me a dirty look.

"What?" I said, innocently.

Tony shook his head, saying nothing.

"He didn't say anything. Are you still hung up on him, Jayne?"

"Yeah, maybe. Can you blame me? There you are, getting your ass handed to you last night by a ... lightning boy or whatever, and Jared takes off to save his own ass. And I'm sure you noticed the old yellow flags already there on the waypoints - *yellow*, same as Jared's flags. Coincidence? I think not."

"I ran away, too," said Becky, softly, guilt lacing her voice.

"Yeah, but that's different. You hung around a while and tried to help, and you're half the size of Jared. He's a big enough guy. He should have stayed to help Chase and Spike ... and you too."

"No use arguing over it now," said Tony. "I think we should go back and check on the others. I wouldn't feel right just walking away, knowing they could be hurt like Becky was."

I sighed loudly. "I had a feeling you were going to say that. Fine, let's get going. Becky, can you walk? If not, we can leave you here. I'll ask our friends to watch out for you." I glanced up at the trees.

"No, I'll come. Like Tony said, I wouldn't feel right staying behind. But can I eat one of your crackers or something? I left my bag back there and I'm starving all of a sudden."

Tony dug out a package and handed it to her.

Becky scarfed the food down without even stopping for a breath.

"Wow, you really were hungry," he said, impressed.

"I know. I don't know why, though. I ate dinner last night, not that long ago."

"I'll bet it's the healing stuff. The trees probably sped up your metabolism or something," he suggested.

We nodded. It made sense.

"Come on, guys," I said, walking now. "We're burning daylight. Let's go."

*****

Becky was able to lead us back to the spot where she had been pummeled by the boy-thing, as the fog lifted from her memory. The trees kept clearing a path ahead of us, helping Becky show the way.

As soon as we got there, we could see that something bad had happened. Becky walked over to where a bunch of plants and ivy had been trampled. "This is where Finn was." There were brown stains on the ground, but no Finn. "That's his blood," she said, starting to cry again.

"Well, he's not here, so that's a good sign," I said. Dead people didn't get up and walk away, even in the forest - or at least I hoped so. I ignored Becky's tears. We didn't have time to wallow in her pain right now. I was very nervous about being here at the scene of the crime. Whatever they had done to set that creature off might be something we were doing right now. I didn't want to face that thing, whatever it was, if we could help it. I liked my face the way it was.

"They're not here," I said, stating the obvious. "What next?"

Becky looked around, a forlorn expression on her face.

"Let's go to waypoint three," said Tony, the voice of reason. "I'm sure that's where they're headed. We'll meet up with them there or on our way to the last one."

"Fine. Let's go."

I walked off with Tony, the way we had come, but Becky stayed put. I went back to her, taking her by the hand. "Buck up, little camper, we'll find 'em."

"But what about Finn?" she said, staring down at the stained forest floor.

"I haven't given up on him yet, so you shouldn't either."

Becky looked up at me, tears in her eyes again. "Did the trees tell you something?"

"No, it's just a feeling I have."

I was glad she didn't ask for any explanation because I really didn't have one. It's not that I was totally bullshitting her, but whatever it was that was bothering me, giving me these feelings of doubt, was too deep in my subconscious to come to my thinking, rational brain right now. Something, something, *something*, was just not right about this whole thing, and I wasn't talking about the fact that we were in a totally bizarre forest with supernatural creatures trying to kill us. Something bigger than all of this was going on. I just didn't know exactly what it was. Yet.

Chapter Twenty-One

WE REACHED THE LAKE AROUND midday. It was gorgeous. Sunbeams hit the surface of the water, intersecting with its still surface to create random patterns of diamond-like sparkles, flashing and twinkling in the light. The water's edge was ringed with a narrow shore and trees. On the far side stood the waypoint obelisk - this one topped with a silver point that shone brightly, reflecting the rays of the sun. We stood at the edge of the trees on the opposite side of the lake.

"Thar she blows," I said. "And when I say she blows, I mean, she *blows*. This whole thing blows. It blows the big honkis."

"What exactly is a honkis?" asked Becky, sounding a little more chipper now that we'd actually succeeded in reaching our nearest goal.

"A honkis, my little friend, Beckster of the Land of Tampa, is a penis - a dick ... a prick ... a schlong, a dong, a wanker ... a johnson, a trouser trout, a ... "

"Um, excuse me? Jayne?"

"Yes, Tony?" I asked innocently.

All I got was expectant bug-eyes in response.

"What? Does my penis talk bother you?"

Becky giggled and said, "Dong."

I couldn't help but laugh. "Dong? That's all you got is *dong*?"

Becky stuck her chin out. "No, I got more. How 'bout ... *wiener*."

I shook my head. "Pitiful. You and Tony are perfect for each other."

Becky looked over at Tony shyly, her face going red.

Tony pretended not to hear us, walking out of the trees towards the lake shore; but I saw the back of his neck going red too.

Hmmmm. Maybe when we were done fighting for our lives and getting our asses kicked by supernaturals, they could go to the movies or something.

My matchmaking was suddenly interrupted by a howling coming from the trees on the other side of the lake. We all stopped walking towards the obelisk, and instead, carefully and slowly regrouped back at the edge of the woods.

I shook my head angrily. "Mother*fucker!* If it's not one thing, it's another. Did that sound like a wolf howl to you guys? Because it sounded like one to me." I was pissed. We just couldn't catch a break.

"Yeah," said Tony, quietly and intensely, "that definitely sounded like a wolf howl."

Becky just nodded her head up and down quickly, her eyes big and round and looking particularly gruesome with remnants of bruising around the edges. She looked like she had done a particularly bad job applying some goth makeup.

"And what are the chances that this wolf is a garden variety wolf? Anyone?" I looked at Becky and Tony for feedback.

"Not good," said Tony.

At least I could count on him to be honest, even if it wasn't really what I wanted to hear.

"Can the trees help us?" asked Becky, looking up.

"I don't see how," I said. They could communicate feelings to me and respond to my requests doing plant stuff with their branches and leaves, but as far as I knew that was the extent of their capabilities.

"We need to get to that waypoint," said Tony, frustrated.

"Let's just go, then. We'll keep our weapons out and our eyes open. Stick close to the trees.

"Shouldn't we stick close to the water?" asked Becky.

"Yeah, that way we have more room to maneuver, and we can see anything coming out at us from the trees," said Tony.

Any other time I would have agreed with them, but based on my newfound relationship with the green stuff in the forest, I was feeling much more secure being with them.

"I feel more comfortable with the trees; I can communicate with them." I looked out over the water. It seemed so beautiful and peaceful - just like this forest had looked on our first day in it. I continued, "Not to mention the fact that the Loch Ness Fucking Monster could be swimming around in that lake looking for its next meal."

Becky and Tony looked at the lake with new eyes. They both turned back to me, nodding reluctantly in agreement. If nothing else, this forest had made us a lot more open-minded about what *could* be. Never say never in the Green Forest.

"Let's go."

We took our weapons out and circled the lake, staying just inside the edge of the trees. We got halfway around before we encountered problems.

"Jaaayyyyne," said Becky nervously, her eyes on the lake to our right.

"What?"

Becky grabbed my arm. "There's something moving in the water."

I looked at the lake but saw nothing. "Where?"

"There," she said, pointing to the center, directly across from where we were standing.

A wolf howl split the silence around us. It came from inside the forest, just to our left, and it wasn't far away. We weren't quite surrounded yet, but we had only two directions left to choose from - forward and back.

"Jayne, it's close," said Tony.

A second howl pierced the air, this one of a different timbre.

"There's more than one!" said Becky, panic in her voice.

Then a chorus of howls split the air.

"There's a whole fucking pack! Get up in the trees," I urged.

I glanced towards the lake, second-guessing myself, wondering if we should go in that direction; but then I saw something just barely cutting through the surface of the water - a long trail of something, coming towards the shore, just next to where we were.

Trees, I need you. Help me and my friends get up in your branches. We need to go very high in one of the Ancients.

I decided that the old trees, the ones that had super big trunks, were going to be called the Ancients from now on. It just felt right. I didn't have much time to think about it, though. I was too busy trying not to get mauled by wolves or eaten by Loch Ness monsters.

The branches of a huge nearby tree leaned down.

"Grab onto the branch!" I yelled.

Becky and Tony obeyed at once, tucking their weapons into their clothes and taking hold of the tree's limb. We could hear something crashing through the forest, coming towards us. I shoved Blackie into my waistband.

Once we had grabbed hold, the tree lifted us up to the next branch.

"Get on!" I yelled, panic in my voice. At this distance above the ground, which was still too low, I could see gray and black shapes darting between trees deeper in the woods, coming in our direction. "Faster!"

Another branch lowered to meet us, and we all grabbed on desperately. We were lifted up again, now about twenty feet off the ground. I didn't know if it was going to be high enough.

More.

Another branch came down and we all climbed aboard. Becky didn't get a good grip though, and started to slip. She screamed.

"I'm falling!"

Tony grabbed her wrist and pulled her hard. She used the leverage to get a better grasp on the branch.

"Thanks," she said breathlessly, lifting herself up, once again secure.

Now that we were higher up, but still not so high that the view below was obscured by other branches and leaves, we could see what we were dealing with. A pack of wolves reached our tree and circled below.

But of course these weren't normal run-of-the-mill wolves. They were wolf-*people.* Wolves in as much as they had fur everywhere, wolfish looking heads, tails and big fucking teeth - people in that they stood on two legs and had hands - but with sharp claws on them. *Werewolves.* They were snarling and jumping up on the side of the tree, trying to grasp the lowest branch.

I had moved to the inside part of the branch so I was against the tree's trunk. I hugged it for all I was worth. *Don't let the wolves in the trees, don't let the wolves in the trees; protect us, protect us, protect us.*

"Jayne, what are you doing?!" Tony shouted in full freak-out mode.

"She's talking to the tree, dummy!" retorted Becky. "Give her some space!"

I opened my eyes in time to see Tony looking sheepish.

"I'm just asking it to keep the wolves out of the trees and to protect us," I explained. I didn't want Tony to feel bad. This was a lot to process, so I was totally cool with any one of us losing our minds.

"How's it going to keep the wolves out of the trees?" Tony asked, looking down.

One particularly persistent wolf was jumping up, over and over, trying to reach the lower branch. He was coming disturbingly close.

"I'm not sure; hopefully we won't have to find out."

No sooner had I said that, than the wolf succeeded in grabbing that friggin' branch, to the absolute jubilation of his pack mates who were now snarling and howling all at once. The wolf on the branch fixed us with a hungry look, saliva dripping out of the corners of his mouth as he flexed his biceps, slowly lifting himself up and hooking his arms over the branch.

"Jayyynnne!" moaned Becky, near hysteria.

I could tell that the wolf thought he had it in the bag, a savage smile curling up the edges of his mouth, when all of a sudden the tree next to ours swung one of its branches over and whacked the ever-loving shit out of that wolf, right on its stupid wolf head. The blow momentarily stunned him. He looked around not realizing where the assault had come from, naturally assuming it was from us. He roared his displeasure and doubled his efforts to re-establish his hold on the branch and continue his upward movement.

But my lovely trees had other ideas. Now two large branches from neighboring trees swung over, their wood protesting with groans and cracks that rang out through the forest. They were beating him about the head and shoulders, causing him to yelp and snarl in frustration. Then our tree shook its branch up and down, making it impossible for the carnivorous beast to hold on, especially when combined with the beat-down from the other trees. The wolfman fell to the ground, landing on his back, stunned.

The other wolves stopped their snarling and growling for a minute, gathering around their fallen pack-mate, sniffing the air above him. He sat up and shook his head, trying to get rid of what I hoped was one hell of a headache. Then he looked up at us with the most malevolent stare I've ever seen. He was even madder than that hag had been when I stole her boyfriend away.

He growled at the group and they renewed their efforts to get us down from the tree; only this time, they were more subtle. They just circled it, growling. The look their bruised leader gave us said it all: they were going to wait us out. We had to come down eventually.

It was then that I realized how bad I had to pee. This was going to be a long friggin day.

Chapter Twenty-Two

"WHAT TIME IS IT, TONY?" I asked. I knew he didn't have a watch, but that didn't stop me from expecting him to know the answer.

He looked out over the calm water of the lake, gauging the sun's position by the reflections he was seeing. "About five o'clock, give or take."

"I have to pee like a friggin' racehorse," I said to no one in particular.

"Me too," said Becky.

"Me three," said Tony.

I looked down. All of the wolves were still there. "At some point I'm just gonna have to pee on those fuckers."

"That'll make 'em happy," said Tony, tiredly.

I'm pretty sure he thought I was joking, but I wasn't. I really had to go.

"Jayne, you probably shouldn't," cautioned Becky.

I sighed. I didn't even know how I was going to work it, mechanically speaking. At the least, I'd have to pull my pants down and dangle my hoo-ha over the branch, giving the wolves a perfect view of the Golden Palace of the Himalayas. That was just too embarrassing, although there was a sort of poetic justice to peeing on your enemies when they weren't able to get to you. And it wasn't like they would kill me less painfully if I *didn't* pee on them. Either way, I was going to die if they got their paws on me. *Might as well pee on 'em,* I decided.

I started to unzip my pants.

Tony went into panic mode. "Jayne, do NOT wiz on the werewolves."

I looked down at the wolves, deciding that it wouldn't technically be my fault if I warned them first. "Hello, werewolves? Excuse me!"

A few of them glanced up.

"Yoo hoo! Werewolves! Hairy motherfuckers! Yeah, *you!*"

The one who had gotten bonked was looking up now.

"Yo, listen, I gotta pee. You know, take a piss? So I'm gonna unleash up here. You might wanna look out below, if you know what I mean."

I watched in mid-unzip, while their leader, the one we had smashed, stood up and looked me in the eye. A shimmering formed around him, kind of outlining his body.

"What's he doing?" asked Tony. "What's that ... stuff around his head?"

"How the fuck do I know? Maybe he's going to turn into a vampire now."

We watched as his features quivered and changed. They became less wolfish and more mannish.

Becky whispered, "I think he's turning into a guy ... "

Sure enough. Where there was once a wolf standing, there was now a man. A very naked one. A very *hot* naked one.

He snarled at me.

A very hot, naked, *angry* one.

His voice was gruff. "What are you saying, human girl?"

I cleared my throat, now a tad nervous. It's not every day that I spoke to a totally hot naked man who I was getting ready to expose my parts to - and piss on.

"What I said, is that I have to pee, so if you don't want to get pissed on, I suggest you move your hairy asses out of the way."

His eyebrows screwed up as he processed what I said. "You are going to urinate." He said it like a statement, not a question.

"Yes, that would be the technical term for what I'm about to do."

"And you are telling us because you do not want to urinate on us?"

"Yes, that's the idea."

"You realize that we are going to kill you and eat you, yes?"

"Well, that did actually appear to be your goal - so yes, I am fully aware of your plan to kill and eat me and my friends. Not that I'm on board with this plan, mind you."

"Do not be foolish. You have no escape. We will wait for as long as it takes. You will have to come down eventually."

"Yeah, well, when I come down I'm going to have to kill you, so maybe you should take this opportunity to move along. I'm pretty sure the Loch Ness Monster's going to be paying us a visit soon, anyway."

He frowned. "Who is this monster you speak of?"

"The one in the lake."

The wolf looked out towards the water. "The Lady of the Lake has no quarrel with The Wolf."

Ah, so it was a Lady of the Lake and not Nessie. *Cool.* A chick I could handle.

"Yeah, well, I have weapons and I have friends, so I don't plan on being your next meal. Not today. Not ever."

The naked wolfman smiled. "You are brave."

I smiled.

"And stupid."

I frowned.

"Go ahead with your urination." He growled at his pack and they all moved away from the base of the tree. He was still looking up at me.

"Um, could you tell them to turn around?"

He looked at me, confused.

I signaled with my finger, turning it in the air. "Give a girl some privacy, would ya?"

He shook his head, but turned his pack around.

Imagine that - a werewolf who lets a girl pee in private. Little bits of coolness in my totally fucked-up life. This place was full of surprises.

"Come on, Becky, now's our chance."

Tony didn't waste any time either. We all dropped our drawers and peed for what felt like five full minutes.

As soon as the sounds stopped, the wolves returned, although wisely avoiding the areas too near the drop zones.

Now that I could think of something other than my full bladder, I had some questions. "So, wolfman, what are you exactly? A werewolf?"

He looked out into the forest, saying nothing.

"We're kind of new to this whole supernatural thing, so I was just curious. Maybe you're a shapeshifter. Do you turn into a vampire at night?"

The wolfman spit in disgust. "Vampires ... "

"Ah, so you're not a werevampire."

"Do not be foolish," he yelled, angrily, looking up at me. "There is no such thing as a werevampire." His eyes glittered with anger.

"Yeah, sure. How foolish of me not to know that." I rolled my eyes. This guy obviously didn't get out of the forest much. "So, do you know Mr. Dardennes?"

"All in the forest know Dardennes," was his curt response.

Now we were getting somewhere. Tony and Becky were listening attentively.

"What about Jared Bloodworth, do you know him?"

Becky shot me a dirty look. Tony just looked off into the distance, shaking his head.

The wolfman spat on the ground again.

Hmmmm, interesting. "So you *do* know him?"

"Human, stop this useless interrogation. Come down here and save us the trouble of coming up there. I will make your death less painful."

I stared him in the eye, giving him my 'take no shit' look. "No, I don't think so. Not today. Not tomorrow. Not *ever.*" In hindsight, the stare-down I gave him was probably not the wisest thing to do to a werewolf.

The wolfman snarled, shaking his head violently. We watched in disgusted awe as he changed from a man back into his wolf form. It was horrible and amazing all at the same time. He was agitated, and his anger got the rest of them all riled up. They were pacing under the tree again, several of them doing the vertical jumping stuff once more.

"Jayne, if enough of them start getting up here, I'm not sure that the trees are going to be able to beat them off," said Tony.

He was right. We were in a shitload of trouble, and I had probably made it a tad bit worse by antagonizing their leader.

Suddenly, one of the wolves yelped in pain, dropping to the ground. I looked down, trying to see what the hell was going on. "Can you guys see what's happening?"

"No!" said Tony, desperately searching for clues as to what was freaking the wolves out.

And freaking out was definitely what they were doing. All but one of them were lined up at the base of the tree, facing into the woods, snarling and growling. The fur on their necks and backs was standing on end, their ears flattened, tails held straight out behind them. The one on the forest floor wasn't moving, and it had an arrow shaft sticking out of its body.

"That's a fucking *arrow!* Finn's here!" I yelled.

Becky shouted, "Finn! We're in the tree! Be careful, there are seven of them!"

Another wolf yelped and fell, then got up, shaking its head and whining. It took two steps sideways and then walked face-first into the tree. It turned around, obviously confused, now walking towards the lake. One of the other wolves went over to it, nudging it in the side with its nose. The injured wolf looked up, sniffing the air, but apparently blind. I could see blood oozing out of its eyes and down around its ears. *What the hell?*

"Becky!" came a voice from the woods.

Spike!

Becky answered. "Spike! I'm here. I'm with Jayne and Tony in a tree near the lake!"

We heard the distinctive sound of a flying arrow as it entered our little area and then buried itself into another wolf body. The beast went down without a sound. The pack was down to four wolves now, the one with the eye problem - no doubt a victim of Spike's slingshot - having stumbled down to the lake, of no use to their cause anymore.

"We need to get down and help them," said Tony, putting his hand on the head of the axe that was sticking out of the top of his belt.

"Shit," was all I could think to say. He was right. We couldn't sit here on our grandstand and watch our friends get maimed, or possibly killed, trying to help us. I put my arms around the trunk of the tree. *Help us down.*

I could tell the tree didn't like this idea. I knew it would never deny my wishes, but I could sense a sorrow or empty feeling where normally all I felt was joy and abundance. The tree offered branches for us to climb down with so we could join our friends.

The wolfman leader looked up and saw what that we were coming down, weapons in hand. Then he looked off into the forest at our approaching friends. His head swiveled back and forth a couple more times. I could tell he was doing some wolf math in his head, trying to calculate his odds of winning.

A gunshot rang out and one of his comrades fell stone dead right next to him. That made the wolf math a lot easier. He let out one sharp bark at his pack and they all took off, running away from our tree and our friends, back in the direction we had come from.

Seconds later, we reached the lowest branch and Spike, Chase, and Finn showed up under our tree. Spike flashed me the most amazing smile I'd ever seen, even for him. "What's up, guys? Mind if we join the party?"

Chapter Twenty-Three

I JUMPED DOWN FROM THE last branch and ran to Spike, jumping into his arms, wrapping my legs around him, too. Having multiple near-death experiences apparently made me less inhibited.

He hugged me back fiercely, putting his face in my neck and inhaling deeply, sending shivers up my spine and down to my special places. "Nice to see you too, Jayne," he said softly.

Sliding down his body so I could get my feet and brain back to earth was nearly mind-blowing. *Holy hotness.* He smelled and felt so damn good. I smiled back at him and then turned to Chase. I walked up to him more sedately, laying my head momentarily on his chest as I hugged him around the waist.

He reached around and awkwardly patted me on the back. "Hey. You okay?"

"Yes. And damn glad you're alive, Chase." I pulled back and smiled, noticing that he couldn't help but smile back.

His face had a slice on one cheek, but looked surprisingly good, considering the beat-down he had probably received from that thing Becky had told us about.

I stepped over to Finn who already had Becky fawning all over him. His shirt was covered in old blood and smelled none too pretty.

"I'll save the hug for later when you don't smell like death warmed over."

Finn smiled weakly at me. "Yeah, I'll take a raincheck."

Becky turned to me, alarm in her eyes after having peeked under his ragged shirt. "Jayne, you have to do something to help him."

I saw Chase raise his eyebrow at that, but of course he said nothing.

"Dr. Jayne, calling Dr. Jayne," said Spike, imitating a hospital page. Becky frowned at him and Spike had the good sense to look adequately chagrined. "Sorry, not a good time for jokes." He swung his slingshot around, whistling nervously.

"Nice shot, by the way," said Tony, looking pointedly at Spike's weapon.

Spike gave him an upward nod of his chin. "Yeah, thanks. I'm getting pretty good with this thing. Nothing like a life or death situation to help speed up the learning process."

"I think you blinded that wolf," said Tony, respect lacing his voice.

"Yeah," said Spike, sounding a little sad, "not the best way to go, but what was I supposed to do?"

Becky walked over to him and put her hand on his arm in a comforting gesture. "You did what you had to do. We're grateful. They told us they planned to kill and eat us, so don't feel bad."

Finn looked up from my amateur inspection of his chest, which had revealed a big, nasty-looking hole. "What do you mean, 'they told you'?"

Becky answered. "Well, they weren't just wolves, they were werewolves. One of them changed into a guy and had a conversation with Jayne. He pretty much told us their agenda then."

Finn shook his head. "Jayne-Girl, you are somethin' else, you know that? My momma would'a just loved you. She always liked girls with sass." He was smiling, even though I could tell he was in pain.

I stood up straight and took his hand. "Finn, I think maybe I can help you, but it's gonna be a little weird, so I just need you to go with it and don't give me any shit until it's over, 'kay?"

"You gonna do a little voodoo on me, or what?"

"Yeah, something like that - minus the sacrificial goat."

"Whatever. I'm beyond arguin' at this point. Just put me outta my misery if you can't fix me. I've done gone about as far as I'm gonna go."

I pulled on his hand. "Just a few more steps, and after that I won't make you walk anymore unless you want to." I led him over to one of the Ancients. I knew I was going to need some big guns for this one.

"Can we watch?" asked Becky, eagerly.

"Yeah. But I need you to keep an eye out for those wolves and the bitch from the lake."

"Bitch from the lake?" asked Spike.

"I'll tell you later. Just assume she's a mean-ass motherfucker if you see her coming and shoot her in the eyes."

Spike barked out a burst of sudden laughter but took something out of his pocket and put it in the pouch of his slingshot. He was locked and loaded, apparently.

I looked Finn in the eyes. They weren't very bright and he looked really tired. His skin was a pale gray, the sheen of sweat making it look even worse.

"I feel sick," he said softly.

"Finn, I need you to put your hands on this tree with me."

He had questions in his eyes, but lacked the strength to ask them. He reached over to put his hands where I showed him. He was leaning his cheek and upper body on the tree, the rest of him remaining on the ground among its roots. I went behind him, kneeling down so I could wrap my arms around him from behind and touch the tree above his arms.

He sighed. "This is nice. Cuddlin'."

I nipped his ear.

"Ow! What was that for?"

"We're not cuddling. You're getting healed. Now shut up and feel the energy."

I sent out my request. *Trees and all creatures connected to us, I need your healing power for my friend.* I felt the responding surge almost instantly.

Finn had started to complain. "I don't know what yer ... " Then he suddenly went silent.

I couldn't tell if he was feeling the energy or not, but I sure was. This tree was big time - a granddaddy of a tree. The energy was a heavy rumbling, deep and dark green-blue, coming up from the center of the forest, channeling power from trees, plants, creatures, the lake, the air, *everything*.

"Finn," Becky asked, a look of concern on her face, "what's wrong, sweetie? Why are you crying?"

"I ... it's just ... I can't ... "

"Shhhhh," I said, whispering because it was all I could manage, "we're almost done." I could feel the Ancient reeling the energy back in to its lowest level, which was apparently all I had experienced up until now. My heart was in my throat. I knew why Finn couldn't get his words out. The beauty and the power and the awesomeness of it all ... it was too much for our puny minds to comprehend. I was hoping I hadn't fried his brain, putting him on this tree. *Maybe I should have picked a smaller one.*

The tree disconnected all but the most tenuous link. I knew it wasn't a rejection - just a signal to me that its business with Finn was done. I didn't want to overstay my welcome, so I pulled us both away from the trunk, wrapping Finn's arms around his torso with mine on top.

I looked at Becky, since I couldn't see Finn's face. I mouthed the words, *'Is he okay?'* at her.

She nodded her head, amazement and relief written all over her face.

"I'm letting you go, Finn, okay? Don't fall back."

Tony stepped behind us to help me up and make sure Finn didn't pass out and collapse onto the forest floor.

Spike and Chase stood off to the side, speechless.

Tony eased Finn back against the tree.

Finn's eyes were closed, but his color already looked better. His cheeks were a nice, rosy pink and he had a very peaceful smile on his face.

Becky came and leaned over him. "Finn, are you okay?"

"Yep," he said lazily, "I'm just enjoyin' the moment right now. Jus' gimme a minute or twenty."

I stepped away, brushing myself off again. Seemed like I kept getting covered in forest crud. I looked at my hands. My nails were a disaster.

Spike and Chase came over to stand with me.

"Soooo, what was *that* all about?" said Spike, a neutral look on his face.

Chase just looked at me questioningly, letting Spike do the talking.

I looked down at my feet, a little embarrassed; I don't know why. "Since we've been here, I've kinda discovered I have a connection to the trees or something."

"A connection, huh? Like how so?"

"I don't know - a connection. I touch the tree, I talk to the tree, the tree answers." I shrugged my shoulders. That was the essence of it, anyway.

"So you say, like, 'Hey tree, fix Finn,' and the tree is like, 'Okay, shazam, done.' "

"Not exactly, but that's the idea. I don't really use words so much as I use images or feelings. It seems to work."

Finn slowly stood up and ran his hands all over his body, breaking out in a huge grin before suddenly grabbing Becky and lifting her up high, making her scream in surprise and delight.

"I'd say," said Spike. He looked up at Chase and I saw them exchange a look.

Chase lifted his shoulders. "Could come in handy."

I play-punched Chase in the shoulder. "Chase, you are the master of the understatement; anyone ever told you that?"

"Yep."

Spike and I laughed. Chase even smiled a tiny bit. We walked over to join the others. It was time to get some flags tied to waypoint number three. I was *almost* hoping the lady in the lake would come out to dance so we could kick her ass too. *Almost*.

Chapter Twenty-Four

I TOOK A FLAG FROM each of the others and walked over to the obelisk to tie them on. Chase had retrieved Becky's bag from where she'd dropped it after getting attacked, so luckily she had her flags back.

We all saw Jared's flag there, but none of us said anything. As far as I was concerned, my suspicions had been confirmed. Two yellow flags - one old and one new. He was working with the enemy. I wasn't sure what everyone else's opinion was, but I didn't care anymore. So long as he stayed the hell away from Tony and me, he could go on running around and hiding every time a creeper showed up. Maybe I'd see him at the finish line so I could smack him with my stick.

I turned from the obelisk to face the others. Everyone but Chase was looking at me. I walked over, intending to discuss our plan for waypoint number four, but I got distracted by the look on Chase's face as I drew even with him. He was staring out at the lake, mesmerized.

I shrugged. Who knew what went on in that guy's head? My mom always said that still waters ran deep, so maybe Chase had a lot more things going on than I realized. But if he did, he rarely showed signs of it. He reminded me of a military recruit, just waiting to take orders. I ignored him in favor of making our plan.

"So, what's next?"

We all stood there looking at each other, none of us wanting to be the first one to speak. I think seeing Jared's flag on the waypoint had kind of bummed them out or something.

I sighed. It sucked being the only one with their proverbial shit together. "Listen guys, we have some options. We can stop for a while; we can eat; we can stay here for the night; we can keep truckin'. Just tell me what you want to do and I'll do it."

"I'm starved," said Finn, rubbing his belly.

"Yeah, I was starving too after I had a dose of tree-healing," said Becky.

Tony was looking through his bag. "I don't know about you guys, but I really don't have much food left." He pulled out the last meal packet he had - mystery beef - and a half bottle of water. He looked out towards the lake, and I could almost see his mind working. We needed more water.

Before I could interject with my theories on drinking water from a lake that allegedly had some lady living in it, I was distracted by the look on Tony's face.

He opened his mouth and yelled, "Hey, Chase! Where are you going?!"

I turned in time to see Chase walking towards the edge of the lake. He didn't answer. He just kept moving towards someone standing in the water. Someone wearing a long, white, flowing dress - a lady.

"Fuck balls, it's the bitch in the lake!" I ran towards Chase to intervene.

The woman raised her hand towards Chase and he obediently returned the gesture, continuing forward, his feet now nearly touching the water.

I reached his side and nudged him. He didn't look at me; he just took another step forward.

"Hey, big guy, where ya goin'?" I asked.

No response.

I grabbed hold of his outstretched arm, pulling on it a little, but he just shrugged me off.

I ducked under his arm and stepped in front of him, putting my hands on his chest to stop his forward movement, my feet now in the water. "Just hold up a minute, Chase ... what's your hurry?"

He just kept walking forward, still in some sort of trance, pushing me ahead of him and deeper into the water.

"A little help here, guys!" I yelled, straining with the effort of keeping this human bulldozer from drowning himself, which is what I figured the Lady's plan was for him. She was like a siren or something, luring him into her watery lair.

Screw that - not on my watch!

Becky came running over to help me. She stood in front of Chase too, pushing with all her puny might.

"Where are the others?" I grunted out, my feet slipping farther into the water, dredging up some muck on the way. I could feel it going into my Converse. "This ho-bag is ruining my sneakers. She's gonna pay."

"I don't think the guys are going to be much help," said Becky, mysteriously.

I snuck a peek around Chase's arm and was thoroughly alarmed by what I saw. Spike, Finn, and Tony were all staring out at the lake, their eyes glazed over.

"Sonofabitch!" I yelled. How is it that we could take out a pack of ferocious werewolves with a slingshot and a couple of arrows, but a watery bitch floating in the lake was going to kill all my guy friends

with a look? This was *totally* fucked up. Guys were so vulnerable sometimes.

I slid down to my knees, taking Chase's legs in my arms. Then I sat down in the muck and wrapped my legs around both of his as best I could, like I used to do to my dad when I was a little kid and he wasn't yet a flaming asshole, trying to keep him from going out the door to work. I had to get in contact with the ground and keep Chase from moving at the same time.

I put my hand down in the water, touching the shore beneath. *Green things, help me. Grab my friends. Pull them away from the water.* I pictured ivy and vines coming out from the forest and winding themselves around the guys and then dragging them back away from the lake. I left Becky out of the vision, even though she was pretty much zero help at all right now. No need to truss her up along with them. Maybe she'd come in handy later. She still had her knife.

The forest must have felt my urgency along with my instructions. The vines crawled across the ground at a much quicker speed than I would have thought possible. They reached the guys' feet and then traveled upwards, slithering like snakes up their legs and torsos, weaving around themselves and wrapping the guys like mummies as they went. I made sure The Green knew its goal was to hinder and not strangle. It was alarming to think how quickly my plan to protect could turn into a hangman's noose if I wasn't very clear about what I wanted.

Now that I thought about it, though, strategizing using images was better than using words. When I thought in language and then matched my images to words, like I did the night I asked The Green to protect Tony and me, I failed to take into account that my specific words don't consider other scenarios. It was fascinating, this whole topic, but I didn't have time right now to mull it over or analyze it further. First, I had to immobilize the guys. Then I had to kick this watery bitch's ass.

There was a thud as Tony's body hit the ground. He was struggling to get up, but his arms were now restrained at his sides. He was tangled in vines from his ankles to his shoulders. A second and third thud vibrated through the ground as Spike and Finn went down. Finn didn't struggle much, but Spike was pissed. He really wanted a piece of that waterlogged ass I guess. *Stupid guys.*

More vines had made their way to Chase, so I scooted away to let them do their thing. He was covered up to his armpits by the time I got to my feet, and they were beginning to make some headway in drawing him back away from the lake and its beckoning resident. I was covered in watery muck from the waist down.

"Fuck me, I'm wet *everywhere,*" I said with disgust. I had my head down assessing my soggy clothes, so I didn't see exactly what happened next.

"Jayne!" screamed Becky, a violent splashing making its way to my ears.

I looked up and saw the aftermath of my critical planning error. The Lady was close to the shore and had Becky by the hand, pulling her out into the water. The Lady was just floating, but she was floating backwards, dragging a struggling Becky behind her.

Chase was being pulled away from the lake and back towards the forest by the vines. I called out to The Green to come and help Becky, but the vines stopped on the edge of the water, gently bobbing up and down with the rhythm of the waves created by Becky's still fighting form. She was up to her shoulders now, heading out to deeper waters.

"Becky!" I screamed, making to go in after her. The vines, which moments ago had refused to go into the water, suddenly awakened and grabbed me, wrapping their leafy arms around my legs, stopping me from going farther.

I slapped at them, grabbing and pulling as hard as I could to get them off. The more I tried to escape, the harder they wrapped themselves around me. More vines came to join the party. Pretty soon I was going to look like one of the guys - a green mummy.

"Let me go! I have to get her!" I sobbed.

"Jayne, help me!" Becky screamed in sheer panic.

I had to do something, but apparently swimming after her was a no-go, thanks to my ropey green friends. I tried in that moment not to question their loyalty - they'd never done anything but help me, so I had to believe they were doing that now.

I let them know that I wasn't going to go in the lake, turning to head back to shore. They loosened their hold on me and I ran back to where Finn had fallen, finding his bow and arrows lying next to him on the ground. I picked them up and tried to hold the bow, and at the same time, load an arrow. It was much harder to do than it looked.

I considered freeing Finn from the vines, but his eyes were still glazed over. I couldn't trust that he would help me and not go drown himself.

I sent a mayday message out to The Green, not expecting there to be a plant out there that knew how to shoot bows and arrows, but I didn't know what else to do. I stood on the shore of the lake, tears streaming down my cheeks as I watched Becky's face begin to disappear below the surface of the water, her eyes confirming the fear she felt as she approached her watery death.

"Becky! I'm sorry!" I screamed. I hated myself at that moment for being so powerless.

The bow and arrow were jerked from my hand. I started to fight, thinking one of my other friends had escaped and was going to follow Becky in, but it wasn't one of them. It was a small person, not much bigger than Becky herself, dressed in clothes that can only be described as camouflage, even though it wasn't a military variety. His shoes were more like moccasins and made no sound as he stepped one pace away from me. He lifted the weapon and, in one swift motion, notched the shaft in place, drew back the string, and let the arrow fly.

It sang through the air, hitting its intended target, piercing the heart of the Lady of the Lake. She let out a harrowing screech - it sounded like the cry of a thousand desperate, tortured souls. It was horrible. I covered my ears, trying to keep the sound away. I knew without question and without being told that too much of it could drive a person mad. I was already thinking that this world really sucked just hearing her screech one time - that was some powerful negativity coming at me. The Lady sunk beneath the surface, her deep crimson blood pouring down her gown and coloring the water around her. She kept her eyes locked on mine, even as the water rose up and covered her head. I saw anger in her eyes, and a silent promise of vengeance.

I anxiously watched the water for signs of Becky. My vines, sensing perhaps that I was again considering a water rescue, slithered up my legs. I absently brushed them away, knowing they were wasting their time because I'd never make it. The Lady was down, but I hadn't actually seen her die. The look on her face had said that she'd like nothing better than to get her clammy hands on me.

The place where Becky had disappeared was calm. A few bubbles rose to the surface, which instantly got my hopes up, but then nothing followed. No waves, no ripples, no more bubbles. No Becky.

"Is she gone?" I asked.

The man next to me didn't answer, so I looked at him. He nodded at me in silence.

I dropped my face into my hands and sobbed. The man pulled

me away from the edge, pushing down on my shoulder when I drew near my vine-entangled friends. I lowered myself to the ground, not thinking, just grieving.

I knew if Becky hadn't come out of the lake by now, she was never going to come out. She was gone and it was all my fault. I had chosen to help the guys, but left her unprotected and vulnerable. The sobs racked my body. She was only a kid, tiny and unable to fend for herself. I should have taken care of her. I should have known better than to leave her out there.

My heart was breaking. I hadn't known Becky that well, but I did know that she was a good person. She was always happy, always positive. She was like a girl version of my Tony. That realization made me cry even harder. When had our lives become so fucked up? One day I was worried about a trip to the principal's office, and the next, I was watching a really great kid getting drowned in a lake and my friends being hypnotized into nearly committing suicide.

I felt a movement nearby as one of the guys bumped up against me.

"Jayne, what the hell's going on?" asked Tony, struggling against his bonds. "Why am I all tied up?"

Spike spoke next. "Yo, not so sure I'm okay with the S&M. Can someone untie me please?"

Finn was still just lying there, I assumed too weak from his recently healed injury to protest too much.

Chase struggled in silence, not managing to get very far but not due to lack of effort. He grunted with the strain he was putting into breaking the vines.

"Just stop, Chase, I'll let you go."

I sent a request out to The Green to release my friends, and they were freed within seconds. I thanked the vines for their help, because without it, I'd no doubt be mourning the loss of five friends and not just one. But one was more than enough. I started crying again.

The guys sat up, rubbing the circulation back into their arms and legs. Tony scooted over to sit next to me, laying his arm across my shoulders. Spike came to my other side, putting his arm around my waist. Chase stood, gazing out at the water.

I looked up and saw what he was doing through my tears. "Chase, turn around!" I yelled, panic in my voice.

Chase turned to look at me with a questioning expression.

"There's a fucking siren bitch in there who already hypnotized you once. Don't look out there because I'm not fucking coming after you again." I was furious, but not at him. I was more angry with myself than anyone or anything else.

Chase came back to stand in front of me. "Where's Becky?" he asked softly.

I dropped my head down, unable to look at them. "She went into the lake. She's not coming back. I couldn't save her." I threw my head up, disgusted with myself and yelling in frustration through my tears. "Correction! I *could* have saved her, but I *didn't*. She's dead because of *me!"*

The pain overwhelmed me, crushed me. I couldn't think straight. I needed to get back into the forest and far, far away from this lake - this place of death. "Get me away from here," I begged.

Tony and Spike helped me stand.

Chase stopped for a minute, opening Becky's bag. He pulled out her flare and her flint, sparking it until it caught and lit the end of the flare. He held it up above his head and aimed it out over the lake. I watched it fire off its bright red light and send a signal soaring up into the sky. It was too late for a rescue ... I knew that. The thought had me crying all over again. Chase threw the spent cartridge down on the shore of the lake.

The guys bent down, collecting our weapons, including Becky's knife that had been dropped near the water's edge. Seeing it brought even more tears to my eyes. I had so many of them rushing out I could hardly see anymore. Even so, I ran to the edge of the lake and picked up the cartridge. I don't know why, but I just wanted to keep it.

"Leave it. So they can find her," said Chase, softly.

I stopped walking and just dropped the cartridge where I was standing. *So they could find her dead body.* A horrific thought. I doubted they'd even bother. It was their fault it had happened. Theirs and mine.

My friends led me into the forest, away from the lake and towards the waypoint, gently guiding me finally to sit under a stand of trees. Within seconds, leaves were falling all over me. I paid no attention, only barely registering their soft caresses sliding across my arms or brushing my head before tumbling in slow motion down my back to the ground. Soon I was nearly buried in the sympathies and condolences of The Green.

My sobs quieted down bit by bit. I was aware of the guys standing nearby, talking in low tones. The only thing I cared about right then was making sure none of them was walking back to that fucking lake. I didn't have any more tears left to cry for them.

Tony noticed that I had stopped and came over, crouching down beside me in the pile of leaves. "I know you're not better, but are you good enough to walk? We think it's best if we get out of this area before nightfall."

I wiped my nose and eyes off with the sleeve of my sweatshirt, nodding. I hated to leave Becky's final resting place, but the farther away from that witch in the water we were, the better off we were all going to be. I wished that I had the luxury of giving in to my feelings of revenge, because that bitch had it coming to her. The world was now short one awesome kid, and that just wasn't right. But we needed to leave this place and finish this nightmare test.

I stood to join the guys and, suddenly remembering my short-statured savior, looked around to see where he was.

"What are you looking for, Jayne?" asked Spike.

"The guy who shot that bitch in her evil, rotten, slimy heart."

"Uh, what guy?"

"There was a guy here. He took Finn's bow and arrow and shot her. I couldn't do it - I couldn't work the damn thing." I tried not to feel shame about that fact. It's not like I'd ever held one before. "Maybe I should've had you teach me, Finn."

Tony nudged me. "Stop torturing yourself. You had no way of knowing."

He was in my head again, but this time I wasn't mad about it. It was lonely in there right now, and I could use the company.

"Well, whoever he is, he's not here now. It's just us guys," said Spike.

Minus Becky, was all I could think. My depression settled over me like a heavy, dark cloak.

Chapter Twenty-Five

I TRUDGED ON, WALKING BEHIND Chase and Spike and in front of Finn. Tony walked next to me whenever the terrain would allow it. They were boxing me in, protecting me as best they could. I knew if something attacked us right now, I'd be of no help at all. All I wanted to do was lie down and sleep for the next ten years. Maybe by then I'd be able to forget all this madness.

I alternated between feeling helpless and sorry for myself, and being pissed and ready to kill any of the people of One Eleven Group with my bare hands. In those moments, I was feeling pretty confident that I could even take Ivar down. Rage had a way of bringing on the adrenaline and superhuman powers for me - or at least, the illusion of them.

Superpowers. That reminded me of the interview and the meeting we went to two days ago. *Was it just two days ago?* The beginning of the lies. My superpowers sure would have come in handy here in the forest. I hesitated in my thoughts. I kind of *was* using superpowers - at least in my interactions with The Green. *I* wasn't doing anything myself, but I was involved. Something was bothering me, something my subconscious was seeing that I wasn't. I think I was just too exhausted from the emotional pain and fatigue to focus. I had to get my mind off it for a little while. Maybe it would come to me later when I wasn't trying to think about it so hard.

I hummed one of the tunes Spike had played in the warehouse. He looked back at me and smiled, reaching out his hand to touch my shoulder. It felt nice, the contact. These kids were nice people; they didn't deserve this shit any more than I did.

My thoughts were interrupted when Chase stopped and pulled out his map. Tony, Finn, and Spike joined him, looking over his shoulders.

I sank to the ground, staring off into space. I could feel the hum of The Green below me, reaching up through the earth to connect. It was as if it could feel my sorrow and was trying to heal my heart. But there was no way to do that. I cut off the link so I could be alone.

Tony came back and sat down next to me, drawing his knees up to his chest. "Hey," he said, searching my face.

"Hey."

"How're you doing?"

"Not good."

He reached out and stroked my arm. "I know. Do you want to stop?"

"I really don't care anymore," I said. And I really didn't. Go, stop, sleep ... it didn't make any difference.

Tony got up and went back to the others. They conferred for a little while and then went around, gathering bits of wood. After a few minutes, Tony came back and explained.

"We're going to stay here for the night and then head out really early in the morning to reach the last waypoint. That okay with you?"

I shrugged. I couldn't care less.

"Do you think you can get the trees to protect us tonight so we can all sleep? I think Finn especially needs it."

"Probably."

"If you can't do it, no one will mind. We understand, just tell us if you can't."

I got angry with his patience and unspoken forgiveness that I didn't feel I deserved. "Fine! I can do it! Just leave me the hell alone!"

"Uh, that'll be a *no* on that," said Tony, sitting down next to me again.

"I'm serious, Tony, get the fuck away from me." I wasn't in the mood for his niceness or his easy acceptance of me right now.

"So you can sit here all alone and feel sorry for yourself? Nope, I don't think so."

I caught Spike and Chase stealing glances over at us, which only made me madder. Angry tears welled up in my eyes. "Screw you, Tony. I'm *not* feeling sorry for myself."

"What do you call it then?"

I shoved him away.

He tipped over on his side but then sat back up. "You're gonna have to do better than that," he said boldly.

I started to boil up inside and a message of bad intent formed in my mind. I could picture The Green tying Tony up and hanging him upside down from a tree branch.

"Ah, ah, ahhhh," Tony scolded me, wagging his finger back and forth like a mother to a child. "No fair using your powers for evil. Superheroes can only use their powers for *good;* you know that. It's Good Guy Rule Number One."

The evil image dissipated out of my mind as quickly as it had appeared. "I'm not a fucking superhero, you a-hole."

"I beg to differ," said Tony softly. "Without you, we would all be dead right now."

The tears came down my cheeks then and my throat closed up,

making it hard to talk or even breathe. "What about Becky?" I said hoarsely. "I didn't save her, and I could have. I *could* have, Tony, but I didn't!"

Tony threw his arms around me, pulling me close, and I let him do it because I just didn't have the strength to fight him off anymore. The leaves were raining down again.

"Shhhh, shhhhh ... I know you're upset ... devastated. But you have to know this was not your fault. You did *not* put Becky in that water, and you did *not* make her walk in too deep. That was the Lady in the Lake and no one else. You may have a connection to the green things in this forest, but you cannot read minds and you cannot tell the future. Stop blaming yourself. It's actually kind of arrogant, if you think about it."

I pulled back away from him, looking at him fiercely. "Arrogant? Are you fucking *kidding* me?"

"No, I'm serious. Do you really think you're so amazing that you can save everyone from everything? *Please.* None of us can do that. We have to work together as a team. We knew that on day one. It was your dumb idea in the first place, remember?"

I huffed out a pissed-off breath of air, but he did have a point. I was awesome, but on the other hand, I did suck at lots of things - shooting a bow and arrow for one. That brought my mind around to the guy who *could* shoot a bow and arrow, Robin Hood or whoever that guy was who had materialized out of nowhere and sank that soggy bitch in the lake. And Finn ... he was also a good shot.

I wiped my face off with my sleeve for the umpteenth time and tried to clear my gooey throat. "A-*hem* ... so, what? ... Is this your tough love speech?"

"Yeah. How am I doing?"

"Too fucking good," I said, letting out a half laugh, half sob.

Tony put his arms around me again, squeezing really hard. "We're gonna get through this, you'll see. Just hold it together for a little while longer."

I nodded my head into his shoulder. I was going to hold it together for just a while longer, alright - until I saw Dardennes again. Then I was going to unleash on his sorry ass. He was never going to know what hit him.

*****

We went to sleep that night with a powerful, and I hoped, very clear request for protection sent out to The Green. My dreams were filled with Becky looking at me, her face crazy with desperation as the water rose up over her head. I must have called out to her in my sleep because at some point in the night Tony shushed me and then laid down to sleep right next to me.

I woke up the next morning once again covered in leaves. I was super warm because I had not only Tony next to me, but also at some point Spike had come and joined the party. I was sandwiched between the two of them. On another day in another place, this might have been very, very interesting, but not today.

Once I realized where I was, I sat up quickly. I couldn't help but let a tiny piece of me wish Becky would be there in a pile of wet clothes sleeping at my feet. But she wasn't. I didn't even want to think of her spending the rest of eternity in the depths of that miserable lake.

I stood up and did some jumping jacks to clear my mind of those horrible images. Then I searched around desperately for a semi-private spot to do my business.

"Hey, guys, I'll be right back ... gotta go pee."

I disappeared around some trees, going as fast as I could. I got back in time to see zippers going up. Apparently, the guys didn't worry about hiding to do their thing. *Lucky jerks.*

I pulled out and ate the remaining food from my pack and swallowed the last of my water. "Well, we'd better find this last waypoint today, because I'm outta grub." I stuffed the wrappers back in my bag and then tried to work my fingers through my tangled hair. I gave up and put it back into a ponytail with my rubber band.

Finn had been carrying Becky's bag along with his. He took the time to go through it, moving its contents into his. "Becky didn't have much left herself. We can share it later."

The thought of eating her food depressed the shit out of me. *And the day had started out so well ...*

Chase walked to the base of a tree, looking up its trunk to the branches above.

"What's up, Chase?" asked Spike.

He responded, giving one of the longest replies I'd heard from him so far. "I'm not sure which direction to go."

I stood up. *Might as well make myself useful.* "I'll go up and see."

Chase backed away from the tree, while Finn and Spike watched with rapt attention. This was new for them. They knew I was going to do something with the tree, but they didn't understand exactly what. Tony realized what was coming, so he backed up even farther.

I rested my hand on the trunk and made my connection, sending my images out to The Green. The branches moved in response to my requests. I stepped onto the nearest one, steadying myself before reaching for the next. The only sounds I heard were the swishing of the branches and the creaks and groans of the wood as the tree strained to do my bidding. The guys were totally silent, watching in awe as I was hoisted up to the higher levels.

I soon reached the top and was happy to see that the last waypoint appeared to be less than a day's travel from here, heading due south. I tried to get a feel for the forest in between here and there, but it was impossible. The only thing I could see was that it was dark. Very dark. The trees were denser there, tighter together. They appeared almost black. The waypoint was in the dead center. I almost turned to go down, but then I looked again. Something wasn't right, but what was it? I looked at the forest around the waypoint. Nothing was happening. It was totally still.

Wait a minute ... That is the problem. The forest around us and the sections farther away from the fourth waypoint moved ever so slightly with the wind, an occasional bird bursting in flight through the canopy only to glide and float back down into it somewhere else. Not so, for the section of forest we would be entering soon. I looked for a while longer, but nothing changed. That forest was utterly still, frozen in place but without ice. I got a really bad feeling about it. I climbed down carefully, putting together in my mind how I could relate what I'd seen to the guys.

I explained my concerns to them as best I could, and could see from their expressions that they were as worried as I was. "We need to go in ready for anything," I said. "I have a feeling that whatever's in there will make the whore in the lake look like our fairy friggin godmother." Using the W-word to describe the thing that killed Becky made me feel just a tiny bit better. I only used *that* word when it was absolutely necessary, and this was one of those times. I looked out in the direction of the water. *Lake whore, lake whore, lake whore!*

We walked due south, and it wasn't long before we were in the darker forest. We could tell the difference just by looking around us. The forest wasn't green anymore. The tree trunks looked black and gray instead of brown. The leaves were faded out husks, none of them fully green. The ground beneath our feet crunched, being dry and brittle instead of spongy like we were used to from the other parts of the forest. There were no normal sounds here. The birds, if they were here at all, were sleeping. Or dead.

I moved closer to Tony who was already walking next to me. I took his hand, and he didn't even blink. He was probably as freaked out as I was.

We made our way slowly through the forest, trying to make as little noise as possible. Occasionally, one of our steps would snap a twig, and there was always a bit of crunching as the dry, dead leaves crumbled beneath our feet. I was constantly on edge.

After a few hours of trekking, we heard another distinct sound - my stomach, growling loudly. Spike turned around and smiled at me. "Anyone up for some lunch, by any chance?"

I smiled, embarrassed. *Stupid stomach.* I didn't have any food left.

Finn dropped back to walk next to me, pulling some crackers out of his bag and handing them to me wordlessly. One of Becky's flags fell out and onto the ground. The food was Becky's, I could tell from the look on his face and how he was trying to act all casual. I bent down and took her flag, shoving it in my pocket.

Part of me wanted to refuse the food, but I was so hungry, I couldn't. And I knew that if it were me in the lake, I wouldn't want Becky to starve when she could eat my food. I took them and tore open the wrapper. They were dry but did the trick. I shoved the wrapper in my bag and kept on walking.

The others took things out of their bags and ate as we walked. A bottle of water got passed around and I took a sip. It tasted stale. I couldn't wait to have a nice, ice-cold soda when we got back. I was never much of a soda drinker before, but I would have killed for one right then, especially if it was Dardennes or Ivar standing between me and the bubbly beverage.

I grinned evilly as I thought about that - stabbing one of them with my stick and then causally walking over and taking a nice, long drink from an ice-cold glass. This hunt was making me a little more primal than I used to be. I wondered if that was a good thing or a bad thing. My thoughts were interrupted by Chase stopping up ahead. We gathered around him to see what was going on.

"What's up?" I asked.

"I think we need another bird's-eye view," said Chase, looking around the forest. He didn't look happy.

"Okay, no problem. You look worried about something," I said, searching his face for clues about what he was thinking. I had to do that a lot with Chase because he so rarely expressed himself. But looking at him now I got nothing, other than concern. He didn't respond to my comment.

I walked over to a tree that looked like a good candidate, placing my hands on the trunk to make a connection. I inhaled sharply at the unpleasant sensation, causing the others to look over, and jerked my hands away, shaking them off and rubbing them on my jeans.

Tony came over. "What's up?"

"I'm not sure. I was going to talk to this tree, but something weird's going on."

"Here, let me do it with you," said Tony, putting his hands on the tree. He didn't pull his hands away, he just waited for me to start hugging.

I stepped over, putting my hands on his and the trunk. I immediately felt the same feeling - a sharp, tingling, coldness ... an emptiness. After the joy and positive energy that had come from The Green, this feeling was especially unwelcome. It was like an abomination of the beautiful tree communication that I had quickly grown to love and expect from the forest.

Tony pulled his hands away, a stricken look on his face. "That was *awful.*"

"I know," I whispered. "I don't know what's happening. I don't think I can communicate with this tree." I looked around. "Any of them."

The others walked over. "Something wrong?" asked Finn.

"Yeah, the trees here are messed up," said Tony.

I shook my head, very sad for some reason. My despondency reminded me of Becky. Why did everything have to suck so much right now? "I can't talk to them. There's something wrong with this part of the forest. It's not dead, it's ... hurt. It's been blackened. Something ... or someone, has nearly killed it."

"How can you kill a forest?" asked Spike.

"I have no idea. I just know that when I put my hands on that tree, I got some very unhappy vibes. The trees aren't the source of it. They're merely communicating what is all over this area ... in the ground, in the living things ... maybe even in the things that aren't quite living."

"What the heck is that supposed to mean?" asked Spike, looking a little nervous.

"I don't know. Really, I don't. I just get sensations and feelings from the trees, and that's the only way I can describe what was there in my mind. There are things here, I think, that aren't quite alive and aren't quite dead. And they are not nice things, if the pain I'm getting from the trees is any indication."

Tony had been quiet, thinking to himself. He glanced up at all of us and then around at the nearby trees. I saw a momentary look of panic spread across his face.

"Out with it, Tones; what's on your mind?"

He reached up and scratched his head - a dead giveaway that he's trying to avoid saying something.

"Say whatever it is that you're thinking or I'll make you touch that tree again." We didn't have time to mess around with hurt feelings. I was prepared for Tony to say something I wasn't going to like.

"It's just ... I'm worried that your tree whispering isn't working. The last few confrontations we've had - all of them, actually - kind of went our way because of your help from the trees and stuff. Without them, I'm not sure we would have made it this far."

"Hey, we helped with the werewolves. Don't forget my awesome slingshot skills," said Spike, feigning offense.

"Yeah, but all of us would be with ... well, in that lake right now, if it wasn't for the vines from the forest."

All of the guys nodded. He was right.

Tony got a pensive look on his face. "Jayne, you said that you were feeling things all around us, not just in that tree, right?"

"Yeah ... "

"So how far does that communication link go, anyway?"

I shrugged my shoulders. "I have no idea. Far maybe ... not far ... I don't know."

"Do you think it's possible that you could connect and reach out past this darker forest and into the green one around it?"

Tony was onto something. This felt right on so many levels. First, the selfish girl in me wanted to connect back up with my peeps in The Green, just so I could feel good again. This dark forest was seriously bringing me down. Also, I'd seen the trees heal two seriously wounded people. Maybe they could do it for trees too.

If it was possible to help this place cast off its dark mantle of ugliness and *evil* to be green again, I had to try. It must have been green at one time. I didn't see how else any plant could survive here. Mushrooms and moss maybe, but that's about it.

The last reason for trying this little experiment was probably the biggest priority in my mind. We needed to figure out where we were so that we could get the hell out of here and head back home, hopefully five hundred bucks richer, although the money had kind of ceased to matter so much. My life was worth much more than that. I shook my head thinking of all that I'd risked for a mere five hundred bucks. *Ridiculous.* It made me hate Dardennes all over again. I'd like to tie him up to one of these trees and unleash that hag on him ...

Tony cut into my thoughts, being all practical and shit. "Come on, Jayne, let's get this done. We're all going to help, aren't we guys?"

They looked at each other, faces revealing their unspoken doubt that they could be of any assistance.

"It might help to have more hands in the mix. Let's go see," I said.

I picked the biggest tree in the area - an Ancient that towered above the other trees around it. Its body was heavily ridged. I could fit my entire hand sideways between cracks in the scabby-looking bark. I debated between a big tree like this and a smaller one, thinking maybe the younger energy would be better, but then I decided to go with the Ancient. Surely this thing had seen some crazy shit. Maybe it had a deeper connection to The Green. That was my hope, anyway.

"You guys go hug that tree."

They all just stood there staring at me.

I shooed them away. "Go on! Go hug the tree! After you get set up, I'll come over and find a good spot."

They all moved to obey, but I could tell they thought I was nuts. Finn had felt the power before, more than any of them, but even he was a little skeptical.

I stood there, arms crossed, tapping my foot. "I don't have all day ... "

They grumbled a bit but moved over to the tree. They each leaned in to give it a tentative hug.

"Man, oh man, I wish I had my cell phone so I could take a picture of this for the Sierra Club's newsletter." I wasn't even sure if the Sierra Club had one, but if they did, this would be an awesome cover shot. I stepped over to join them, finding a spot in between Chase and Spike where I could hug the tree and touch a piece of each guy's arm. "Here goes nothin'," I said as I made contact. I was immediately assailed by the darkness and cold, the pricks and tiny piercings that were putting invisible marks on my skin.

"Oh, *shee-it* that don't feel good *at all*," said Finn.

"Damn, this is depressing," said Spike.

Chase and Tony said nothing. Tony was doing some deep breathing, probably trying to control his reaction.

I blocked out their voices and faces so I could focus on the connection. I'd never before searched through the link for anything specific; I'd always just let it carry me wherever it wanted, more on the receiving end then the searching end. I smiled as I realized I was just about to wish for a Google search engine. Now *that* would be convenient.

I let my mind wander the connection, searching for other links branching off. *Ha, ha, branching off, get it? Shit, this was no time for puns. Concentrate, Jayne.* There was definitely an energy here. I had been wrong before when I had said it was dead. It was just that it was a different energy. I realized with a sickening feeling that it was a dark energy - dark as in evil ... worse than the hag and the watery whore. They lived in The Green. Whatever was here, its home was darkness.

I stretched my mind farther out. I rushed past shadows of things I couldn't see clearly - things I knew I didn't *want* to see clearly. They sensed the presence of my mind, my energy, and reached out. Screeched. Tried to connect with me. I slipped by as quickly as I could, blocking off the tendrils of energy that tried to make their way into my presence and to coax me into theirs. I didn't want to even think what would happen to me if one of them managed to get through. *Who knows if I'd ever be able to get out?* I squeezed the arm of the nearest guy - I think it was Chase. He squeezed me back, and I could feel the reassurance in his touch. It was then that I realized I could feel the guys with me. They were like an anchor, keeping the most essential piece of me back there with them. It made me feel more secure, and I used this confidence to reach out even farther, towards a faint green light that I could sense was up ahead.

I knew the exact moment when I broke through the border of the dark forest. The light and love waiting for me in The Green was unmistakable. I didn't stop at the border, though. I continued searching, touching tree after tree after tree. I touched the vines, and the bushes and the grasses. I touched the leaves and the needles and the flowers. I touched everything I could reach and sent out my request. Bring your love and energy back with me, into the Dark Forest, and heal this tree. From there, we can heal them all.

This energy I was calling up, I knew was of the infinite variety. I couldn't exhaust it. Once I brought it back, it would feed on itself and spread. I knew this because I realized what this green energy was. It was our oneness ... the thing that connected all living creatures to one another. It was *love*.

I traced my way back to the Dark Forest, led there by the strong support of my human friends. They felt The Green's arrival before it got there.

"Here it comes," said Finn excitedly.

"Here comes what?" asked Spike in hushed tones.

"Wait for it ... ," said Tony, enthusiasm coloring his voice.

And then we were there. Me and the energy from The Green.

The tree we were hugging shuddered.

Then it groaned.

Black leaves fell all around our heads, covering us from ground to knees.

The branches waved back and forth as the green energy coursed through their fibers.

The roots buckled in the earth under our feet.

And then the tree itself started to shake and twist. We could hear a cracking begin, and Tony was thrown to the side.

"Everyone off!" I yelled. The groaning was getting so loud, it was difficult to hear anything else.

We all staggered back, Tony getting to his feet and joining us. We moved away, as far as we could without leaving the tree alone.

"Is this what's supposed to happen?!" yelled Finn.

"I don't know! I really didn't know what to expect!"

Chase put his hand up, blocking me from going back towards the tree. He wasn't even looking at me, it was an automatic reaction. I smiled as it reminded me of my mom. When I'd ride in the passenger seat of our car and she'd have to slam on her brakes, she'd throw her arm across my chest to protect me from going through the windshield, as if she could defy the laws of physics with her puny resistance. It wasn't the eventual success of the maneuver that mattered; it was the thought. I knew now that even if Chase never said anything, I was important to him. And I realized at the same time that he was important to me ... they all were. If we ever got out of this living hell, we were still going to be friends, I was sure of it.

The tree cracked down the center, drawing my attention back to our problem.

Uh-oh, this doesn't look good.

A green glow came from the center of the fissure. It spread out of the tree's core and then to the bark, moving up and down from there to cloak the tree entirely in green energy.

We watched as new leaves came out of new buds on the branches. They unfurled in fast-forward time, opening to greet the sun that surely awaited them, so they could nourish this gigantic, majestic tree.

There was a bright flash of green again, as a thin bolt of energy left the tree and struck another one nearby. Our eyes were jerked over to that tree now, watching as the same process began there.

Tears filled my eyes. This was better than I'd hoped for. The visceral energy was leaping from tree to tree, bringing a healing light to each of them. They were being reborn.

A rumbling sound was coming from the first tree, out of the crack that remained in its center. And then a roar.

It was not a tree roar - I was pretty sure a tree couldn't make a roaring sound like *that*. Whatever was making that sound was not happy and was ... *in the tree?*

I no sooner had formed that thought, than a black liquid began to seep out of the crack. A dark mist rose up from the liquid, and a form began to take shape.

We all reached for our weapons, which we'd had the forethought when we were walking earlier to stick in our belts or across our backs. I reached into my backpack, pulling out my flag and quickly shoving it in my pocket. "Get your flags out! Leave the bags!" I yelled. If my instincts were right, we were about to get the hell out of there quickly. I didn't want to lose the five hundred bucks - or my life - because I'd lost my flag somewhere. The others rushed to do what I said, securing their flags in their own pockets.

Whatever this was, it was definitely not good. It was blackness, something that had been inhabiting that tree when it was near death. And now it had been released.

The form continued to solidify, fed by the black molten goo and smoke collecting at the base of the tree. After a few moments, the dark liquid abruptly stopped oozing out, and the green energy moved from the branches down to the trunk and sealed the great crack, leaving the tree whole and unbroken now, beautiful healthy branches and leaves reaching up toward the sky.

Standing upright at the base of this majestic reborn tree, however, was what appeared to be a fully-grown, black, horrible-looking monster. It was covered in spiky, leathery skin glistening with goo. And it was staring at us with blood-red eyes.

Chapter Twenty-Six

A GLOB OF DROOL FELL out of the black monster's mouth and dripped down its chin, falling to the ground at its feet. My gaze followed it down and saw a tendril of smoke rise up from where it fell in the leaves below. I felt sick to my stomach. *Acid drool. Faaaantastic.*

I heard the unmistakable rumbling sound again, this time coming from a tree next to the big one with the monster in front of it. The black liquid and smoke were bleeding out of this new tree now, too. All around us, the trees were cracking, releasing the demons that had been trapped there, probably a very long time ago if the dark state of this forest was any indication.

I heard Finn's voice, but it made no words - just a sound. "Ahhhh ... " It sounded like the beginning of a song.

"What the hell?" asked Spike. "What *are* those things?"

"Orcs would be my guess," said Tony, sounding much calmer than I was feeling.

"What the fuck is an *orc?"* I asked angrily. I was feeling very strongly at that moment that Dardennes should have warned us that 'obstacles' could mean 'acid drooling orcs'. That was just common decency.

Tony sighed. "Didn't you guys watch Lord of the Rings?"

"I did," said Chase.

I glanced at Chase and saw him squeezing the handle of Becky's knife in one hand and the handle of his gun in the other, never taking his eyes off the monster.

"Any chance you can put the breaks on that green energy, healing thingy?" asked Spike with a nervous laugh.

"I'm not sure. But I don't think I should. Yes, it's releasing these ... things ... these ... orcs or demons or whatever; but if the trees are green, maybe they can help us."

"Not sure that's gonna matter too much if we have an army of these monsters against us. Vines and branches are okay for Ladies in the Lake, but probably not so much for these guys."

Spike had a point, but something told me it wasn't right to stop the awakening of the forest. It wasn't that I was willing to die for green trees or anything. My self-preservation instincts were alive and kicking, telling me to get the fuck out of there right now. But my trees hadn't let me down before. They'd even sent Robin Hood or whoever he was to help me once, so I had to keep the faith ... and probably kill off some orcs in the meantime.

The first orc we had released seemed to finally wake up to his situation. He was free of the tree that had kept him imprisoned, and there was a group of smallish pale things - us - standing in front of him.

The drool was freaking me out. "God, it keeps salivating. I think it's hungry."

"Wouldn't you be? Trapped inside that dang tree for who knows how long?" said Finn.

That was a cheery thought. I was going to be dinner, or maybe just an appetizer. Chase was more main course material.

"Stay close," said Chase. "We need to keep our backs together. If one of those gets behind us, we're done." He raised the gun up and took aim at the monster who'd taken its first step towards us.

I was just about to make a wisecrack when the thing lifted up its head and let out the most awful sound I'd ever heard. I'd thought that the water whore had the worst voice ever, but no ... this guy's was *the* worst. It sounded like a demon dinosaur. Not that I'd ever heard one of those, but it was what I imagined one would sound like. It nearly made my heart stop with fear.

Answering roars came from all around us. There were now at least thirty green trees, spewing black stuff, and ten of those piles of sludge had turned into fully formed, agitated monsters.

"*Fuck me.* This isn't possible! There are hundreds of trees in this place, *hundreds!* We don't stand a chance!" I was losing whatever cool I had left.

"Don't freak out," said Chase, the voice of reason. "We need to stay calm. Use your weapons. Go for the throat. Try to stay away from them as best you can. I think they move slow. If we can start running, we can outrun them back to the Green Forest."

"I think we should run towards the waypoint," said Finn. "How far into the Dark Forest is that last one, Jayne."

I wracked my brain trying to remember what the forest looked like when I was up in the tree. "Um, the waypoint is in the center of the dark area. Once we get to it, we'll have to go for at least a few hours to get out."

"Maybe Dardennes and his buddies will be waitin' for us there," said Finn, hopefully.

"I'm not sure that they know about or will be prepared for this little monster problem that we'll be bringing with us," said Tony.

With our luck, Tony was probably right. We couldn't expect Dardennes and his group to do anything to help us. All they'd done from the start was put us in harm's way.

The other monsters suddenly roared from behind me. The first orc roared back and then advanced toward us.

"Stay together!" yelled Chase.

I held up my sharpened stick. "Blackie, don't let me down!" I yelled, just at the moment when Chase and the monster started fighting.

The thing reached out to grab him and Chase brought his knife down, slashing the beast's hand.

I was jostled from behind and turned in time to see a slightly smaller orc, though still a foot taller than any of us, start grappling with Spike. Spike's slingshot was no help to him in this type of close-quarters combat. He landed one punch, though, at least throwing the orc back a few paces and giving Spike a temporary reprieve.

"Give me your gun!" I yelled at Chase. He handed it over without question. I turned and pushed it into Spike's hand. "I don't know how many bullets there are, so do what you can."

Spike nodded his thanks at me before shooting the orc right between the eyes when it advanced again. It stood there for a second before going down at Spike's feet. Spike shoved its shoulder with his foot, causing it to roll over and away.

One down, ninety-nine to go.

The sounds of battle rang out around me. The guys had enveloped me in the middle of them, not letting me out to fight and not letting any monsters in to eat me. While I appreciated the sentiment, I knew I was an asset they had to use. I bent down and put my hand to the ground, checking to see if I had any connection to the newly green trees around us. I could sense something there, but it was weak. There hadn't been enough time yet for all of the things around us to come alive - with the exception of the monsters, of course.

Two orcs dropped in quick succession, arrows protruding from their gooey black bodies. One staggered away from our circle with its arm hanging, nearly severed by a blow it had received from the axe - the axe I was happy and proud to see drawing luminous blue streaks in the air each time my Tony swung it. The hum it emitted as it swooped through the air made my heart swell. It was obvious the orcs didn't like that axe one bit. They shied away from it whenever they heard its hum.

Shots rang out. An orc that had nearly grabbed Finn fell onto its back, thick blood coming from its neck in a gurgling, black tar-fountain. I worked to keep the bile in my stomach where it belonged.

The orcs were slow. It was the only reason we were still alive right now. I wasn't sure if they were always this way, though. Maybe they were still tired from being cooped up in trees all this time. We needed to press our advantage. Soon we were going to be out of bullets, arrows and energy.

"We need to try and run to the waypoint," I yelled. Maybe Dardennes would be there to help. I didn't think so, but we had to do something. If we stayed in this forest, in this spot, we were sitting ducks just begging to be exterminated. I didn't want even a single drop of that nasty acid drool to touch me if I could help it.

We went farther into the forest, staying back-to-back, moving as a group. The guys continued to fight the orcs off, while I kept trying to get a jab in with my stick when one of them got close. I wasn't very successful because the guys kept pushing me back, keeping the orcs at a distance.

Then all of a sudden, one of the orcs broke through our circle. He knocked Finn over like he was a piece of paper and came right for me. I didn't think twice, holding Blackie out in front of me, ready to meet him head-on. When he was less than a foot away, I saw his skin up close and feared that there was no way Blackie was going to penetrate that stuff. It looked like alligator hide.

Much to my surprise, Blackie didn't just penetrate it; it sunk in like a red-hot poker sliding into a stick of butter. The orc looked down, and the green light coming from my stick reflected off the slimy skin of its face. It lifted its eyes to mine and snarled, reaching its arms up. But they only made it a few inches before that glowing red light in its eyes went dark.

The orc's body went slack, and I jumped to the side as it fell to the ground, keeping a hold of my weapon. I looked down at it and saw that it was covered in black goo. The green light was still coming from inside, working to burn off the black orc blood. Within seconds, my stick was back to normal, no longer gooey and no longer glowing.

"Holy bat balls, did you *see* that Tony?!"

Tony was too busy to answer, throwing his lightsaber axe all around, slicing and dicing orcs left and right.

I stepped outside the ring of guys, confident now that my badass Blackie and I could do some damage of our own. I stood with legs spread wide, Converse sneakers gripping the forest floor beneath me. I pushed up the sleeves of my sweatshirt, quickly wiping under my nose for good measure. "Come on, you smelly bastards. Let's dance."

One of the smaller ones took me up on my challenge. He strode over, moving a little faster than the others. I could see Chase getting annoyed with me out of the corner of my eye.

"Get back in the circle, Jayne!" he ordered.

"No!" I yelled, a fever in my brain. "I'm gonna kill me some orc!"

I kept Blackie hidden by my wrist, revealing it only when the orc got close. I faked left, acting like I was going to run by it, with the intention of stabbing the orc in the side with my right hand as I passed.

My plan would have worked perfectly if the fucking orc hadn't closelined me. It stuck its arm out, making instant and direct contact with my face as I tried to run by. I went down like a ton of bricks, my stick never touching anything.

Another orc was right behind the one that had dropped me. It grabbed me by the legs and pulled. I found myself sliding across the forest floor, being dragged farther and farther away from my friends. I finally found my voice and screamed, Blackie slipping out of my hands to land in the leaves.

I kicked as hard as I could, twisting my body around and around, trying to get the orc to let me go, but the fucker had his claws good and tangled in my shoe laces and pant legs. The orc seized the front of my sweatshirt, lifting me up off the ground, and putting me into an unwelcome bear hug, pinning me to its disgusting body from behind.

The smell coming off that orc body was somethin' else. Four-day-old desert roadkill crossed with the world's worst body odor had nothin' on this guy. It was so bad I started to retch. The monster squeezed me to make me stop; and I did, but only because my olfactory nerves had gone numb. The smell was seriously that bad.

I heard some roaring and grunting as the orcs communicated with each other. Heads gestured to my friends still fighting valiantly. I felt so fucking horrible at that moment, knowing they had been doing so well, and then I had to go and screw it all up. Chase had told me to get back, and I didn't listen. He was going to hate me forever. I'd never get to kiss Spike. And Tony ... what was going to happen to my Tony?

The guys stopped fighting and the orcs backed away. One of them, a big one, was gesturing towards me. The orc that held me moved forward, showing the guys that it held me prisoner. I tried to tell them I was sorry, but the orc squeezed the breath out of me. I almost passed out before it loosened its grip. I used my eyes to transmit as much emotion as I possibly could. *I'msorryI'msorryI'msorry.*

One of them grabbed some old, black vines from the forest floor and came over to me. It pulled me roughly from the other orc's grasp and shoved my shoulder to turn me around, grabbing my hands and securing them together with the vine behind me. I was now officially a prisoner of war.

The orc grunted and gestured to his friends, holding up a vine. Its intent was obvious: *tie up the others like the girl.* Now we were all going to be prisoners of war. On the bright side, though, they weren't eating us. Not yet anyway.

The guys put down their weapons and submitted themselves to our captors. Tony tried to fight a little, and one of them smacked him so hard he went down in an unconscious heap. He was so still and dead-looking, I couldn't help but cry out. The orc that had been holding me cuffed me on the side of the head, making my ears ring.

"Why you sonofa ..."

It hit me again, only harder this time, dropping me to my knees.

Spike shouted, "Stop talking, Jayne!" He ducked when one of the orcs came over to shut him up and took a hit to the shoulder.

The orc behind me pushed me, signaling me to get up and start walking.

I stood my ground. I wanted to walk with my friends. I tried to run over to them, awkwardly because my hands were tied behind my back, but I didn't make it far. One of the orcs tripped me, and I went down on my face, my mouth instantly filling with forest muck. I was lying on my side, trying to spit it out, when a pair of leathery, disgusting orc feet appeared in my vision. The last thing I saw before the lights went out was that leathery foot drawing back to kick me in the head.

Chapter Twenty-Seven

I SLOWLY CAME TO, INITIALLY only hearing grunts and shuffling sounds, then eventually able to open my eyes. I found myself in a clearing, still inside the Dark Forest. I was tied to a tree, or rather, I was hung from a tree. The vines that had secured my hands behind me had been replaced by vines that bound my wrists in front. These handcuffs were then attached to another vine dangling from a tree branch above me. I had just enough play to sit with my hands suspended at about shoulder-height. I probably should have been grateful that they had moved my hands to the front of my body or that they hadn't hung me from the tree, but I wasn't grateful at all. I was pissed.

The trees here were green, but only newly so. I could tell from all the black and gray leaves on the ground that the trees had recently morphed into the beauties they were now. I wondered how many orcs currently made up the enemy forces - probably a lot. I was seriously regretting the rejuvenation of the forest.

In the center of the clearing was a fire. Something was roasting over it; it smelled like bacon. My eyes were still a little fuzzy, but if I squinted, I could see a little better. The thing hanging over the hot wood coals didn't look like a pig, or even a deer. It looked like ... like ...

holy shit, they're roasting a dwarf!

A large branch had been jammed down his throat and out his back end. An orc stood to one side, turning the speared dwarf from time to time, like a pig on a spit. I turned my head immediately, thoroughly repulsed by the sight, trying not to barf.

I looked around the camp in a panic, the fear rising up to stick in my throat. I was pretty sure we were going to be the next few orc meals. Nearby, I could see Tony and Finn, tied up like I was. Finn was closest. He had blood under his nose and on his chin, like someone had popped him one. I saw him looking at me, and I got ready to yell out to him, but the panic on his face stopped me. His eyes were bugging out and his lips set in a thin line. He shook his head very slightly, telling me silently to shut the hell up. I did faintly recall the orcs didn't like it much when we talked. Maybe that's why Finn had a bloody nose.

I mouthed the words, *"Where are Spike and Chase?"*

I followed Finn's eyes across the camp. The guys were on the other side of the fire from us. I had to look past the roasting dwarf to see them. They were also tied up, both looking at the ground. Chase had some bruising around his face, and Spike had a cut on his cheek that had bled down to his jawline. It seemed as if none of them had gone quietly.

I could see Tony on the other side of Finn. He was either sleeping or still unconscious. If he'd been unconscious this whole time - and I wasn't sure how long it had been, but at least an hour - he could be seriously hurt.

Silently I asked Finn about Tony, *"Is Tony okay?"*

I tried to read Finn's lips, but it looked like he said, *'They like him again.'*

Like him? Then realization dawned. He hadn't said *'like'*, he'd said, *'hit'*.

Fuck. I sent up a silent prayer to the universe that Tony didn't have a concussion - or worse.

The orcs were scattered around the camp. Occasionally, a new one would wander in from farther out in the forest. My guess was that they were newly-freed ones, formed from the goo released by the trees. They grunted and growled at each other. The biggest one, the one Chase had cut on the hand at the beginning of our battle, seemed to be in charge. *Yeah, that's just perfect.* I had released the leader with that first Ancient tree. *Fucking brilliant.*

No matter where I tried to look, my attention was repeatedly drawn back to the fire in the middle. My brain entered into an otherworldly level of panic. A real human being ... dwarf being ... was roasting over a fire. My friends and I were tied up and sure to be next. Would they kill us first before they stuck the branch down our throats and out our ass cracks? Or would the branch do the work? Would we still be a little alive when we went over the fire like rotisserie chickens? My mind wouldn't let it go. The panic was real and overwhelming. I whimpered, unable to stop myself.

The nearest orc came over to me and smashed me in the head with its fist. Some of the spittle from its mouth swung out in an arc and landed on my arm, leaving a burn mark as it slid off. I wasn't sure if the nausea I felt was from the beat-down, the bar-b-cue, or the drool.

When he hit me, it spun me around so I was facing outside the clearing. *At least I don't have to look at that poor dwarf anymore.* But I also couldn't see Tony or the others. I forced myself to do some deep breathing, to keep the panic from rising up again.

A movement out in the trees caught my eye. Someone was there, and it wasn't an orc. The size and coloring wasn't right. I squinted to see if I could figure out who or what it was. The flickering light from the fire made it difficult to see what was beyond our circle of trees.

Then I saw a movement nearby, just beyond the tree I was dangling from. The figure slowly and cautiously crept closer. It moved near enough now that I could see its features in the light of the fire.

Jared! My eyes nearly fell out of my head. *Jared is here!* My heart soared. I didn't give a flying fuck if he was in league with Dardennes at this point. He couldn't possibly be on Team Orc. I was pretty sure no one was in cahoots with these barbarians, seeing as how they'd eat a dwarf and all. Probably their smell discouraged friendships, too.

Jared put his finger to his lips, signaling me to be quiet. I slowly turned and got Finn's attention, jerking my head slightly towards the tree I was attached to so he'd look back. He stared at me in confusion, not understanding what I was trying to tell him. I took the heel of my shoe and slowly wrote J-A-R-E-D on the forest floor in front of me. As soon as he read it, I kicked the dirt around to erase it. I was pretty sure these grunting orcs couldn't read, but just in case ...

I turned to look at Jared again, getting up on my knees to ease the numbness in my hands. Finn turned too, also looking at Jared. Jared held up Becky's knife and pantomimed cutting the vines around our hands.

I nodded my head in happy agreement. *Get me the fuck out of this nightmare.* Jared must have been behind us, following our trail. I remembered Chase dropping the knife in the leaves during our earlier battle.

Jared was trying to give us his plan, charades-style. It was more than frustrating. I thought what he was saying was that he was going to go around and release all of us quietly, and then we would get up and run together. Sounded like a plan to me, or at least the beginnings of one. The question was, where were we supposed to run? I kept mouthing, *"Where?"* to him, but he wasn't getting it.

It soon became clear to me; this plan wasn't going to work. I plopped down on my butt, resigned to the fact that we had a half-assed plan that barely had even a miniscule chance of being successful. I started to shift my body, aware that my butt bone was now resting on something hard, lumpy, and very uncomfortable. But just before I shifted, I felt something. A tingle.

A tingle in my butt? Suddenly, I realized what it was. The Green. I was sitting on a root that had grown up above the surface of the ground.

I used the toe of my left shoe to push the shoe and sock off my right, and scooted over so my bare foot could touch the root. Now I could feel the connection much stronger. The link was difficult enough to make here in this dark place, and my clothes had been dulling the sensation.

I sent out a tentative request, the beginning of a conversation, just with this tree. The Green was there. It was new, fresh, and just starting to awaken, but it was definitely there.

Finn was looking at me, frowning, wondering what the hell I was doing. He must have seen the smile on my face, because he smiled a little back at me. He probably thought I was happy about Jared - or that I had finally cracked under the pressure.

Things were looking up. We had Jared with a knife and I had a connection to The Green. Now I just had to figure out how to use it to our advantage. I thought it might be worthwhile to try a little experiment. I didn't bother trying to mime this to Jared. He wasn't aware of my little secret yet, and explaining my connection to The Green with charades would be impossible.

I connected into The Green using the link I had with my foot. I imagined a vine grabbing the foot of an orc off to my left, with the plan to trip it.

I didn't see the vine, but less than a minute later an orc got up from the group sitting near Chase and started walking to the edge of the trees. It got two steps and then went down, face-plant style - victim of a vine tripping. Bummer for the orc because its face-plant at that particular spot put it partially into the fire. It jerked back, roaring, its black skin bubbling and smoking where it had touched the flames.

The stench that rose up from that bar-b-cued orc was even worse than their natural body odor. I could see why they weren't cannibals. *Double yuck.* My eyes watered at the awfulness. I even saw Chase and Spike get repulsed looks on their faces, and Chase didn't usually react to that kind of thing.

The burned orc got up, looking around to see what had caused it to trip, but the vine had long since disappeared back into the forest. The only thing there, several paces away, was Chase. The orc took one look at him and roared. Spike cringed at the sight and sound, but Chase sat stoically. He was one badass dude, that Chase.

The orc turned sideways while it was roaring, and I could see its mouth in profile. There was spittle dripping from its gnarled, pointed teeth and drool sliding down its chin. Boy, was it pissed. And now, since I had once again done a very bad job of considering the consequences of my actions, it was pissed at Chase. Even though there's no way Chase could have done it, the orc was going to blame and punish him for tripping it.

It took two long strides towards my friend and backhanded him. Hard. Chase flew to the side, as far as his bonds would allow, and then swung back the other direction like a human pendulum. Anger blazed in his eyes, fresh blood dripping down his cheek from the gash that had opened up over his cheekbone again. The orc wasn't finished with him yet, though.

Spike and Finn watched in horror at the violence playing out before us. Spike ducked with every hit, as if he were the one being beaten.

Jared used the distraction to sneak up behind me and cut the vines around my wrists. Before heading off to Finn, he whispered closely in my ear, "Pretend like you're still attached. Don't let them see you're free until I get everyone. Get ready to run *that* way." He signaled the direction that was behind the biggest group of orcs, all sitting down having some sort of powwow together - probably planning when they were going to eat us. I wasn't so sure I wanted to run in that direction, but there was no way to communicate that to everyone, and the worst thing we could do was get separated. Jared had already left me, moving on to Finn.

I kept my hands together, like they were still connected, but my eyes immediately went to Chase. He was getting his ass royally kicked by the burned orc and there was nothing he could do about it. Now he had another bleeding gash, this one over his eye. I could see him trying to blink the blood away. Spike wasn't looking anymore. His head hung low, but I could see him still flinching every time Chase was hit.

I felt horrible that I'd made this happen. Yes, it had provided a great distraction for Jared, but it wasn't worth it. I had to figure out a way to help Chase, but part of me was panicked that I'd make the situation worse again. Unfortunately, the gift of future sight had not come with the gift of talking to The Green.

Suddenly, I saw my chance. Another orc was coming across the clearing, obviously hyped up by the violence he saw. He was nearly jumping with joy, and making motions with his hands like he wanted in on the action. He stood just behind the other orc, ready to take his turn.

I quickly communicated with The Green, asking for another tripping. The vine came out of the trees, moving rapidly across the ground towards the second orc.

Don't look down, don't look down, don't look down. I kept chanting fervently to myself until the vine secured itself around the second orc's feet, effectively tying them together.

The first orc took a step back from beating Chase to catch its breath, and the second orc took a step forward to begin its turn at the fun game called 'Beating the Shit Out of Chase'; but its feet didn't cooperate as expected. The orc's arms went out, flailing and searching for something to stop its fall. They made contact with the first orc, whose back was to the entire scenario and who didn't expect to be touched, or, in this case, tackled.

The first orc spun around, shoving the second one to the side, causing it to land in the fire, face first. But the second orc had managed to grab the first's arm, and didn't let go. The first orc found itself pulled into the fire too. It stumbled, looking for something to grab, knowing it was about to be burned again. The only thing there was to grab onto was the dwarf on the spit. The orc grabbed it, intending to right itself, but the spit wasn't strong enough to hold it.

The stick holding the roasting dwarf split, sending both the orc and the dwarf into the flames and hot coals below.

The group of orcs that were sitting off to the side grunting and conspiring jumped up, enraged that their dinner was being compromised. A few of them came stalking over with angry strides to take care of the problem.

The second orc got pulled from the edge of the fire by its feet, its face a mass of bubbling blackness, its screams of pain and rage ringing out through the forest. Another orc grabbed Tony's axe that was leaning against a nearby tree and hacked the screaming orc's head off, throwing the axe off to the side when it was done. It landed where the other unguarded weapons were.

Black goo spurted out of the headless orc's neck, sizzling as it landed among the coals. The audible anguish of the second orc had ceased immediately, but the first orc's screams and roars continued. I barfed a little in my mouth, spitting it out on the ground next to me. Seeing gore on television was one thing; seeing orc beheadings live was a whole other deal altogether.

I looked over in horror at the group of orcs that were mobilizing in the direction of the fire, but my attention was distracted by the sight of our weapons leaning against a tree where the orc had thrown Tony's axe. I put my foot on the root and sent out a message for the vines to take our weapons and pull them into the forest behind Tony for safekeeping. I could get them later as we left, knowing I was going to grab Tony before I did anything else. I turned my head towards the action for a second and when I looked back, the weapons were already gone. *Good ... one less thing to worry about. Thank you, my Green friends.*

Two more orcs pulled the first orc off the dwarf body and began beating the shit out of it. I didn't know if their victim was roaring and screaming from the painful burns or the beat-down it was getting, but scream and roar it did. I covered my ears with my hands to block out the sound, forgetting I was supposed to still be tied up. I quickly moved my hands back to the vine dangling above my head.

Jared was behind Chase now. He'd cut the vines from Finn, Tony, Spike and me. Tony was still out cold. I agonized for a brief moment about what a bad sign this was, but I knew I couldn't take the time to really freak out about him now. Hopefully, there would be time to worry later, if we were lucky. Right now, I had to figure out how to get him and the rest of us out of here.

Jared hesitated, trying to get to Chase without being seen. The orcs were fighting very close by, some of the bodies even falling at Chase's feet. He took a chance and darted out, cutting the vine above Chase's hands and leaving him with the knife before melting back into the trees.

Chase used it to cut the vines from around his wrists, balancing it between his knees and sawing with four quick strokes.

I looked over at Finn and grabbed his attention. Then I pointedly looked at Tony and then back at Finn. Finn looked at Tony, then me, nodding his head. I took this to mean he understood that I wanted us both to grab Tony when it was time to go.

It was almost time. I caught flashes of Jared through the trees as he headed back to Tony, which made me feel a little better. We'd be able to move Tony with us faster if we could trade off carrying him. Between the rest of the guys and me, maybe Tony wouldn't slow us down too much.

I sent one more message out to The Green before I quickly slipped my sock and shoe back on. Luckily, the orcs were too caught up in their bloodlust to pay any attention to what I was doing. I didn't have time to formulate the idea in my head, really, so I hoped The Green knew what I wanted and that I hadn't forgotten to consider any consequences that could backfire on us.

As soon as Jared came through the trees behind Tony, I made my move. Finn was one step ahead of me. We grabbed Tony's very still form and dragged him back into the trees. Our weapons were there, vines wrapped around them. I reached down to retrieve them, the vines dropping off as my hand made contact. I tucked the gun, stick and axe into my waistband; the bow and arrows I slung over my back. Spike's slingshot wasn't there.

One of the orcs saw us and immediately roared. I didn't stick around or even look back to see whether the other orcs paid him any attention; I just took off running next to Finn and Jared who were going as fast as they could, dragging Tony between them.

We made a wide circle around the camp of orcs, hoping to come out on the far side, just as Jared had instructed. Chase and Spike weren't with us, so we had to go that way if we were ever going to hook up with them again.

The sounds of crashing and pursuit reverberated behind us.

"They're coming!" I yelled, panic reaching up into my throat, nearly choking me. The adrenaline was pumping, and I felt like I was going to vomit again. My legs were tired. They didn't want to move as fast as I needed them to.

Finn was huffing and puffing, his face bright red and sweating. He and Jared were trying to get through the trees and brush and over fallen logs as fast as they could. Tony's dead weight was a serious problem; especially it seemed, for Finn.

I could still hear the orcs behind us, but occasionally I'd hear a loud thump and then a roaring that sounded like rage. Hopefully, that meant my plan was working, and with any luck, it would give us more time to get away.

We had finally reached the spot that Jared had designated as our meeting point. We were behind the area where the group of orcs had been sitting and grunting at each other. Chase and Spike weren't there. We stopped for a minute so Finn could catch his breath. Jared wasn't even winded.

After a minute or two, we started running again, heading in the direction Jared told us was towards the last waypoint. I had no reason to doubt him now; without him we'd still be sitting around that fire and Chase probably would have been beaten to death. Jared had redeemed himself in my eyes. Whether he'd needed to, I still wasn't completely certain, but it didn't matter now. We were getting the hell out of there.

The sounds of orc screams grew more distant. Finn shook his head as he jogged along. He tried to talk, but couldn't, too out of breath. "Stop ... for a ... sec ... ," he gasped.

I took over holding Tony for Finn as he bent over to get his breath. I looked at Jared to see how he was faring, but he seemed fine. He was barely out of breath, hardly breaking a sweat. *Man, is he in shape or what?*

"Why haven't they ... caught us yet?" asked Finn, still gasping for air.

Jared had a confused look on his face. "I have no idea. I expected to have them on our heels the whole way back."

"Back? Back where?" I asked, suddenly suspicious again.

Jared sighed, but it was no use lying. "Back to the final waypoint. I've already been there."

I knew it. "Why didn't you just leave?"

"Because I was worried about you guys." He shrugged his shoulders.

His answer made sense. It's what I would have done - it's what Tony and I *did* do when we had Becky with us. My throat tightened at the thought of her, bundled up by my feet that one morning. Poor little thing ...

I cleared my throat and continued. "Well, I set up a little plan of action as we were escaping which is probably why they've been slowed down; but they're only delayed. It's not going to keep them away forever."

The light bulb went on for Finn. "Ahh, I see. Okay, then, let's get going."

Jared looked at us, confused. "I don't get it. What's going on?"

"I'll explain later," I said. For some reason I still didn't want him to know. I trusted him, but then again, I didn't. I felt like he was keeping secrets, so I had no regrets about keeping some of my own.

Finn took Tony from me, and he and Jared set off jogging again. I followed behind, the sounds of our pursuers still echoing through the trees behind us.

Chapter Twenty-Eight

WE STOPPED SEVERAL TIMES SO Finn could catch his breath. The trees around us were all green. I wondered how many orcs had come from this area of the forest.

Jared looked around him, shaking his head in what looked like disbelief.

"What's wrong?" I asked.

"When I came through here before, all these trees were black. They were all dead. Now everything's green - I don't understand what happened."

"It's because Jay... "

Finn didn't get the rest of his sentence out because I kicked him hard in the shin.

"*Gol durn it!*" he yelled limping around, nostrils flaring as he kept the pain in. "Jayne, you sure are lucky you're a girl, that's all I got to say right now." He shot a dirty look in my direction and then limped away.

I did my best to plaster an innocent smile on my face.

"What were you going to say?" asked Jared, looking at us suspiciously.

"He was going to say that it's probably green because it *rained*." I nodded my head to add believability to my story. "It rained, you know, pretty hard. Like, for hours."

"Huh," was all Jared would say. He wasn't buying it, but he knew I wasn't going to fess up. And now Finn wasn't either, thanks to the lump on his shin.

We all heard a moan coming from the area by our feet.

"*Tony!*" I squealed, bending down to touch his face.

His eyes were open, and he was looking up at us. His hand reached up to touch his head. "I feel like I got hit by a bus."

"You kind of did," I said, "only it was an angry orc with the strength and attitude of a silverback gorilla."

He closed his eyes in pain. "Don't remind me. You mean those things weren't part of a nightmare I was having?"

"No, they're real, all right," said Finn. "Real as the two inch hairs growin' off the end of my granny's chin."

I looked at him aghast. *Ew.* And I thought orcs were gross.

"Help me up," said Tony as he struggled to get into a sitting position.

Jared and I grabbed him under the arms, helping him stand.

He swayed on his feet a little but soon shrugged off our help. "I'm ready to go. Where are we heading? Did we get to the finish line yet?"

"No, we're on our way to waypoint four."

"Where's everyone else?"

"Hopefully, Chase and Spike are headed this way too. We lost them when we escaped from the orcs."

"Where'd you come from?" Tony asked Jared, his eyes narrowing.

"I followed you guys to the orc camp."

"He's already been to the last waypoint," I explained. *Let Tony noodle that one through.*

"What's it like? Is Dardennes there?"

Jared sighed. "You'll see."

I didn't like his answer at all. "You know, I'm getting pretty fucking tired of all these secrets, Jared."

He looked at me, a small smile playing on his lips. "Seems like I'm not the only one with secrets, Jayne."

I raised my eyebrow at him. *Touché.* "Well *fuck you* anyway - I don't want to know what's there. If Dardennes is smart, he *won't* be."

"Jayne!"

"What, Tony? He's been lying and sneaking around this whole time. I don't even know why he came back for us. For all we know he needs us or something. Or he's leading us into something worse."

Tony looked nervously at Jared. "Listen, Jared, she's just tired. She gets kinda cranky when she's tired. Just ignore what she's saying right now." Then he ducked, waiting for the smack he surely deserved.

"Don't talk about me like I'm not here, Tony. And you're just lucky you have a concussion right now, because otherwise I'd smash you one. I'm tired, yes, but I speak the truth. Unlike *some* people around here." I looked pointedly at Jared.

He shrugged his shoulders and turned around. "What was that sound?"

"Stop trying to change the subject."

"Shhh!"

I frowned, but shut up, listening for whatever he was talking about.

Then through the trees behind Jared walked Chase and Spike.

"Oh, thank the lord!" I exclaimed, running over to them and grabbing them in a three-way hug. Actually, it was me hugging them and them hugging me back, but they didn't hug each other. *Guys.*

"How did you find us?"

Spike answered with a smile, "It was kind of hard to *not* hear you, actually."

"You have no idea how happy I am to see you." I couldn't handle losing another friend, I really couldn't.

"We missed you too, Jayne," said Spike, giving me an extra squeeze, his fingers spread out on my back. I put my face in his neck and inhaled deeply. *Damn*, he smelled good.

I released Spike and then looked up at Chase. "Damn, they sure did a number on your face, didn't they?"

"Don't know; can't see it."

Spike laughed. "Trust me, dude, they did."

I looked in Chase's eyes, truly sorry for the part I'd played in that. "I'm so sorry I caused that to happen."

Chase lifted his hand and gently touched the side of my face. "It wasn't your fault."

The tears came up in my eyes, much as I wanted them to stay hidden.

Chase grabbed me in a bear hug. It was kind of like the orc hug, being as how Chase is so big, only it wasn't like the orc hug because it was warm and soft and kind ... comforting. I didn't want to let go. Apparently, neither did he. After a bit, my body started to heat up, and I'd be lying if I said it didn't feel pretty damn good.

I was brought back to Earth by someone clearing his throat.

"*A-hem*, okaaay then. So, where to now?" said Spike, staring at me and Chase.

I stepped back out of Chase's embrace.

He was staring at me, searching my eyes.

I looked away and my gaze landed on Spike. He was also staring at me, not smiling but not mad either - just searching. The close quarters scrutiny from the two of them was making me nervous. I moved away and took a deep breath. *Man, is it hot in here or what?* I felt like fanning myself.

"To the waypoint," I said, my composure partially back in place.

Jared said nothing; he just walked. We all followed, one at a time. I stayed as close to Tony as I could. He was a little slow, but he was able to go on his own. I took that as a very good sign.

I tried not to think about Spike and Chase as we walked along. Without the immediate threat of orcs on our asses, my brain had time to analyze, over-analyze and over-over analyze what had happened and what could possibly happen. Sometimes I hated having a girl brain. This was one of those times.

Why did that hug with Chase feel so good? Was there more to the hug than just friends? Why did I think Spike was so hot? Was he really that hot or did this forest mess my hot-o-meter all up? If I liked them, would either of them like me back? Could there be any kind of future with either of them - future being anything beyond this forest? Why were they runaways? Were they really criminals, hiding behind nice-guy exteriors? Was it wrong to like two guys at the same time? When was I going to see Spike's tattoos again? Could I think of a way to get him to take his shirt off? *What does Chase look like without a shirt on? I wonder how I could find out ...*

And on and on it went. Before I knew it, we were entering the clearing of the fourth and final waypoint, deep in the heart of the once Dark Forest.

Chapter Twenty-Nine

THE OBELISK FOR WAYPOINT FOUR was bigger than the others. It too was made of granite, but its base was much wider and the spike on top was black; it looked like it might be made of onyx. It reflected the lunar rays beaming down on us from the sky above. The moon was huge; I'd never seen it look this big before. I felt like I could actually reach out and touch it.

I turned my attention back to the task at hand. It was time to end this bullshit.

We entered the clearing cautiously. I kept my eyes alternatively on the obelisk and on Jared, preparing myself for him to pull a fast one during the last minute of our test.

As we drew nearer, I could see his flag tied to the iron ring on the side of the obelisk. At least he'd told the truth about that part. We were alone, though - no Dardennes, no Ivar, no commando dwarves. *Those bastards better show.*

We each went up to the iron ring to tie on our respective flags. I was last. In an act of defiance, I pulled Becky's flag from my pocket and tied it to the ring too. She deserved to be here with us. I looked back at the guys for their reactions and they were all nodding their heads in agreement.

I threw my hands up in disgust. We'd finished but there was nothing and no one here. "Now what?" I didn't know what I had been expecting, but I had kind of hoped that tying the flags would wake me up from this nightmare. But I was still standing here, still fully in it.

Jared pointed to the front of the obelisk.

"What?" I didn't get it. There was nothing there.

"Read the inscription," he said, softly.

Above our heads, inscribed into the stone and readable by moonlight, were these words:

Speak Your Fondest Desire. Enter To Begin The Change.

"What the hell is this, Jared?"

He just shrugged his shoulders, acting like he didn't know.

Asshole. I lost my temper. It was bound to happen sooner or later. I just wasn't prepared for how violent I felt.

"Aaaarrrrhhhh!" The battle cry ripped from my throat, ringing through the clearing like the call of a banshee. I'd never heard a banshee before, but they couldn't possibly get as pissed as I was at that moment.

I ran at Jared and jumped on him, punching and kicking him as hard as I could. All I could think about was Becky's face as she went deeper into the water, Tony lying slumped over and tied to a tree, Chase getting the shit beat out of him as he sat helpless, the two forest creatures whose lives I'd snuffed out with the point of my stick, and a hundred other things that had happened from the time I got to that warehouse in Miami until now ... and stupid Jared sitting there blowing smoke rings on a bench, asking us if we were lost.

Jared didn't fight back; he just moved to protect his more sensitive parts. It didn't stop me from giving him a good raking across the face with my nails and a nice uppercut to the jaw, before the guys converged on us, pulling me off.

Chase held me in a bear hug, me facing out towards the others. I tried to kick him to free myself but he stood still, not moving. I stopped kicking because it wasn't fair that he get hurt. I didn't have a beef with him - just Jared. It pissed me off they weren't as mad as I was. *We should all be beating his ass right now.*

"No, Jayne. It's not going to happen," said Tony wearily.

I sneered at him. "Back in my head again, eh?"

"Unfortunately."

"Let me go, Chase."

"Promise to settle down?"

"For now."

Chase set me down and let me go, but he kept an annoyingly close eye on me.

"Remind me never to get on your bad side," said Spike, flashing me his teeth. It wasn't exactly a smile, but it wasn't anger either.

"Never lie to me and you don't have to worry about it," I spat back, eyes on Jared.

Tony stood in front of the obelisk, reading the inscription out loud.

"Speak Your Fondest Desire. Enter To Begin The Change ... What does that mean? Do we stand here and say what we want most? What is the change we're going to start?" He looked at Jared. "Do I even want to start something like that? Seems like my life's already changed quite a bit, and I'm really not all that happy about it."

Jared was frustrated, that much was obvious. "Please, be honest with yourselves, all of you. Sure, your lives have changed. But is that such a bad thing? All of you were running from something. I don't know what it was, but it couldn't have been good. So you got into some pretty scary situations; but you made it out - together. You have friends for life here. And you've made some money in the bargain.

You have to agree - life is arguably better for you right now."

I looked at him in disgust. "Say that to Becky."

Jared nodded to the obelisk. "Say it to her yourself."

I looked at the granite spire in front of me. What was he saying? Was Becky somehow associated with this? Was she still alive?

I made a move towards Jared, but Chase was too fast for me.

"Nope. You're staying right here with me."

"Chase!"

"Sorry, Jayne. Let him say what he has to say."

Jared sighed. "Just finish the test. That's all I can say. Just finish."

Jared walked up to the obelisk, standing front of it just below the inscription. He looked up to the onyx at the top and said, "I want to go back to my people."

A grinding sound erupted from the granite. All I could think was that some stinking black muck was going to come out and we were going to have to fight the orcs all over again.

But I was wrong.

A portion of the granite swung in to reveal a doorway. Jared stepped into it, turning to look back at us. "See you on the other side," he said, stepping backwards into the blackness. The door swung shut behind him.

Chapter Thirty

ALL OF US STARTED TALKING at once.

"Where the hell did he go?" asked Spike.

"What in the sam hill?" said Finn.

"I *knew* that motherfucker was in on it with them!" I yelled, finally feeling validated.

"I didn't even notice a door was there," said Tony, sounding more curious than anything.

I walked up to the spot where Jared had just been. I felt along the granite surface of the obelisk, but there were no cracks, no hinges, nothing.

Spike had walked around to the other side of it, doing the same thing. "I don't think he slipped out the back or anything."

Tony stepped up to the space under the inscription. "We might as well do this. It's the only way we're going to get out of here ... unless you guys feel like going through that orc forest again. You know we're in the dead center of it right now."

It was as if him speaking the words suddenly caused it to happen. The sounds of orcs off in the distance came out of the trees and across the clearing to our ears. They were coming this way.

"So, what are we supposed to do, then?" I asked, panicking once again.

"The inscription says to speak your fondest desire. Jared said he wanted to get back to his people. I'll try that," said Tony, bravely.

Tony straightened his shoulders and looked at all of us. "I want to go back to my people."

Nothing happened.

He tried again, louder. "I want to go back to my people!"

"Try something else," Finn suggested.

"Like what?"

Finn rolled his eyes. "Duh, say your fondest desire, not Jared's fondest desire."

Tony's face turned red. "Right. Okay. Um ... let's see ... what is my fondest desire?"

The sound of the orcs' arrival was getting louder.

"Come on, Tony, hurry up!" urged Spike.

I ran up to his side. "Maybe we can go in together and save some time."

Tony looked down at me and made his decision. "My fondest desire is that Jayne be safe."

The door opened, the blackness within beckoning.

Tony and I stepped forward. Tony entered into the blackness, but I bounced off, landing on my ass in the grass.

"What the ... ?"

Tony was inside, looking back at me. "One at a time, I guess. Do it, Jayne! I'll be right here waiting."

The door swung shut behind him.

I looked at Spike, Finn, and Chase in a panic. "Do you guys know your fondest desire? I don't! I'm thinking, but I can't come up with it, I'm too nervous!"

"I have mine," said Finn.

I waved him forward. "You go. I'll come after. Watch Tony's back for me."

"I'm not sure if I feel right leaving a lady behind."

"You're not. I have Chase and Spike here."

"Fine, then." Finn went over and stood at the invisible door. "I wish I could have an ice-cold beer and a chew."

The door opened and Finn stepped through.

Fucking rednecks. If only life could be that simple.

Spike laughed. "Sounds good to me. Ready now, Jayne?"

"No. You go."

Spike looked at Chase. "You good to wait for her?"

Chase nodded once.

Spike stepped up to the door. He straightened his shoulders and said, "My fondest desire is to go home."

The obelisk stood silent, unmoving.

Spike ran his fingers through his hair. "I guess it's some sort of lie detector, eh?" He laughed self-consciously. "Okay, how 'bout: my fondest desire is to get out of this forest."

Still nothing.

I raised my eyebrow. Whatever it was, Spike was either avoiding it or he didn't even know what it was. I could feel his discomfort from here.

He looked over his shoulder in the direction of the orc sounds, which had grown increasingly louder.

"Better make it fast," said Chase.

He turned back to the door and threw his hands up. "Fine! I wish I could kiss the lips of Jayne Sparks!"

I gasped as the door opened.

He turned around, walking backwards into the opening, smiling at me with those amazing teeth. "See you soon."

The door shut behind him.

Chase's eyebrows rose in surprise, but he didn't say a word.

I was too stunned to say anything. The guy could have wished for anything in the world, but what he wanted most was to kiss me? What a horrendous waste that was - all he had to do was ask! *Shit,* he didn't even have to ask, he could have just done it and I wouldn't have complained. I shook my head. Life was so messed up sometimes.

Chase gestured with his head that I was to go next, but no friggin' way was I sharing my heart's desire with him or anyone else. I trusted him and everything, but as I heard what the others said, my wish became clear to me. I was a little embarrassed about how selfish it was, but there was no use denying it. Only the truth was going to open that door. Only the truth was going to set me free.

Chase got behind me, trying to push me gently by my shoulders to the door.

"Chase, you should know me well enough by now. I'm not going until you go."

"I can't leave you here."

"Yes, you can. I have it all figured out. I know my fondest desire. I just don't want you to hear it."

"Is it Spike?"

"What? No, it's not Spike."

Chase smiled. "Do you think we get what we wish for?"

"I don't know. I guess I'm hoping so."

He stepped up to the inscription and took a deep breath. He looked back at me once and then up at the words. "I want to protect Jayne from all the evil."

The door opened. Chase stepped through without a backward glance.

The door shut behind him.

I was blown away all over again. Chase's fondest desire was to take care of me. *Me?* Why not himself? Why not wish for a swig of ice-cold beer, or a soda? Why not anything else? He was always so quiet. How was I supposed to know he felt this way?

The thoughts and emotions kept tumbling through my head. Tony, my best friend in the world, loving, protective, smart ... Spike, the hottest guy I knew with the most amazing sexy smile, happy, positive, musical ... Chase, strong, fearless, dedicated, unassuming, deep. They all were amazing guys who I was more than fortunate to count among my friends. How did I get so lucky?

The sound of a blood-curdling roar filled my ears. I turned in a panic, realizing that I'd wasted too much time. I was no longer alone in the clearing.

The largest orc of the army of orcs was striding towards me, salivating at the idea of eating me alive. I could feel the malevolence coming off of him in waves.

The grass in the clearing was tingling. I could feel it in my feet. The Green was reaching out to me. It was all around me. The trees were no longer black. They were green, alive, connecting and linked. I sent out my last message - keep me safe.

I ran to the front of the obelisk, looking behind me. The orc was still coming, closing in on me. A legion of orcs was behind him, the earth trembling with their footsteps.

"My fondest desire is to be worthy of my friends!"

The door didn't open.

Shit!

"My fondest desire is to be a good person!"

Still, the door remained closed.

Shitfuckshit!

The orcs were fifty feet away, closing in on me. I was desperate.

What was my fondest desire? *Help me!*

I called out to The Green, and seconds later, detected movement out of the corner of my eye. Something was coming from the forest on the other side of the obelisk, opposite the orcs. I took a step to my left, trying to get a better view.

Lining the edge of the trees and moving purposefully towards the obelisk was a group of people. No, not people. Well, yes, people, but not regular ones.

They were smaller, lighter, and clothed in green and brown.

They were tall and thin, wearing cloaks.

They were short and squat wearing commando uniforms.

They were the people of The Green, and they had come armed with bows and arrows, clubs, axes, spears, and slingshots. The Green had sent an army to help me.

Vines came out of the forest behind the orcs, quickly slithering across the clearing to grab at their ankles and take them down. Once down, the orcs were covered in vines, incapacitated, and pulled back towards the forest - away from me.

The Green army fell on the orcs and began annihilating them.

The carnage was unbelievable. Black blood sprayed up and covered anything and anyone nearby. The burning acid saliva hissed as it landed on bodies and the ground. The screams of the soldiers of The Green echoed off the trees surrounding the clearing, as the orcs were able to escape their bonds and use their strength to bludgeon and rip apart some of their attackers.

I stood there, in shock, tears pouring down my face. My heart had stopped beating for I don't know how long and now rushed to get back in sync.

This is all my fault ... IT'S ALL MY FAULT!!

People of The Green were screaming, crying, and dying. They

were being butchered. Small people, big people, short people, tall ones, black ones, green ones ... all of them. Dying because of me.

Just when I thought I wouldn't be able to take another second of it, I felt a gentle touch on my arm. I looked to see who it was.

"BECKY!!"

I grabbed her in a hug so hard I was surprised I didn't crush her bones.

She hugged me back for a second and then pried me off of her. "Jayne, you have to go now. This is not where you need to be."

I was sobbing so hard I could barely breathe, let alone talk. I had to shout to be heard above the noise of the battle.

"Becky! You're alive? You're ... holy shit ... *alive!"* I gasped to catch my breath. "I thought you died in that lake!"

"Things are not as they seem here, but I think you already know that. You must enter the obelisk and finish the test. They are waiting for you on the other side."

"Aren't you coming?"

"I've already been. I'll see you again, don't worry. But it's time for you to go now. You cannot get tangled up in this mess." She gestured with her head to the battle that was still raging on.

She took my hand and pulled me to the obelisk. "Say the words."

"I can't."

"Yes, you can. And don't lie or say something you think other people want to hear. Say what is in your heart - what is your fondest desire?"

I took a deep breath, glancing at Becky and then at the door. I looked again at the inscription there, carved into the stone.

Speak Your Fondest Desire. Enter To Begin The Change.

I closed my eyes, listening to the sound of the orcs roaring and the people of The Green yelling their war cries. Everything was connected. Everyone was here for me and because of me. I already had my wish.

"My fondest desire is to be someone extraordinary."

The door to the obelisk opened, and I stepped into the darkness beyond.

Chapter Thirty-One

THE CORRIDOR BEYOND THE OBELISK of waypoint four was lit with torches set in old metal sconces and brackets embedded in the stone walls - stone walls that were not built with individual blocks of material fitted together, but walls that were carved right out of great pieces of rock themselves. I ran my hand across its surface as I walked. It was slightly moist and smelled of minerals.

After going down the corridor for what seemed like a long time - but was probably no more than two minutes - I saw the gentle, flickering glow of candlelight in the shape of a rectangle up ahead. As I got closer, I realized it was a closed door. The light shining behind it and seeping through the cracks had created an illusion of a glowing shape.

The door had big iron bands on it, holding the wood together and maintaining its shape. There was an iron knocker on the front. It had a familiar face on it, but I didn't make the connection. *How do I know this face?* I grasped it and banged it down on the metal plate resting underneath, three times. The door swung open to reveal Tony standing in the doorway.

I jumped on him, burying my face in his neck and closing my eyes, hugging him as hard as I possibly could. I wanted to be instantly transported back to Florida - back to my horrible house with my disgusting mother's boyfriend and everything. I didn't want to be here anymore.

"It's not that bad, Jayne, you'll see," whispered Tony in my ear.

"Yes it is," I answered, my voice muffled by his shirt.

"Just come in and talk to them."

"No." I refused to let go of him. "There's a war going on out there, you know."

"Yes, we know. Come on ... come inside. They'll explain everything."

I let Tony go. "They who?"

Tony turned and gestured. "They, *them*."

I looked in the room and gasped. Not only were all my friends there, but so were Dardennes, Ivar, Niles, Céline, the Lady of the Lake - otherwise known as the watery whore - the werewolf I had talked to and probably a few of his friends, but I wasn't sure because I'd never seen them looking so un-wolf-like - Gilly, Gander, the vampire, and last but not least, Jared. And he was standing with all the forest people.

"Ha! I *knew* you were in on it!" I yelled at Jared, pissed all over again.

Jared gave me a vague smile and tipped his head.

I looked at Tony smugly. "I fucking *told* you, but noooo, you wouldn't listen."

Tony held up his hands, surrendering to my superior intellect, or at least that's what I told myself. "You win, Jayne, you were right ... about part of it, but not all of it. Come on, let's sit down. They're about to start."

"Start what? Eating us for dinner?"

I shot an evil eye over to the wolves and the lake whore. I didn't care if Becky was still alive. That woman was still rotten to the core, and I knew those wolves would have eaten me if I had come down from the tree. *I wish I'd just gone ahead and pissed on them.*

I took a seat at the massive wood table where the rest of my friends were already sitting. Spike looked at me and smiled, his face turning red. I pointed at him, mouthing the words, *'You're mine later.'*

He raised his eyebrows all cocky-like, welcoming my challenge.

Okay, so it's not all bad right now.

I sat down next to Chase and Tony. Chase nodded at me, and I reached over and squeezed his arm. It was nice to know he had my back. I tried to ignore the other warm feelings that came up when I looked at him. I didn't think I was talented enough to juggle two love interests simultaneously. Of course, I'd never tried, so maybe ...

Tony kicked my seat, for sure vibing me and picking up on my amorous thoughts.

Dammit.

"*A-hem.* Let's get the meeting started, shall we?"

It was Dardennes talking. I gave him my most powerful evil eye. I *so* wanted to get him alone and show him just how appreciative I was of all the lies, deceit, and near-death experiences. He was just lucky as hell that Becky was okay. Now at least I didn't have to avenge her death, which I had been totally prepared to do.

"First, congratulations on making it through the test to the end. We are all very proud of you, as we are well aware of the obstacles you faced."

I snorted at that. *Obstacles, my ass.*

Dardennes continued, pretending he hadn't heard me. "You have all not only succeeded in completing the test and earning your five hundred dollars, you have also qualified for the special bonus that was mentioned by my colleague Céline on your first day at the lodge."

My ears perked up at the word 'bonus'.

"Before I share the details of that with you, it's important that I give you some background. Without it, the bonus would make little sense to you. I hope that you can remain patient with me." He gave me a particularly pointed look, to which I responded with a good rolling of the eyes. "I ask that you hear me out and give my colleagues your due attention as well. We have some history to share with you."

He paused, looking to each of us for some sort of response. We all nodded, now at least curious. History wasn't my favorite subject, but I had a feeling this history lesson was going to be different than the ones I was used to hearing in school.

*****

"Many years ago, thousands of years ago, in fact, there was a special species of human-like creatures on the Earth. Today this species goes by many names, but we call it 'fae'. This species is very similar to the human species, with some key differences, one being that the life spans of the races that make up this species are much longer - for some as long as several thousand years - and another difference being that they all have what *you* would call supernatural abilities. These abilities are supernatural to the human species, but are in fact, quite 'natural' for the fae species." He paused to take a drink of water and let his words sink in.

I felt like Alice must have felt when she fell into the rabbit hole. Yes, when I was in the forest, some next-level freaky shit was going on. Yes, I was now talking to trees. And yes, I just saw an army of orcs being attacked by an army of ... fae. But it wasn't until sitting through this little history lesson that I finally, finally felt like I was in another dimension. That shows how fucked up in the head I was at this point.

Dardennes continued. "Within the fae species are many fae races. You have already met some of them: the werewolves ... "

At this, the pack of guys who I assumed were the werewolves who had treed us the other day, bowed their heads to us.

" ... the gnomes ... "

Gilly and Gander bowed low, and once again I was thankful I wasn't standing behind Gilly. I saw one of the wolves glance over at the wrong time and quickly look away, swallowing hard. *That'll teach him to look at the ass-end of a gnome with a miniskirt on.*

" ... the sirens ... "

The Lady of the Lake looked at us, without making any gesture at all, but we knew who he was talking about.

The big door opened and the guy I had nicknamed Robin Hood stepped through, nodding to Dardennes as he took his place among the fae.

" ... the Green Elves ... "

Robin Hood fae nodded his head briskly at all of us.

" ... the Dwarves ... "

Niles put a fist to his chest over his heart as some sort of warrior salute, no doubt.

" ... the Incubus and his female counterpart the Succubus ... "

From behind Dardennes stepped the vampire guy we had seen attacking Chase. He gave a little curtsy before stepping into the background again.

" ... the daemons ... "

Jared nodded his head at me only.

Dardennes gestured above his head. "And the orcs ... I believe you've met them as well. They're ... a little different ... but obviously not human." He gave us a weak smile, and some of us couldn't help but return it. Mine was of the bitter variety. *Yeah, we fucking met the orcs. One of your little dwarf friends did too, much to his regret.*

Tony kicked my seat.

I turned around and gave him my mean look.

His return expression said, *'Give the guy some slack.'*

I thought, *'Fuck that!'* as hard as I could back at him and stuck out my tongue.

He rolled his eyes at me.

"Don't forget the old hag posing as Samantha," I said resentfully. She was the first being I'd ever killed and I was still pissed they had pushed me into that.

"Yes, she was one of our witches - an unfortunate end, but our colleagues know the risks of participating in the tests. But we will get to that later. For now, let us continue with our history ... Céline?"

Céline stepped forward and picked up where Dardennes had left off. "You may be wondering how the fae came to have these supernatural abilities and the humans did not. Well, actually, if you believe this is the case, then you are of course forgiven for it, but you are wrong. You see, many humans do have these abilities, but they are too closed off from the source of their power to ever put their abilities into practice. There are some humans who have no abilities, that is true; but you would probably be surprised to know how many *do*. How can that be? Well, it is simple: Many of the humans who inhabit this planet actually have abilities like this because they are part fae. Let me ask you ... have you ever experienced a feeling of déjà vu? Have you ever had a dream about something, only to have it or some version of it come true? Have you ever seen someone you thought you knew from somewhere else? Do you ever meet someone and for some reason, get very bad vibes telling you to stay away from them? Do you ever have dreams where you fly above the trees or breathe underwater? Did you ever go somewhere new and feel as if you'd been there before? And finally, have you ever felt that you were special, but misunderstood - on the outside looking in? All of these are manifestations of fae ancestry."

We looked at each other. Even Chase swung around to look at me. I wondered if talking to trees meant something. Apparently my friends thought it did.

"Over the years, many fae have lost their connection to the magic that links them to their abilities." She looked around at our faces. "I see that several of you doubt the concept of magic."

She was including me in this observation, because her explanation was entering the 'too-far fetched to be believable' zone. Actually, we had passed that zone a *loooong* time ago, but I had to draw the line somewhere. Apparently, I drew it at the word 'magic'.

"Humans call sleight of hand and illusion magic. This is a misnomer. Magic is not a trick or something that fools your eyes. Magic is an energy present here on this planet and out in the universe. It is the energy that binds all of us together and to other living things - and even to things that are not living or that are only in a partially living state."

"The fae have a natural ability to tap into this magic without effort. It is, practically speaking, an automatic, involuntary connection that they use without thinking. The magic provides the energy for them to express and use their natural abilities - or as you would call them, their 'supernatural' abilities."

She stepped closer to our table, looking at each of us in turn. "Our species has a division in it, one that has existed for as long as our recorded history goes back. Each of the fae is on one side or the other of this division. There are the Light and the Dark; so we say there are 'Light Fae' and 'Dark Fae'. Some races of fae as a whole tend to belong to one division over the other - for example, the wraithes. They, almost to the wraithe, belong on the Dark Fae side. There have been some Light Fae wraithes, but it is rare. Sprites, on the other hand, usually tend to be Light Fae. Again, there are some exceptions, but they are rare. Finally, there are fae that equally go to the Light or the Dark. For example, there is nearly a perfect division of numbers for the witches - half of them are Light Fae and half are Dark."

"Some, or I should say, many, of the fae actually survive off of humans in one way or another. Some need human energy, some need human blood, and some, human meat. The main difference between the Light Fae and the Dark Fae is that they have opposing opinions about what our role among humans should be and how humans should be treated. The Light Fae believe that our survival depends on anonymity, not revealing our existence, and protecting our own kind, as well as protecting the humans from destruction by fae-kind."

She saw our looks of disgust and quickly responded. "Don't get the wrong idea here - we're not talking about the stuff of horror movies. The Light Fae value human life. They don't take human lives to satisfy their cravings or even their needs."

"Now, the Dark Fae believe that the fae are superior to humans, and as such, believe the ultimate goal for all fae should be to take over leadership of the world and essentially 'come out of the closet', as they say. They don't agree that to maintain the safety of our races we should live in anonymity and in harmony with the humans, with the humans remaining ignorant to our existence. If the Dark Fae were to have their way, humans would eventually be enslaved to them, and used for whatever they could give to the fae - including energy, blood, and meat."

I looked at my friends' faces and they mirrored the revulsion I felt. *Humans as sources of meat? Disgusting.* I thought about the dwarf in the orc camp.

"Apparently, the orcs don't just like to eat human meat," I said.

Céline sighed. "Yes, this is true. There are some ... creatures ...

that have turned to eating their own kind; just as there are some humans on the planet who practice cannibalism."

Dardennes took over the history lesson. "We have reached a critical period in the history of the fae. Our numbers have dwindled, particularly in the Light Fae division. All of the fae you see here today are members of the Light Fae."

That little nugget made me feel a little bit better. I could see on Finn's face he felt the same. I looked at Jared and he met my stare, not looking away. He was proud of who he was, that much was clear.

"The Dark Fae are willing to use certain, shall we say, unsavory methods to maintain their numbers. Since we, on the other hand, have such high regard for our fellow species - the humans - we cannot do these things; it is against our moral code. Therefore, we had to devise other methods to find and recruit members of our species, that is to say, *humans* who may not know that they, in fact, are members of our species. Certain individuals of our kind are suited for identifying and recruiting possible candidates." At this he gestured to Jared who nodded back and then looked over at us.

Chase turned around in his chair again, first looking at me and then at the others. Tony was nodding his head in comprehension, along with Spike.

Finn and I looked at each other with questions written all over our faces. *What exactly does this have to do with us?*

"We have found the best way to identify those with fae blood in their veins is to test for fae abilities in controlled studies ... tests such as the one you have passed - with *flying colors* I might add." He held up each of our flags.

Oh, the irony.

"Based on your performance over the past three days, you have been identified as very likely having fae blood and therefore, fae abilities."

Whaaaat?

Spike raised his hand.

Dardennes smiled. "Spike?"

"Yeah, uh, so what you're saying is that I ... all of us ... are fae?"

"Not exactly. What I'm saying is that it is *likely* that you have fae blood somewhere in your ancestry."

"So, how do you know for sure?"

"We won't know unless you choose to participate in the next step."

Here it comes - I knew it wasn't going to be this easy.

"So ... what's the next step?"

"Once all of you know the story, know what you could be participating in, you will be given a choice. We have in our possession certain ... amulets ... imbued with qualities that will essentially awaken or charge your fae blood and race-specific abilities. If you choose to use the amulet, and you are of the fae, it will bring about your change. You will become a 'Changeling'. Should you choose not to awaken your fae blood, you will be given the money you have earned and sent back to Miami, or wherever you'd like us to take you."

"So, what's the catch?" I asked.

"There is no catch."

"So, you'll just tell us your big secret, we say 'no thanks', and then you just let us go? How do you know we won't tell anyone?"

"Ah, yes, I did actually leave out one piece of information. Thank you, Jayne, for your question. Should you choose not to awaken your fae blood and realize your particular fae race, your memory of this test and everything I just told you will be erased by one of our colleagues who has that supernatural ability."

Finn cleared his throat and sat up a little. "Excuse me, Sir, I don't mean to be rude, but I need to ask: What's in it for us if we decide to do this thing - I mean, not get erased?"

"Another good question," Dardennes answered. "First, you will become what you truly are, the best possible version of yourself. Depending on which race of fae you are - and again we don't guarantee that you *are* fae, just that it is *likely* - you will have supernatural abilities beyond those which you could scarcely imagine or ever experience without your fae blood being charged by our amulets. The things you saw in the forest done by our colleagues are but a fraction of what is possible for many of you."

Céline stepped forward. "You will join our community which is vast and varied. We are in every state in the United States of America and every country in Eastern and Western Europe, Africa, the Middle East, and the Orient, among other places. You will never again feel alone or lost or wonder what your purpose is. We all live and work together as a team. You will have a job, a place to live, and a family."

Niles stepped forward. "Many of you will also be trained to help us in our efforts to build our Light Fae forces and defend our way of life against the Dark Fae when necessary."

Spike spoke up again. "Do we get to choose which race we belong to?"

"No," answered Dardennes. "You have the blood of a certain race in your veins. The amulet merely wakes it up. We can try to guess what your race is by your current human qualities, but we are not always correct - and frankly, some of our races have died out over the years and occasionally we are confronted with a race we've never seen before ... one that hasn't walked the Earth in thousands of years. It's not often that this happens, but we have reason to believe it could happen with one of you." With this he looked pointedly at me. So did everyone else at the table.

Great. I'm a freak in the human world, and I'm probably a freak in the fae world too.

Tony reached over and squeezed my shoulder. Chase nodded at me supportively. Spike flashed me his trademark smile. For sure he was going to be an incubus. There was no getting around those teeth.

Finn was all business. "I think I'd like to discuss this with my friends before I make any kinda decision."

"Me too. And by 'friends', I also mean our friend Becky," I added.

"Fair enough," said Dardennes. "We will leave you to your discussion. In the meantime, food will be delivered and we invite you to relax and enjoy your meal while you talk."

"Ivar wasn't the chef, was he? 'Cause I'm not a big fan of his drinks," I said sarcastically.

Dardennes laughed. Céline and Ivar smiled. "No, Ivar was not the chef. One of our Green Elves was, and I think you will find they have a particularly supernatural skill when it comes to the manipulation of herbs and spices. It will be a vegetarian meal, but I'm sure you will find it more than satisfying."

I was so hungry at this point I would have happily eaten a dried pig's ear.

A door on the other side of the chamber opened and fae started walking in, carrying trays of food, dishes and utensils. Within ten minutes we all had plates loaded with food in front of us and ice-cold glasses of soda - and for Finn, a beer. He got a huge smile on his face when one of the dwarves put it down in front of him.

"Now that's what I'm talkin' 'bout."

I got an ice-cold soda, which was a little freaky, since I didn't remember telling anyone that was what I wanted. They must have a friggin mind reader in their group. *That should provide some interesting entertainment, especially with this bunch.*

Dardennes and his colleagues left, as did the servers and others who had put together our meal. We ate in silence for a few minutes, all of us too famished to talk. And I was also too hungry to worry about the food being poisoned. If they wanted to kill me at this point, well they could just go for it.

The door from the corridor opened and Becky stepped in. We all jumped up from the table and rushed over to hug her. She found herself nearly tackled to the floor in our enthusiasm.

"Wow, guys, I missed you too." Her face was all flushed and she was smiling.

Everyone but me went back to their seats. I just couldn't stop looking at her. "Becky ... I ... ," I couldn't get the rest of it out. I was choking up, tears gathering in my eyes.

Becky grabbed me in a super tight hug. "Shhh, I'm fine. I'm totally fine. I didn't die. I just ... had a little swim, that's all."

I laughed and cried at the same time. "I should have helped you. That watery bitch shouldn't have been able to get you. It's my fault."

Becky laughed, pulling me away from her so she could look at me. "It's a *good* thing I went into that water. I found my fae blood there. I discovered my true race. I'm happy, Jayne. If you hadn't made the choices you made, I may not be here right now. Those awful orcs might have gotten me ... or any number of other things."

"Really?" I said, wiping the tears off my face and the snot from under my nose.

"Yes, really. I'm totally serious."

"So what are you then? A vampire?"

Becky laughed. "No, silly. I'm a water sprite!" Her face broke out in a glorious grin that lit up the whole room.

"I guess I'm not surprised."

"I'm just glad I'm not a fire sprite. That water would have been a big problem for me."

I looked at her aghast, wondering how close I'd come to destroying her fae race thing or whatever.

"Kidding! I'm joking! Just relax, I'm fine, Jayne, geez. Lighten up."

I shook my head, going back to the table. "Fucking fairies."

Everyone laughed, even Chase. I punched him in the arm as I sat down.

"Becky, have a seat. We need to figure this out and since you're already in with those guys, maybe you can help shed some light on this thing," said Finn.

Becky sat down. "Okay, so what do you want to know?"

"First of all," I said, "what is this amulet thing?"

"Well, in my case it was a necklace. I put it on, and then after a few seconds, my fae blood kinda just woke up and I became a Changeling."

"What's the difference between a Changeling and a fae?" asked Tony.

"There is no difference. A Changeling is a fae - just one that's been awakened by the power in an amulet. The really old fae never lost touch with their heritage, so they never needed it."

"I thought a Changeling was something else - like when a fairy stole a baby or something, putting a fairy baby in its place."

"Yeah, a mix up in terminology or some of our history bleeding into the history of humans. In the old days, people used to have babies sometimes that cried all the time and made the moms crazy - so they'd say the baby was not really human, that a fairy had traded babies with them in the night. So they'd leave their baby outside for the fairies to get it, when instead it was probably a wolf or something that took the baby. Maybe some fae did come by and take the baby - or ate it - I don't know. I get stories from them, explanations, but I haven't asked about much more than that. As far as I know, the fae never put their babies in human baby cribs and stole the human one. What would be the point? It would be like a human putting their baby with a group of monkeys to raise."

Tony shrugged. I guess the explanation was good enough for him, although I couldn't help but be a little offended at being compared to a monkey. I didn't really care about the terminology though. I wanted to get to the good stuff.

"If we choose to be erased, how much of our memory gets taken away?" I looked at Tony. "There are many parts of my life I want to remember."

"I didn't have that done, obviously, but my understanding is you will be erased up to the point immediately prior to learning about the meeting at the hotel."

"Is the change painful?" This question came from Spike.

"No. It tingled, but it didn't hurt."

"Did you know how to use your abilities right away, or do you have to be trained?"

"Some are there right away and some need practice. I think it depends on your race. The witches need to learn spells and stuff. Some races are pretty powerful and need to learn how to control it."

"What kind of abilities does a water sprite have?" asked Finn, smiling.

Becky disappeared. She was there one second and the next, she was gone.

"This for one."

Finn jumped out of his seat, eyes like saucers on his face. "Holy shit, girl, you just scared the bejesus outta me!"

Becky giggled, now standing next to Finn's chair.

Spike was pointing at the door and then at Finn and then back at the door again. "You just ... you just ... "

"Yeah, I just kinda disappeared and then reappeared. Like teleporting."

"What's that got to do with water?" asked Tony, my little scientist.

"The air around us is *what* percentage water?" she asked, a little sass in her tone.

Tony nodded in appreciation, smiling. "Ah-haaaa, I see ... "

"Will they tell us what race they think we are before we become Changelings, if that's what we decide to do?"

"Yes; they've already discussed it." She looked a little anxiously over at me.

"Do you know what they said?" I asked, suddenly suspicious.

"Yes, they have included me in all their meetings and gatherings since I became a Changeling."

"Instant trust, eh?" I asked, not sure I believed it.

"Yes. Jayne they were not kidding when they said you instantly become a part of the community. I'm part of a very big, very close, very special family as a water sprite. The sirens and the water sprites are kinda related - like cousins I guess you could say. The Lady in the Lake is really actually very nice. You just have to get to know her. I really hope all of you decide to join too so you can see what I mean."

"So, what's the deal with Jared?" I asked.

Now that everyone finally agreed with me about our traitor friend, they listened intently for her answer.

"Jared is a daemon - not 'demon'. That's a different thing altogether. His race, the daemon, are warrior guardians. He also has a talent for hunting down and finding fae. He goes to cities around the world and finds recruits, bringing them back here for the test."

She twisted her hands nervously. "I know you guys are mad at him; but please, don't be. He's a super nice guy. He has a really important job and he takes it very seriously. He would never hurt anyone on purpose. He's trying to save his people. He wants you all to help. They could be your people too."

The room got quiet. All of our questions had been answered, or we didn't want to hear any more answers to our questions; I wasn't sure which it was.

Finn banged his hand down on the table. "Well, I don't know 'bout you guys, but I'm in. I got nothin' better goin' on in Florida. My family's gone, 'cept for my grandma, and she's gettin' pretty old. My dad's in prison, my ma's dead. I ain't got no brothers or sisters. I don't know what I'll become with this change, but anything's gotta be better'n being a starvin' runaway."

Finn looked at Spike. "What about you, man?"

Spike shrugged his shoulders. "I'm gonna do it, too. Life on the street's not bad, but I like the idea of being a part of something bigger. In Miami I was a part of ... I don't know ... the music scene ... a group of runaways. No offense to you guys, I love you all, but this feels like an opportunity I shouldn't pass up. I want to be the best Spike I can be. Huh ... kinda sounds like a military recruitment slogan." He smiled at me, then looked over at Chase. "What about you, Chase? You gonna join the fae army? Be all you can be?"

Chase looked at each of us slowly, then frowned, nodding his head. "Yep."

We all laughed. Leave it to Chase to bring us all back to what was real. It was a simple yes or no question. *Do we want to be something else?*

Becky was bouncing up and down on the balls of her feet. "What about you, Jayne? Are you gonna do it?"

I'd been hemming and hawing in my mind since the moment we

were told we could choose to change who we are. I had tried to deny it to myself during the test. I had tried to deny it at the door of the obelisk. I had even tried to deny it in this room. But the truth was, my fondest desire was to be extraordinary. I didn't want to be the old Jayne anymore - the one who sat in high school History waiting for life to happen ... the one who feared men coming into her room at night ... the one who looked at amazing things and could only wonder what they might mean. I wanted to be special. I wanted to be more.

"I'm doing it. I just hope I don't turn into an orc."

Everyone laughed.

"I don't think you have to worry about that," said Becky, smiling.

"What about you, Tones, you in?"

I felt certain he was going to do it, only asking him as a formality. We were a team. We did everything together. Tony was my right hand man and my best friend. My brother from another mother.

"Well, I've thought about it, and believe me, it's definitely the opportunity of a lifetime; but I'm afraid I'm going to have to say no. I'm not going to be a Changeling. I'm just going to be Tony. I'm going to go home."

Hate Cliffhangers?

Not to worry! Just go to Amazon, find the next book in the series, click on the "Look Inside" cover of the book, and you'll be able to read the first several chapters of the next book for free. I know, I know ... cliffhangers make you crazy, right? Sorry. I just can't seem to help myself. :)

Other Books by Elle Casey

War of the Fae: Book One, The Changelings
War of the Fae: Book Two, Call to Arms
War of the Fae: Book Three, Darkness & Light
War of the Fae: Book Four, New World Order

Clash of the Otherworlds: Book 1, After the Fall
Clash of the Otherworlds: Book 2, Between the Realms
Clash of the Otherworlds: Book 3, Portal Guardians

Apocalypsis: Book 1, Kahayatle
Apocalypsis: Book 2, Warpaint
Apocalypsis: Book 3, Exodus
Apocalypsis: Book 4, Haven

My Vampire Summer
My Vampire Fall

Wrecked
Reckless

About the Author

Elle Casey is an American writer who lives in Southern France with her husband, three kids, Hercules the wonder poodle, and Monie the bouvier. In her spare time she writes young adult novels.

A personal note from Elle ...

If you enjoyed this book, please consider leaving feedback on Amazon.com, Goodreads.com, or any book blogs you participate in. More positive feedback means I can spend more time writing! Oh, and I love interacting with my readers, so if you feel like shooting the breeze or talking about books, please visit me. You can find me at ...

www.ElleCasey.com
www.Facebook.com/ellecaseytheauthor
www.Twitter.com/ellecasey
www.Shelfari.com/ellecasey

Acknowledgments

Once again I sit here thinking of all the people who helped make this book come alive and be available for my readers to purchase and enjoy. First, I must acknowledge my **readers (Yay readers!)**. Without you, I'd be writing for just myself, and while I find writing soothing and self-fulfilling, it means ever so much more when it is shared with those who have enthusiasm for my characters and their adventures. So thank you, my lovely, awesome, kickass readers, for being there and reading, reading, reading so I can keep on writing, writing, writing. And a special shout-out to those who have left me reviews on Amazon.com, Goodreads.com, and the many, many book blogs out there. You guys are amazing. **Book bloggers** deserve a special note. These ladies and gentlemen read my books and tell people about them or give me space on their blogs to connect with their followers, thereby spreading the word about Elle Casey. My pool of readers continues to grow daily, thanks to you guys, so big hugs for you. I would like to acknowledge also my muse for this series of books, the band **Breaking Benjamin** – keep putting out that awesome music so I can continue to be inspired by you. --- Because I'm an indie author, I manage my own editing, cover art, promotion, etc. But I'm definitely not talented enough to do all that alone, so thanks to those who help me with the business of writing, including **Beth Godwin** and **Maggie** for their copy editing, **CrashandEddie** on elance for my cover art, and **Craig Cowden** for his amazing fae-inspired jewelry. --- And last, but not least, are my friends and family who support me in so many ways it would be impossible to list them all, but they include things like giving me a place to write (Lady Olivia!), taking care of my kids and beta reading (Hoanzie! Mom!), reading my books and telling people about them (friends and family!), and the other authors out there who have graciously sent me encouraging emails and Facebook posts. Thanks to all of you for making it possible for me to be a real, live writer.

18804613R00194

Made in the USA
Lexington, KY
25 November 2012